M000158302

Wild SPIRIT

A SOUL SISTER NOVEL

#1 *NEW YORK TIMES* BESTSELLING AUTHOR

AUDREY CARLAN

Copyright 2021 Audrey Carlan, Inc.

Cover Design: Jena Brignola

Copy Editor: Jeanne De Vita

ISBN: 978-1-943340-20-0

*To **Elaine Hennig**...*
Your medical knowledge is astounding.
Thank you for using your knowledge and talent
to help make this series sparkle.
This book is for you.
I adore you, my friend.

Wild SPIRIT

A SOUL SISTER NOVEL

PROLOGUE

Present day…
Day of the bank heist.

FAMOUS SINGER-SONGWRITER MARC ANTHONY ONCE SAID, "IF you do what you love, you'll never work a day in your life." Apparently that wise man was never a teacher. Especially a teacher to two hundred rotating hormonal monster teenagers who were either the sun in my sky or the bane of my existence. Depended on the day. Today was the latter. After disciplining a group of wayward teens who had real academic promise—but lacked parental oversight—with afterschool detention, I finally was on my way to a weekend of nothing but laughter and love with my soul sisters. After I ran my bank errand.

I parked out in front of Liberty National Bank in the heart of Chicago, feeling blessed I found a spot so close. Grabbing my purse, I angled out of my bright blue sporty Chevy Blazer and clicked the lock on my key fob. I took a moment to appreciate my SUV. It was slick and sleek, and I'd pinched my pennies for a year in order to afford her on a teacher's salary. Thankfully at twenty-eight, I was already tenured at Franklin D. Roosevelt High School as their resident Spanish teacher.

Digging for my wallet, I approached the bank with my head down until I ran smack dab into a wall. A giant, bull-headed, grinning, brick wall of a man who I knew all too well.

"Dammit, Omar! Are you following me?" I pointed an accusing finger and narrowed my gaze.

1

He chuckled and smirked in that infuriating hot-guy way that made me seem a little *mal de la cabeza*.

"It's not uncommon, *chica*, that two people who live in the same city might do business at the same bank." He held up what looked like a zippered cash bag that was stretched full of what I assumed to be money. Which I found odd. Why would he have so much cash on him?

"You didn't answer my question. Are you following me?" I repeated.

He pressed his lips together. "*No, mi lirio*. I am not following you. Though I think it must be fate that brought us to this bank, on this day, at this time. No?"

Hearing him call me "his lily," like the flower, sent a shiver of excitement running through my veins alongside scalding-hot fury. I swallowed against both responses. I'd had a crush on the hulking Mexican-American man since I laid eyes on him a few months ago. Until that day in the church changed everything.

Omar Alvarado.

He was an absolute hunk. Much taller than my five-foot-three stature. He was at least six feet and towered over me. The man worked out, a lot. At that moment he was wearing a perfectly fitted pair of dark jeans and a black T-shirt that defied the laws of gravity as it was so tightly stretched against his muscular chest. Briefly I worried it might split at the seams and fall off his form. Not a bad visual. He was clean shaven and smelled amazing. He wore a black White Sox hat with the emblem on the front, the bill flat and stretched out in that street style that made me swoon. He had a series of leather bracelets on one wrist. Falling between his pecs, a gold cross dangled on the outside of his shirt and glinted in the sunlight. It reminded me of the last time I laid eyes on him.

I held my breath as I assessed the symbol of my faith. I too wore a cross every day. One of my most prized possessions, mine was attached to a dainty, old bracelet that my mother was wearing the day she died in the car crash that took both my biological parents' lives.

I had glimpsed the cross before but didn't realize he always wore it. Actually, I'd never seen him in casual attire that wasn't black cargos, boots, and black moisture-wicking tees or long sleeve shirts. The fact remained—the man looked good no matter what he wore. Bastard.

"Cat got your tongue, Liliana?"

I shook my head on autopilot.

"Why haven't you called or texted me back?" he asked abruptly.

Which reminded me. I was avoiding him like the plague. He was too bossy, too possessive, and too alpha for his own good—not to mention a womanizer. Mama Kerri taught me to be an independent woman who didn't need anyone to fulfill her dreams. She also taught me to be open to love. However she never said anything about lust. And every time I looked at Omar I wanted to lick and kiss his body from head to toe. All thoughts of independence flew out the window at the man who stood before me as I allowed my eyes to drink in his beauty.

Omar Alvarado was everything I'd ever fantasized about. This also being part of the problem. I didn't want to get lost in a man. I wanted to stand by a man's side. Be my own person, not cave to his every whim. My real mother doted on my father as though he were the sun. Did everything a good Mexican woman should. Her words, not mine. She took care of me, the house, the cooking, the laundry, and dressed nice for her husband. When he came home from work, she'd have a Dos Equis, a smile, and a table full of food waiting.

Sure, I liked to treat my boyfriends well, but I was a hard-working American-born Mexican woman who wanted to be doted on just as much as the man I chose to have in my life would expect me to dote on him. Unfortunately, none of the men I dated in the past understood that. Also, the men I dated ended up having concerns about my faith. Mostly because I didn't miss church on Sunday if it could be helped, even when there was a Cubs, Sox, Bulls, Bears or any number of sporting events and games that also occurred on Sundays. I attended church regularly and expected the man I would end up with would share in my faith. I'd been spared on that highway where my parents died all those years ago. I saw things that night that cemented my faith in a way that could never be altered. My faith was as much a part of me as my heritage, the love I had for my foster mother, my biological parents, and every last one of my foster sisters.

"Liliana, why are you avoiding me?" His voice was a deep timber that tunneled its way into my thoughts. "I thought we had something."

I shook off the past and shoved my wild curls out of my face, which never worked because they came bouncing back in place. "Because I don't want to date you!" I fired off, moved around him, and entered the large glass doors of the bank doing my best to leave him behind.

Omar was hot on my heels as I asserted my way through the throngs of people and got in line for the customer service counter. I held my wallet in my hand and crossed my arms, tapping my foot and hoping this wouldn't take long. I was supposed to meet my sisters for a bridesmaid dress fitting at

Kerrighan House where Blessing and the bride-to-be, Simone, would be waiting. But first I needed cash for the fundraiser at school on Monday. The kids I taught were eagerly trying to raise money for a sponsored trip to México that I also planned on chaperoning. I couldn't wait to see the old Mayan ruins such as Tulum and Chichén Itzá. It would be my first trip to México, the land where my grandparents were from. I couldn't wait. I should have just gone to the ATM to avoid Omar, but I didn't like to take out a lot of cash at the ATM, preferring the safety and personal nature of speaking directly to a bank cashier.

"You're lying," I heard Omar say from directly behind me.

I spun around. "No, I'm not! I'm just not that into you. Shocker! Call the press," I blurted hotly, my cheeks heating because I was in fact lying through my straight white teeth as I turned around in an attempt to ignore him.

He made a tsking sound. "You know, lying is a sin." He murmured near my ear, his warm breath teasing the baby hairs at the nape of my neck.

"And I'm sure you know a lot about sinning!" I hissed at the memories of what I saw that day months ago, fueling my fire. Not to mention, the man was a walking, talking, slab of sexy-as-heck sin.

"Oh, big words from a tiny woman," he taunted.

"You realize you are not helping your chances of getting me to date you," I said dryly.

"Is that right?" His tone was filled with humor.

"*Sí*, it is."

He leaned forward as I continued to try and ignore him. His hands came down to my hips and he pressed up against my back. Goosebumps rose on the surface of my skin as my heart pounded and arousal swam thick and hot, straight between my legs.

"Good thing I'm not just trying to date you. No, *mi lirio*, I want far more than to date you. I want to kiss you. I want to make you sigh my name in that sweet tone you use when you're happy for one of your sisters. I want to bring you to my home and worship that sexy little body of yours until you beg me to stop. But more than anything, I want to bring you home to *mi madre* and see her light up at meeting the woman I have chosen for my own."

His words were everything I wanted to hear, but also despised with every fiber of my being. He was such a big, fat liar! It was exactly why I avoided insanely hot Mexican-American guys. In my personal experience, when they saw what they wanted, they were all in. They'd stop at nothing to achieve their goal, and I didn't like feeling like a prize. I wanted a man who would go all-in as partners with me. Two halves of a whole. Not one person lording his strength and power over the other on top of hiding huge secrets, which I knew Omar had.

Renewed sadness washed over me. I wanted what my sister Simone had with Jonah. What Addison had with Killian.

Enough was enough. I needed to handle Omar, once and for all.

I spun around. "You are barking up the wrong tree, mister!" I pointed at his chest, hitting nothing but steely muscle. The man was in insane shape. Probably worked out as much as I downed ice cream, which is why even though I was petite, I still had a big booty.

He grabbed my hand and lifted it to his smiling lips. He nibbled teasingly at my finger. His touch was achingly seductive.

My gaze zeroed in on his and I gasped at the arousal I saw swirling in those endless depths.

"You will be mine one day, Liliana. Stop fighting it and enjoy what's burning just under the surface between us." His words were direct, straight to the point, and filled with desire. A desire I wanted nothing more than to succumb to. But it wouldn't work. I wasn't the woman he wanted. I'd never bow down to him. Never serve in a stereotypical role that I was certain he was used to. And I'd never be the other woman again. Ever. I didn't care how many times he texted, called, left voicemails, or dropped by my house unannounced over the past three months. I can't unsee what I did in that church.

I was able to avoid him all those times, and I'd continue to do so in the future. Eventually he'd realize that I was no longer interested in a romantic relationship. Even though my body didn't agree. Traitor. Arousal was already churning in my gut at the physical sight of him. I soaked in what I could and promptly shook it off. My resolve back intact.

"I'm not the woman for you," I whispered, knowing it was the God's honest truth.

"You're exactly the woman for me. And I'm going to stop at nothing until you feel it too," he whispered, and my resolve quivered but it wasn't easy to forget what I saw three months ago. It was too important. I needed to set the truth free. Tell him exactly what I saw that day that destroyed any hope for more between us.

I closed my eyes and was just about to rebuff him when a series of gunshots rang out.

Both of us twisted around, Omar hooking his arm around my form and pushing me behind his back so his body served as a shield.

I peeked around his massive frame and saw four masked men at the entrance to the building with ginormous guns. Bigger than anything I'd ever seen in real life.

People screamed in terror. Chills raced down my spine and out every nerve ending as the reality of what was happening filtered through my brain.

The bank was being robbed.

I looked at the floor near the entrance to the bank where the men had entered and were currently fanning out. A large white man in a security uniform with blood soaking the front of his chest was down, bleeding out on the white marble floor. He wasn't breathing.

"Nobody move! Everyone, face to the ground. NOW! Or you die just like him," one of the masked men commanded in a no-nonsense tone.

Omar and I fell to the ground and plastered our bellies to the cold marble floor. Fear pumped through my veins hot and heavy as the hairs on the back of my neck rose.

"It's going to be okay, just stay still and be quiet," Omar whispered.

As quick as a flash he slid the bag of what I figured was money across the floor and directly under a table. Maybe the bad guys would find it. Maybe we'd be dead and would never find out.

"You, you, you." One of the men hollered to three cashiers standing behind a glass barrier with their hands up. "Touch an alarm and you all die along with everyone here."

Three sets of faces turned pale, devoid of color as one by one they nodded at the masked man.

Another gunman was rounding up patrons of the bank and pressing them against the wall where you waited for a cashier.

Before I knew what was happening, I was being hauled up by my elbows from behind, my back arching painfully.

I screamed at the top of my lungs as I was yanked uncomfortably to a standing position and held to a stranger's front for only a split second before Omar reacted in a series of combat moves I'd only ever seen in an action movie.

The gunman was down on the ground, his face spewing blood across the white marble tile in a macabre display one might see only in a boxing ring. His gun had clattered to the floor and skidded a distance too far for either of us to reach.

"Don't. Touch. Her." Omar hissed through his teeth, his booted foot pressing on the gunman's neck. Unfortunately, it was a single gunman he disarmed not all four. Before he could react to anything more, there was a new threat behind him dressed from head to toe in black, face covered, holding the barrel of his weapon flush against Omar's head.

"Back off or I splatter your brains all over your girlfriend." He spoke in a calm, emotionless tone that I believed was the absolute truth. This man had no bones about taking a life and probably had countless times before.

"Omar, please." My voice shook.

I watched Omar grit his teeth and lift his hands while taking his foot off the other man. That man jumped up and smashed his fist into Omar's face as I screamed.

Omar took the hit and shook it off like a pro, not showing an ounce of response even though that sucker punch had to hurt.

The man behind Omar shoved at his head and his back with the tip of the gun. "Get against the wall now!" he demanded.

I reached for Omar's hand and interlaced our fingers as we were shoved toward the other customers and pushed roughly to the floor, my knees hitting the marble painfully. Omar tried to grab me and soften the blow, but it was too late. I scrambled forward and pressed my back to the wooden counter. Omar wedged himself half in front of me with an arm around my hips holding me close to his side.

The gunman that Omar had taken to the ground held his weapon on the frightened customers, his blue gaze a fiery brand on me and Omar as if ready to dole out retribution for Omar taking him down.

"Get the cash and let's go!" one of the men yelled.

Sirens were ringing in the distance, but the crew didn't seem to be fazed. Gunmen continued forcing crying cashiers to fill their bags with the money in their drawers. Another gunman ordered entry into the vault. I continued to listen intently, hope filling my veins as the sound of sirens got closer. Salvation only minutes away.

I watched in horror as cop car after cop car flew down the road, sirens screaming as they blazed a trail right by the bank, clearly on a different hunt. My shoulders slumped and desperation sank deep into my heart. The jerk gunman in front of us started to laugh maniacally. Omar wrapped both his arms around me, and I pressed my cheek to his chest, letting the rhythm of his heartbeat soothe the ragged edges of fear just enough to keep the tears at bay.

Which is when another gunshot rang out loud enough to pierce my ear drums and set my teeth chattering. Screams bounced off the walls as the pungent smell of iron filled the air.

Another body dropped to the floor.

Chapter
ONE

Five months before the bank heist...

THE WORLD WAS CRUMBLING DOWN AROUND US ALL AGAIN. A short time ago Simone had survived a tragedy that ended in the loss of my sister Tabby's life and the torture of our sister Addison. Now it seemed as though it was all happening again, only Addison was the target. My family had been through hell and back and it didn't look as though we'd find peace any time soon.

Addy was about to leave for work, and I *needed* to see her face, hold her close before she left. After finding out last night that someone had murdered a woman who looked just like my soul sister, I wasn't taking any chances.

The news reported that the victim had not only been strangled, but she'd also been burned down her forearms the same way Addison had been tortured when she was kidnapped by a madman. We were barely healing from the tragedy Simone had gotten caught up in. She'd been a near-victim of a serial killer who crawled into the back seats of unsuspecting women's cars and strangled them. That monster had taken Addy and Simone, and our dear sister Tabitha had ended up taking a bullet to the chest as she singlehandedly took out the predator. She lost her life saving theirs.

And with this newest threat barreling down on all of us,

I never took for granted when I'd see my sisters of the soul again.

"Wait, wait!" I called out as I dashed down the stairs of Kerrighan House where we were all huddled up, courtesy of the newest threat against Addison.

I crashed into her at the front door, and she wrapped her arms around me, her familiar scent filling my nose and helping to settle the uneasiness swarming my senses.

When I felt connected to my sister, I pulled back and frowned. "I didn't want you to leave without saying goodbye."

Addison cupped my cheek and smiled softly. Before she could say anything, a manly grunt interrupted our moment.

"Oh." Addison lifted her chin to a hulking male who had been standing silent next to us. "This is Omar, your bodyguard. He'll be taking you to and from work today along with Charlie and Gen."

I frowned. "Bodyguards... ¿Qué? ¿Por qué?"

"Blessing's doing." She sighed.

"That girl." I rolled my eyes. The protective side of our sister Blessing had been piqued and there was nothing any of us could say or do when she was in such a state. Blessing could be hard as nails. To an outsider, she was a sleek panther. Driven, focused, set on a path toward achieving nothing but success. When it came to her foster sisters, she was a kitten. Sweet, loving, playful, and devoted to our family. Our Blessing lost her family in such a violent way at the age of only ten, and then losing Tabby, it wasn't surprising that she'd taken our protection to extremes. She protected what she considered hers and we were definitely her sisters by choice, love, and devotion.

The man next to us moved his massive arms behind his

back and held them there. Which is when I truly noticed all that was Omar the bodyguard.

Heat infused my cheeks as I stared slack-jawed at the magnificent man in front of me. He was much larger than me, but most people were. My sisters called me "Sprite" for a reason. Standing at only five foot three, I was several inches shorter than all of them. Standing next to Addy I seemed miniscule in comparison.

Only this man was something else. Muscular biceps stretched the fabric of his black athletic T-shirt to the very limits. The hem dug into his warm brown skin as though trying desperately not to tear against such bulk. My gaze flowed down his wide chest that went into a V-shape at his waist. I could actually see the ridges and indents of what had to be a washboard stomach through the tight fabric. On his lower half he wore black cargo pants and matching boots, but it wasn't the imposing nature of his size or clothing that unnerved me. It was his sleek, gorgeous face. Rigid jawline, slashes for cheekbones, and dark, arching eyebrows that haloed the prettiest deep brown eyes. My own were milk chocolate brown, but his, they were melted brown sugar, searing with intensity as we both stood silent and looked our fill of the other. His hair was cut short at the sides with long black layers slicked back and swept off his face on top. If he were wearing a suit, he'd have no trouble fitting in as a put-together businessman with that chosen hairstyle. His lips looked plush, with a plumper bottom one that would be fun to suck on and snap back playfully.

My blood warmed and seemed to pump faster as the images of touching all that muscle, trailing my fingertips along such golden skin, invaded my mind. The more I took in, the more I realized he was simply the most handsome man I'd ever laid eyes on.

Trying to hide my visceral response, I pushed a lock of unruly curls behind my ear, checked that my flirty sundress wasn't out of place after my dash down the stairs, and slowly looked up into those brown sugar eyes. "Um, *hola*. I'm Liliana."

He smiled, and I swallowed slowly while letting out a breath I'd been holding since this vision of male perfection entered my sphere of recognition.

Addison's voice broke me out of my reverie. "Well, I'm going to leave you two to your introductions. See you later?"

My automatic response was to nod dumbly. "*Sí*. Um, *te quiero*. Be careful and check in. I'll be worried if you don't."

Addison pulled me into her arms once more then kissed my cheek. "I love you too, Sprite. Have a good day with your hunk."

The hammering in my heart slowed to a dull thud as I refocused on the matter at hand. Her words filtered through the fog, and I put my hand to my chest. "He's not my hunk..." I lost my ability to speak further. How dare she put me on the spot! We'd be having a talk when she returned. I narrowed my gaze and was about to come back with a rebuttal when Omar waded in, shocking me to my core.

"I could be," Omar murmured, a sinful grin plastered across his handsome face as he scanned my body from tip to toe.

"What?" My gaze slashed to him.

"Bye!" Addy called out, and then slipped outside where the paparazzi was waiting. The disgusting vultures had been hounding Kerrighan House since the press got wind of the connection the murdered woman had to Addison. That wasn't much of a surprise. This latest horror came on the heels of Simone's high-profile case. She'd been pursued by a serial killer and was rescued by the FBI.

To make matters worse, Simone's biological sister was Sonia Wright-Kerrighan, United States Senator from Illinois. Both Simone and Sonia were our foster sisters, two of the eight girls Mama Kerri took in when circumstances in our childhoods left us in need of loving homes.

Addison was tortured for a short time by Simone's serial killer, but when he was caught, we thought all of this was behind us. The murder of a woman who looked just like Addy, the most well-known plus-sized fashion model in the business, basically meant that we were all screwed, our lives once again turned upside down and inside out.

I gritted my teeth and held out my hand. "Liliana Ramírez-Kerrighan." All of us foster sisters had taken the Kerrighan name along with our given names. It was a sign of loyalty, love, and honor for the woman who raised us and helped shape the women we were today.

Omar took my hand with his beefy one. The instant our palms touched I felt an interlocking sensation that filtered from my hand up my arm to my chest. Rightness. It was an overwhelming feeling of *rightness*. Something my biological mother talked about when I was very small. A flash of memory washed over me at the touch.

"Mi hija, when you find your other half, a sense of rightness will flow through your veins and pierce your heart. Be aware, my Liliana, the simplest touch can change your life."

I pulled my hand back so fast it was as if I'd been burned.

"Omar Alvarado. I'll be guarding your body for the

foreseeable future." His lips split into a sunny smile. "Definitely not a hardship," he added, his gaze all over my form as though it were a caress.

My ire replaced all the sexy shimmers I'd been feeling at his presence and amazing good looks. I put my hands to my hips and glared. "Not exactly professional behavior for a hired bodyguard," I fired back.

His lips twitched. "There is nothing professional about the way my body is responding to you, *mi lirio.*" He stated boldly and matter of fact. Calling me "his lily" as though he had the right.

I let my mouth drop open as shock invaded. "Wow, you are a total player, aren't you?" I pressed my lips together and straightened my spine lifting me to my absolute tallest. Not that it would even scrape against his height. The man had to be close to six feet and I was barefoot.

Omar tilted his head, lifted his hand, and petted his bottom lip with his thumb. That move alone would normally have me fanning my face. Not this time. I was too annoyed by his blatant interest.

"I most definitely want to play with you, *chica.*"

A stiff wind could have plowed me over where I stood. The man was a menace. An infuriatingly sexy menace that I wanted to throttle as much as I wanted to kiss. Stupid hormones. Why did God have to send me the perfect man in looks and stature to watch over me, yet be impossible to handle without wanting to stick him with a knife!

I hissed under my breath, my fury about to hit epic proportions when my sisters Genesis and Charlie bounded down the stairs and stopped in the entryway.

Charlie's red ponytail continued to bounce while Gen was

digging through her briefcase looking for something. Her body was encased in a classy cream-colored business suit as she was a social worker in downtown Chicago and believed in dressing for success. Charlie wore jeans, a baby doll tee, black high-top Converse, and a smile to work. She operated a youth center for wayward kids and runaways who needed a safe place they could hang out, take some classes, and fill their bellies, among a wide variety of other activities.

"We're here. We're here," Charlie gasped a bit out of breath. "Sorry, Lil, we didn't know until twenty minutes ago that we needed to be ready earlier so you wouldn't be late to school."

I glanced down at my watch and noted the time as Omar was introducing himself to my sisters and asking whether or not he'd be escorting Aurora, Genesis's daughter who we called Rory, to school too.

"Rory will be staying here with Mama Kerri," Genesis explained.

"*¡Mierda!* I have to get to first period." I rushed over to where I'd left my leather backpack and slipped into a pair of high-heeled cork wedges that had two gold leather bands across the top of my foot and one slim band around my ankle. I almost always wore heels to school because I hated the fact that most of the teenagers were taller than me. And I was hell on wheels in a pair of heels. I could run in the damn things if needed and would have to prove that fact today in order to be on time for work.

I snapped my fingers. "Come, *¡rápido, rápido!*"

Omar shifted right into business, opening the door as the paparazzi went wild, screaming questions at us like maniacs.

"What do you know about the backseat stranger!"

"What about the new murderer!"

"Is it a copycat killer!"

Omar led the three of us to a blacked-out SUV, shuffling me into the front seat and my sisters into the back.

Thankfully the school wasn't too far from Kerrighan House. Omar barely pulled up to the school when I jumped out the door and ran full tilt into the building, escaping him, my sisters, and all of the unwanted feelings that annoying man brought to the surface.

I exited the building after a long day of teaching children a second language that in most cases, they didn't exactly *want* to learn, but had to in order to receive the foreign language credits they needed for graduation.

Maybe I should switch to college-level? I pondered the option, my head filled with the day's lessons and how some of the kids just couldn't sit still in order to pay attention and learn the content I'd spent hours preparing for them.

Thankfully, all the teenagers had already left school for the day. The second the last bell rang, ending the school day, they were **poof** gone within a blink of an eye. I usually stayed until four-thirty most days because I didn't want to bring my work home if I could avoid it. The two hours after class usually was enough for me to finish grading the previous day's work and plan for the next day's curriculum, but not always. It was true, what they said… A teacher's work was never done. Not until summer break. And we needed that time desperately by May/ June. Two to three months to decompress from nine months of shaping children's minds and behaviors over the course of a school year was no cakewalk. What I wouldn't give for each child's parent or parents to spend a single day teaching in my shoes. One day was all it would take for those people to run screaming. Maybe then we'd get more parents participating and better pay. I snort-laughed at myself while the visual of parents racing from the building with their hands waving in the air as they escaped their own kids spun through my mind.

"Yo!" I heard called out.

I finally looked up and assessed my surroundings, having been lost to my thoughts.

"Not smart, *chica*. You didn't even look around when you exited. Anyone could have assaulted you. Plucked you right up and into a car without anyone being the wiser."

I scowled and pointed up to the cameras on the front of the school, feeling rather triumphant.

"Did cameras stop the last guy from taking Addison or Simone?" He countered with no hint of malice, no I-told-you-so's in his tone. Just facts being stated so that I could come up with my own conclusion.

He had a point, the brute.

"I'll be more careful in the future," I stated feeling properly chastised as he opened the front passenger door of his SUV. Not wanting to sit next to him, I went to the back, jerked open the door, tossed my backpack inside, and climbed into the vehicle, slamming the door once I was in.

Omar chuckled, shut the front passenger door, and made his way around the car to the driver's side. Once he was inside, I pulled out my phone so I didn't have to talk to him or look at his handsome, smug face.

Before long he pulled up to the youth center to pick up Charlie.

He turned around in his seat. "Stay put. Unless you want to follow me in? The glass in the car is bulletproof and I'll lock the doors behind me."

I chanced a glance up. "I'm not a dog you can ask to sit and stay. But I'm good here, outside of your presence, thanks."

"Winning you will be fun, *mi lirio*. I look forward to the chase." He grinned and then exited the vehicle.

"Try not to let the door hit you in the *culo* on your way out! *¡Idiota!*" I huffed, then read the text from Mama Kerri in our family group chat asking one of us to pick up Epsom salts. With all the stress she'd been under between Simone, losing Tabitha, and now Addison being unsafe once again, our Mama deserved a relaxing bath with some healing salts. I'd also scraped the dregs of my mascara this morning and threw the tube out. I needed another.

I spun around and smiled, seeing the Walgreens right across the street. I checked the building in front of me but saw no sign of Charlie and the brute. Charlie was known for dragging her feet. The woman would be late to her own wedding one day.

He told me to stay put. *Like a dog,* I reminded myself.

"Psshh. I'm not going to let *un hombre importante* tell me what to do. When to sit and stay. I'm my own woman." I spoke under my breath and pushed open the car door, looking once more for Charlie and Omar. They were still inside. I could be in and out of Walgreens before they got back.

Feeling mighty proud of myself, I checked both ways for cars and ran across the busy street.

Quick as lightening, I got two tubes of my favorite mascara, a large bag of lavender-scented Epsom salts, a sucker for Rory, and a bag of Skittles for myself.

I couldn't have been more than five minutes. But when I exited the Walgreens, I found Omar leaning against the back of the SUV facing the store with his monster-sized arms crossed over his chest, a big vein protruding down the front of his forehead, and his eyes hidden behind a pair of black sunglasses. His lips were pressed together so tight they were white in color against the brown of that scrumptious skin.

"*¿Qué? What?*" I asked, trying to sound nonchalant, even though I knew he was furious.

His nostrils flared as he moved around the car and opened the front passenger door when he knew I preferred the back so I could be away from him.

"I'll sit in the back, thank you…"

"Get in the car before I put you in the car!" he said through his teeth, leaving the front passenger door wide open.

"How dare you speak to me like that! You're not the boss of me!" I ranted, getting ready for our next verbal fight.

"So help me God, Liliana…Get. In. The. Car." His tone was fire and ice and not meant to be thwarted.

A shiver raced up my spine at the severity of his request. Still feeling put out, I stomped my way to the car, tossed my purchase into the front seat, and hefted myself into the tall vehicle.

Omar watched my every move and shut the door once I was safely inside.

"Um, you're in troubleeee!" Charlie cackled from the back.

"*¡Cállate!*" I spat back at my sister who was smiling so huge she looked like a ray of pure sunshine.

The second Omar got in the car and backed out of his parking spot, he went off.

"Do you have any idea what could have happened to you!" he roared. "A murderer is after your sister. A murderer who cares nothing for human life other than getting whatever sick and twisted fix he gets from killing innocent women."

"I just went to the store across the street!" I tried, but he was having none of it.

"It took Wayne Gilbert Black less than three minutes to get Addison Michaels willingly into his car. Then he kidnapped your sister and tortured her! That is not happening on my watch, *chica*. Not now, not ever. No man will touch one curl on your infuriatingly pretty head!"

"Shoot, girl, he told you." Charlie snickered from the back seat with a wiggle of her neck and shoulders for effect.

I jerked my head around and shot lasers from my eyes.

She put up her hands in a placating gesture. "Sorry, sorry. I'm minding my own business. Just looking out the window. Nothing to see here. Oooh look, pretty trees over there. And a guy with a giant belly washing his car with no shirt on. Nice."

I groaned under my breath. My temperature started to rise as irritation filtered through my blood stream.

"Do you understand why you can't just walk off? Do you? If I hadn't seen you entering the store as we exited, I wouldn't have known where you were." His face was a mask of anger. "I would have alerted every member of my team to your absence. Called the police, your family…" He shook his head and flicked the blinker with more strength than was necessary.

"Okay, okay, I didn't think it was a big deal." I tried to soften my tone but apparently it was the wrong thing to say.

"Big deal? I could have lost my job!" he roared again.

My skin started to prickle and my own frustration rose like a boiling pot that was about to foam over.

"If you had made it clear to me the importance of staying in the car instead of treating me like a pet or small child, maybe I would have listened." I used my best teacher voice possible. "I'm an adult and expect to be treated as such." I positively seethed beneath my skin but did my darndest to keep my cool.

"I didn't think I had to. The dead body with your sister's picture clutched in her hand should have been enough. *¡Dios mío! ¡Mujer me vas a volver loco!*" Omar switched fully into Spanish.

"I'm making you crazy? Maybe you should ask for a different security detail. It seems the feeling is absolutely mutual."

He pulled near the front of the building where Genesis worked and stopped the car.

I watched fascinated as he closed his eyes, his fingers gripping the steering wheel so tight his knuckles were white before he released them and stretched them out as he took a calming breath.

"If you would be so kind to stay in the car, meaning, do not leave the vehicle, I would be grateful. I'd like to keep my job and your safety is my number one priority." He plastered a fake smile to his expression and stared into my eyes. "How's that?"

A jaunty snort filtered from the backseat but Charlie didn't say a word.

I huffed and looked down at my nails as if checking my manicure. "Better. Needs work," I said flippantly, not ready to give up the fight. My temper and stubbornness were legendary and had zero boundaries. I let it fly often. Which is why Mama Kerri always said I was the "Wild Spirit" out of her chicklets. My fire couldn't be contained. She said the man for me wouldn't combat my fire but let it fuel him, not snuff it out.

My comment had him shaking his head and laughing heartily, his body language relaxed once more, his anger gone as quickly as it came, like lighting a candle and blowing it out. The deep timber of his laughter wove through the surface of my skin and dug in, sending tendrils of pleasure through my system.

I clenched my thighs and firmed my jaw. "Don't you have somewhere to be?" I blinked rapidly trying to stave off my body's response.

He inched closer to my face so that his nose was only half a foot away.

"There is no place I'd rather be than sitting in a car sparring with you, *mi lirio,* but I have a job to do. We shall continue this later. Perhaps in a more private setting," he added with a saucy wink.

"What? No! Are you kidding me?" I fired back as he left the car and beeped the locks leaving me dumfounded in my seat.

"Shit, Lil, the sexual tension between you two is straight fire! Are you gonna hit that or what?" Charlie leaned forward between the front seats.

"No!"

She frowned. "Why not? He's hot. He's your type. And he's sooooo into you." She grinned and waggled her eyebrows suggestively.

"He makes me so angry I want to punch him in the face and stick a rolled up dirty sock into his stupid sexy mouth so he will shut up!" I spun in my seat to look her in the face.

She nodded. "I could totally see that, but you also want to bang him. That's obvious to him, and to me."

I gritted my teeth and growled. "The next time you ask

me to help one of your Spanish-speaking kids at the center the answer is no!" Which was a total lie. I'd help any kid in need just like I was helped by Mama Kerri and my sisters of the soul after I lost my parents.

She snort-laughed. "Whatever you say, Sprite."

"Don't call me, Sprite!" I snapped as the back passenger door opened and Genesis entered with a serene smile and tired eyes.

Neither Charlie or I spoke as Omar got settled into the car and I astutely ignored him and his delicious-smelling hint of an earthy cologne.

"What did I miss?" Genesis asked.

Charlie took her hand with hers and stared out the window. "Don't ask, sister. Don't ask."

Chapter
TWO

Two weeks later...
Four and a half months until the bank heist.

EVERY DAY FOR THE NEXT WEEK I WAS DRIVEN TO WORK AND picked up by new nemesis Omar the Ogre as I had dubbed him. Since our battle on day one of his protection, he'd upped his game. And when I say "upped," I mean the man was going all out to not only piss me off, but to ensure I'd rue the day he came into my life.

Basically, Omar was not only the best-looking man on the planet, but he also apparently enjoyed my brand of crazy. It went something like this:

Tuesday, when I purposely planted my booty in the back seat so he couldn't mess with me from the front, he proceeded to engage the child lock mechanism. So, when we got to my work, and I tried desperately to bail out like a bat out of hell, he grinned manically and smoothly took his time exiting the vehicle and walking around it. This had Thing 1 and Thing 2, Genesis and Charlie, cackling like hyenas who were watching the play-by-play as though it were their most favorite television show and they were enjoying every minute.

I growled harshly as Omar smirked and eventually opened my door. Before I could alight from the vehicle like a trapped animal who'd just been uncaged, he coolly grabbed my hand

and held on tight as he walked me to the front entrance of the building.

I'm pretty sure steam was shooting out of my ears while my entire face was enflamed with anger and embarrassment. Not only had my plan been foiled, but we'd made quite the scene. After he walked me to the door, he lifted my hand and kissed the back.

I bared my teeth and hissed.

On a gorgeous, all-white smile, he said loud enough for everyone to hear, "Have a great day at work, *mi lirio*. You look beautiful. See you later." Then he dropped my hand and sauntered back to his ride with a swagger that could not be denied. I couldn't help but watch his tight buns and muscular back move and flex as he left.

All of this to the widening eyes of several of my coworkers who were also arriving, and too many kids to count. A group of girls from my second period class called out, "Woo hoo! Ms. Ramírez has a hot man! *¡Muy caliente!*" If I wasn't so pissed off, I would have been proud of their use of Spanish in such an accurate and casual manner.

Wednesday was no better.

On Wednesday I tried to ignore him completely. This had the adverse effect of him trying harder to pester me. Starting with my hair. As we approached the vehicle, this time I didn't fight him leading me through the throngs of paparazzi to the front passenger seat because I wouldn't be fooled twice by the child lock. The paparazzi scattered and left us when the Kerrighan House door opened across the way as Simone was leaving for work with Jonah.

I groaned under my breath as my door was opened.

However, when I was entering, Omar randomly tugged on my long, braided ponytail.

"What is this? A horse tail?" He flicked it to the side.

I snapped my head around and glared. "It's a hair extension. Don't touch," I warned.

He tipped his head and boldly batted the long braid so that it swished along my back.

"¿Estás loco?" Are you trying to make me hate you! Never." I clenched my teeth. "And I mean never touch a woman's hair."

He ignored my request and ran his hand down the length of the braid. If I was being honest, I enjoyed his touch, but more than that, I liked watching his face as he attempted to figure out the magic behind the fact that I now had long hair instead of the shoulder-length natural curls I wore normally.

"I like this horse-tail style. It gifts me a full view of your pretty face." He ran his fingers from my temple down the side of my face to my jaw then petted my bottom lip with his thumb. I shivered under his touch, which was the opposite of how my brain wanted me to react. Stupid traitorous body.

"Explain this extension? Is it your hair that you can put back on?" he asked again.

I let out a grumble. "¡Dios mío! Have you been living under a rock for the last twenty years?" I nudged him out of my way with my hip and got into the car, completely avoiding my body's reaction to his sweet caress.

His face still held a confused expression as he shut the door, walked around the car, and entered silently. The quiet continued for all of five seconds until we hit the end of the street, when he looked at me, with brows furrowed.

"How does this work? This tail?"

"Lord help, me!" I sighed and closed my eyes while shaking my head.

Genesis and Charlie laughed from the back seat which seemed to be all they'd contribute to our morning ritual of Omar taking us to work each day and picking us up in the afternoon.

"Some women, like me, enjoy having different hairstyles. It makes me feel good. I buy the hair extensions to match my natural hair color and then wear them whenever I want to feel and look different. Today I'm feeling sassy, hence the long braid."

"Hmm, sassy. You are definitely that, *mi lirio. Mi madre* would approve. She wants her son to have a woman who speaks her mind." He grinned.

My chest squeezed and my heart started to pound at the mention of his mother.

"I have zero intention of meeting your mother, so the point is moot." I pulled out my compact from my backpack and touched up my powder.

When we arrived at school, I tried to exit the car quicker than him, but it didn't work. The man might have been as smooth as silk, but he moved as fast as a ninja, appearing at my side before I'd even stepped my high-heeled foot out of the car.

To avoid the handholding he'd forced yesterday, I purposely held onto both the straps of my backpack. This move had Omar placing his hand at my lower back and leading me to the front entrance. The man was incorrigible.

"Looking forward to picking you up later. It's the best part of my day," he stated suavely then gave me one of those hot guy salutes with two fingers flicking away from his forehead while I narrowed my gaze and held my tongue. Several sighs and "how sweets" came from the teachers who had classes near the entrance where I'd been dropped off.

The compliments continued at pickup on Wednesday afternoon along with the dragging me from the building. This was when I came up with a brilliant plan. The only way to get rid of one man was to find myself another. Or at least the illusion of one.

I put my plan into place on Thursday morning as we got into the car. I swiftly pulled out my phone and dialed my sister Sonia. Even though Mama Kerri had requested all of us be at her house for the duration of the danger surrounding Addison, Sonia always left for work at the crack of dawn. The United States Senator took her position seriously and felt it important for her to be at the office before any of her staff, setting a good example for the rest of her team. So, when I called at seven fifteen, she likely had already been at work for the better part of an hour.

"Hey, Lil. What's up?" she asked, her voice sounding winded.

"What are *you* doing?" I returned.

"Picking up coffee at the cart for the executives' meeting me in fifteen minutes, so unfortunately, I don't have a long time to chat."

"No problem. I just wanted to give you the okay to have Quinn set me up on a date with his friend," I announced clearly.

The air in the car instantly turned thick and heated. I pressed the button to roll down the window to let some fresh air in. It didn't help. The air was crackling with an energy I feared. I glanced at Omar as I pressed the phone closer to my ear.

His jaw was set, and those plush lips compressed into a thin line as he stared straight ahead. The muscles in his arms were activated and bulging, the veins rising against his lovely, smooth-looking skin.

"Excuse me? Did I hear you right?" Sonia reiterated.

"*Sí*. I want to go out on a date with Quinn's friend. Tell him he can give Alejandro my number along with the message that I look forward to receiving his call."

That tension in the car hit maximum affect and sweat beaded at my hairline. I shifted my head, pointing my face at the window to allow the cool air to calm any lingering frustration and anxiety I may have had at the very blatant move I was making.

"Uh, I thought you were…seeing the bodyguard? At least that's what Charlie and Genesis claimed. I'm confused."

I looked right at Omar's handsome face that currently looked beyond pissed off, and I smiled. "Nope, I'm not seeing anyone. Charlie and Genesis were misinformed," I stated while turning around and shooting daggers at both women.

Thankfully, they had the smarts to look away and keep their mouths shut. They knew if my temper let loose, no one was safe.

"All right, if you say so. I'll let Quinn know. He'll be happy to set you up. Expect a call soon."

"Excellent. *Gracias, hermana*. Have a good day at work. *Te quiero*."

"Love you too. Bye!" Sonia said before hanging up.

The rest of the ride was made in dead silence. Mission accomplished.

When Omar walked me up to the entrance of my school there was no hand holding. No gentle touch to my lower back. He didn't even look at me, just opened the door and waited until I entered when he turned around and left without a single look back.

As much as I wanted him to lay off, I wasn't prepared for how crummy I felt at losing his attentions. It was such a weird feeling of loss that I couldn't quite wrap my head around the foreign sensation.

By the next day, I was determined to clear the air with Omar because nobody wanted to start and end their day or their weekend with negative energy pressing on them at all sides.

What I didn't expect was for Omar to hold a wicked grudge.

When I tried to chat him up in the car on Friday morning, he simply looked at me and shook his head. The second attempt at conversation had him turning on the radio and outright ignoring me.

"Boom, bitch!" Charlie taunted from the backseat.

"Remember I know where you sleep, *hermana!*" I fired back.

Charlie shrugged as Genesis smiled softly and focused on her phone. Mama Kerry had Rory today which always seemed to put Genesis in a harmonious mood. I think knowing Rory was safe in the arms of her grandmother gave her a sense of peace that was needed right now that things were so up in the air.

"Any news from your end on the case?" I asked Omar.

He couldn't ignore a direct question about our detail. That

would be unprofessional. Not that he'd been all that professional to date.

"No. You need to ask Agent Fontaine or Agent Russell about the status. I have no new information at this time." His words were succinct and sharp as a knife.

"So, business as usual?" I prodded, wanting to smooth things over a little. Even though I pulled out all the stops yesterday regarding the date with Quinn's friend, who had actually called and set up a date for the following Friday, I didn't want any of us to continue to be uncomfortable in Omar's presence.

Instead of responding, he simply nodded.

I rolled my eyes, crossed my arms, and sighed.

The rest of the ride was weighted with an angry energy I couldn't shake.

Did I do the right thing?

With that type of man, so alpha and all about winning me, I couldn't let my guard down, not for a second. Those types wanted the happy little woman, at home, making dinner, taking care of the kids, and doting on them when they got home from work like a good little wifey. Sure, I wanted to do all of those things, but I wanted to do it with a partner. A man who would put as much into a life together as I would. A mate who wouldn't expect me to bow down to his needs while forgoing my own wants and desires. I'd had those types of relationships and they stifled the life right out of me. After José and then Anthony, the last two men I had long-term relationships with that ended horribly after two and three years respectively, I wouldn't put myself into those scenarios again. I'd already wasted five years of my life on alpha males.

Not that it mattered anymore, because Omar the Obstinate was now officially ignoring me.

I decided I didn't care and had finally gotten the response I wanted after a week of his advances.

The plan worked... Maybe a little too well.

After a nice weekend of hanging with my sisters at Kerrighan House, pretending our lives weren't flipped on their asses, I decided to attempt once again to mend the tension between me and Omar. Even though the man treated taking us to and from work as though he were babysitting three children who weren't capable of thinking for themselves. Each day we received the same damn reminders:

Don't leave the building for any reason.

If you have meetings outside of work, contact Holt Security and someone will shadow you.

Do not eat lunch out with your coworkers. They are not trained to protect you.

No, you can't drive your own car to and from work.

That last one straight pissed me off. I was tired of being treated like a helpless child. I wanted my life back. My beautiful blue Chevy was getting absolutely no action and I loved my car. It was my baby. The first brand-new, expensive thing I'd ever been able to buy for myself as an adult. And I couldn't drive her.

The more this situation wore on, after already having dealt with it months ago from Simone's ordeal, I'd had it. Add in the infuriating sexy bodyguard who now ignored me completely since I agreed to a date in his car last week, and you had a woman who had hit her limit.

I was a walking, talking, time bomb, by Wednesday, when our school had a half day that crept up on me, and I was suddenly out of school early and not able to leave as I desired.

I called Holt Security and was immediately connected to Omar.

"Yes, Liliana, how can I help you?" He stated politely, but with a hint of annoyance in his tone.

I bit down on my tongue before I let how I really felt fly. "I forgot that today was a minimum day. I'm already out of school. I'm going to call an Uber or have a friend here take me home. I just wanted you to know..."

"Absolutely not. Stay where you are, inside the building. Do not take a step outside. It's unsafe."

I gritted my teeth and took a slow breath. "Fine. I'll wait for you outside at the curb. A friend will wait with me."

"Are you even listening to me! Stay inside. I'm not going to say it again," he barked.

My temperature rose so quickly at the force within his demand there was no possible way to staunch the flow of anger spewing out of my mouth as I said, "I'm not a child, Omar! Stop treating me like one. I'm a grown adult..."

"Then act like one, Liliana, and wait patiently for me to get there." I swore I heard a short, rough chuckle as he paused. "I sure wish I could see your face right now. You're cute when you're mad." And on that note, he hung up on me in the middle of the conversation.

Cute.

Did that man just call me cute while chastising me?

It took three angry breaths before I dialed up my sister Addison. I was D-O-N-E with Omar and his antics.

"Hey, Liliana. What's shaking, sister? Aren't you supposed to be in school teaching?" Addy asked.

"Minimum day. Which I forgot to mention to my big, stupid brute of a bodyguard, so now I'm stuck waiting *inside* the hallway of the school. Because Omar the Ogre won't let me drive my own stinking car to and from work," I complained, needing to offload on someone who would understand.

"I'm sorry my situation is messing with your life. I know how much this sucks." Her voice was filled with sadness which made me feel like a selfish cow.

Addison had it so much worse. The criminal that was after her was killing innocent women. And here I was griping about a man who infuriated me as much as he turned me on. The last I'd not admit to anyone. I sighed, letting go a little of my anger. "It's fine. All for one, one for all. But I'm done with Omar the Obstinate. Can't I have someone else?"

"Is he really mean to you? Saying things he shouldn't? What?" she asked, real concern coating her tone.

"No. He babies me like I'm a child at my own school! *¡Es ridículo!* I mean, I know that none of us are safe, blah blah, I get that. He takes it to the extreme. Won't even let me stand outside with another teacher to wait for him to arrive."

The fire that was building within me started to blaze again. I wasn't helpless. I could take care of myself.

"Hmm, have you talked to him?" she asked.

Have I talked to him? Was she kidding? Does she even know me!

"¡Por supuesto! ¡Lo hice! ¡Simplemente me ignora!" I went off in Spanish. I could no longer refrain from blowing up, my

36

emotions a tether to my body that had snapped back like a rubber band.

"Sis, you said that in Spanish. Now tell me again after you've taken a breath with me. Okay? Inhale fully and hold it at the top."

I ground down on my teeth and inhaled fully.

"Now release it slowly." She instructed, and I followed along. "Better?"

I did actually feel a little more centered. "*Sí, gracias.* What I was saying was, yes, I told him he was irritating me, and he just ignored me. Which he does, all the time. Again, like I'm *una niña*, a child! He just ignores me and looks at me with that smug smile on his face and tells me I'm cute when I'm mad!" My voice rose as my temper reached boiling.

"Cute?"

"*Sí*, it's infuriating," I spat, thinking about how I was ready to wail on him the moment he arrived if he so much as said a single word more to make me mad.

"Honey, he told you that you were *cute* when you were mad?" She asked again.

"*Sí*, are you listening to me?" What the hell? I pounded on my phone. Was this thing working? *Jesús, María y José.* "Is this thing on?"

Addison's laughter rang through the phone. "Yes, I'm listening. I'm all ears, in fact. And what I'm hearing is that your bodyguard likes you."

"Psshhh." I huffed and shook my head as I paced the front entrance inside the building. "This is simply not true, *mi hermana.*"

She groaned and then called out, "Hey, babe, if a guy tells a woman that she's cute when she's mad, what does that mean? Hold up, Lil, I'm putting you on speaker phone." The sounds of the room entered our call. I could hear pans clanking and what might have been bacon sizzling in the distance. "Okay, Killian, what does it mean?"

I waited not at all patiently, glancing regularly through the glass of the front entrance doors as I listened and kept up my pacing.

"I'm no expert but if it were me, I'd assume that the guy is into the woman. Cute is another way to say pretty in my experience." Killian's manly timber entered the conversation.

"See! That's my take too. Lil, the guy is into you."

"He is not into me!" I groaned and put my hand into the wild curls bouncing all over my bare shoulders. "All you sisters all goo-goo gah-gah for your men think everyone is in love with everyone. *Qué estúpido*. Simone asked me a similar thing yesterday. Aye!" I saw Omar's ride roll up. "And now here he comes, pulling up his blacked-out SUV acting like he's the President of the United States. *Dios mío*. I've got to go." I tugged on the door handle forcibly, jarring my shoulder in the process.

"Wait, wait! You didn't tell me whether or not you're into him too?" she asked on a rush.

"And I'm not going to! *Adiós*," I yelled and hung up.

I was stomping on my super high-heeled sandals when Omar met me in the middle of the walkway. Thankfully school had been out for a while so there wasn't a person in sight.

"I told you to wait inside." He pointed an angry finger at the front door.

"And I told you that I'm not your child, your dog, or your woman!" I pointed right at his chest.

"If you were my woman, I'd have you over my shoulder, my hand burning a fiery imprint on that fine ass, after which I'd drive you home, toss you on the bed, and punish you properly," he growled.

"You did not just say that!" I jerked my head back and put my hands to my hips and let my mouth fly. "I'd like to see you try!" I screeched before planting my hands flat against his massive chest and pushing as hard as I could to get him away from me.

He barely stepped back a foot before he moved at the speed of light, hooking me around the waist and tugging me up and against his chest, my feet dangled in the air as we were face-to-face, nose-to-nose.

"Don't tempt me, *mocosa!*" He grinned and nipped my bottom lip in a quick bite that startled me stupid for a moment. While I was shocked from head to toe, he placed a wet, warm kiss to the lip he bit. "*Lo siento*, babe. It had to be done."

I kicked my feet wildly and he finally let me down. I shoved the hair that fell into my face away and glared. "Don't call me a brat!"

"Don't act like one, and I won't." He moved to reach for me once again, but I backed up several feet.

"Also, don't you kiss me again!" I blurted, not sure if that was my true feelings or not. Either way, if he put that mouth on me again, I'd be toast. I'd melt into a pool of bliss and let him run the show. All he'd have to do was put his mouth on me and I'd do whatever he said. The exact opposite of what I wanted.

He shook his head and grinned. "Now *that* I can't promise, *mi lirio*. Now come on, I need to get you home, I was in the middle of a case I have to get back to." He reached for the backpack I dropped when I shoved him.

Thinking back, I actually couldn't believe I shoved him. I'd not done that before, but the man made me so crazy, I lost myself to the moment.

Omar hooked my bag over one shoulder and grabbed my hand, interlacing our fingers. He tightened his hand on mine as he looked across the street, then sidestepped, putting his body in front of mine.

All thoughts of our argument, the bite, the kiss, him bodily lifting me up, disappeared as a sliver of fear sizzled down my spine and I pressed my hands to his back and peeked around his frame.

"What do you see?" I whispered.

"Someone is taking pictures of us." His voice was tight, devoid of emotion and the earlier playful way he fought with me.

I followed his gaze and a man wearing all black, running away from us, disappeared around the corner of the building across the street cutting off our view.

"Let's go." He grabbed my hand again and led me to the front seat. I didn't say a word just followed along and scrambled into the SUV as quickly as possible.

When he got in the car I asked, "Do you think it's the, uh, bad guy?"

His lips pursed into a scowl as he surveyed the entire area.

"I don't know. Maybe. Then again it could have been the paparazzi. Have you seen them follow you to school before?"

I shook my head. "They haven't really been that interested in me. Mostly Simone, Addy, and Sonia. Besides, I wouldn't think paparazzi would hang around a high school, would they?"

He shrugged and maneuvered his vehicle the opposite way from the direction we usually took home. "I don't know. Paparazzi are unpredictable but not as unpredictable as a murdering lunatic. Do you now see why I get so frustrated with you, Liliana? I want you safe. Always. Everything I've done this past week and a half is to ensure your safety and well-being, and you've fought me the entire way." His tone held a level of exasperation that had me evaluating my behavior. I was being a brat.

"I'm sorry." I swallowed down the fear and stupidity that had been fueling my fire earlier. "I really am. Seeing that man, knowing he was taking our picture scares me. Now I'm super freaked out." Tears filled my eyes, and I crossed my arms over my chest and ran my hands up and down my biceps trying to warm my suddenly chilled skin.

Omar reached out and took my hand. He lifted it to his mouth and kissed the back of my fingers. "I'm going to keep you safe. Trust me."

I licked my lips and nodded. "I trust you."

Chapter
THREE

The following Saturday...
Just over four months until the bank heist.

THE REST OF THE WEEKDAY WITH OMAR HAD COME AND GONE without problem. I gave in. Completely. After seeing that man taking my picture from across the street, I fell right into line. Omar continued to tease me but kept it mostly platonic. This confused me as much as it gave me relief.

On one hand, he was still the overprotective, overbearing brute who brought me and my sisters to work and told us what to do and what not to do. On the other hand, he was tasked with keeping us safe and he was taking that role seriously. Maybe too seriously, but what did I know. I'd already lost Tabitha to a madman, and almost lost Simone and Addy at the same time. Now Addy was in danger again, as were the rest of us.

The press and FBI were leaning toward the latest suspect being a copycat serial killer. Someone who was infatuated with the Backseat Stranger, as opposed to the theory that had been suggested that the person was the partner of said criminal. Both sisters claimed they'd never seen another man when they'd been kidnapped by Wayne Gilbert Black. Which meant we were dealing with an unknown individual

42

who had already killed three women that looked shockingly like my sister Addison.

I rubbed my arms up and down to ward off the goosebumps as I stared at the miniscule wardrobe I'd brought to Kerrighan House.

"Girl, you stare a hole through those clothes any harder there won't be nuthin' left." Blessing snickered as she sauntered in looking like a million dollars. She wore a sleek, form-fitting ribbed tank dress that fell to mid-thigh and hugged her curves. She'd paired it with multiple long gold necklaces, a fat gold bangle wrapped around her bicep, and flirty gold shoes. Against her shimmery ebony skin, she looked amazing. Then again, Blessing always looked incredible. She was a fashion designer who was becoming more well known by the day. Her designs were already in fancy boutiques all over the world. With the project she had going with Addison right now, her designs could end up in big department stores such as Macy's and Nordstrom.

"I want to sparkle like you." I gestured up and down to her gorgeous outfit.

She cocked an eyebrow. "Why?"

I rolled my eyes. "You mean you don't already know?" I huffed. "I'm going on a blind date with Alejandro, the friend of Quinn's that he's been dying to set me up with."

Blessing tipped her head to the side and frowned. "I thought you were hot for the bodyguard?"

I clenched my teeth and flapped my arms against my sides. "Why does everyone keep saying that! I'm not hot for Omar."

"But he's your type. As in, look up a picture of Liliana's perfect male in the book, and there you'd find a smiling picture of the bodyguard. Why are you fighting it?"

I sighed and dropped onto my childhood bed and lie flat next to where she sat; her arms braced behind her holding her upright. Her dark curls were let out in a natural beautiful 'fro that complimented her stunning features and piercing coal-black eyes.

"Let's count the ways," I announced, sarcasm coating my words. "He's too bossy." I put a finger down. "Too manly." Second finger down. "Too protective." Third finger down. "Too alpha, and aggressive." I tightened my hand into a fist and was about to continue with reason number six that I shouldn't lust after the hunky bodyguard when Blessing cut in.

"He put his hands on you?" Her voice rose and her chin lifted.

I shook my head. "No. Well, technically yeah. The other day he lifted me up and off my feet, plastering me to his chest. Then he proceeded to bite my lip then kiss it better. In front of the school. All in order to shut me up! Can you believe that?"

She shook her head. "Damn, sis." She waved a hand in front of her face as though she were fanning herself. "That's a sexy as hell move. What did you do?"

I narrowed my gaze. "I kicked my feet wildly until he released me."

She rolled her eyes and sighed dramatically. "Of course you did."

"What do you mean, of course I did? He bodily lifted me up and off my feet in the middle of an argument and kissed me quiet!"

Blessing grinned wide then started laughing. "The visual is awesome," she blurted.

"I hate you."

She snorted and then put her hand to just above my knee and squeezed. "You hate that you love me so much!"

I sat up abruptly then got up and stood before my closet. One at a time I assessed what I had available then slapped the hanger to the side in annoyance as I rejected each item. "Are you going to help me get ready for my date or what?"

"Uh, am I your sister who lives and breathes fashion? Pah-leese. Move!" She stood on her slinky heels and looked through everything. "Where's he taking you?"

"Bavette's Steakhouse or something like that."

Her eyebrows rose. "Fancy. Boy's about to spend some dough on you to-night, sis. Average steak price there is around seventy-five dollars."

"*¿En serio?* Why would he spend that kind of money on a first date? And a blind one at that. He doesn't even know what I look like?"

She chortled. "I'm sure Quinn showed him a picture of you. And girl, aside from that temper, you are a damn fine catch."

I glared and put my hands to my hips. "I don't have a temper, *hermana*. I'm fiery. Passionate. All Latinas are."

Secretly, I think Omar enjoyed my fire. Liked being called out on his alpha-overprotective nature. My guess is he appreciated the art of arguing with passion. My mother and father used to argue and bicker every day. Usually about me, my school, food, their friends and anything in between. They were one another's everything.

My mother used to tell me, *"If you're going to do things right, mi hija, you do it with your whole heart. With all your passion built up inside of you. Then you will always get the best results."*

I lived by that motto my entire life and wasn't about to change it for a man.

"You can't say all Latinas are fiery just like you."

I stared at her for a long minute. "Do you know any that are not passionate by nature?"

She twisted her lips and then shook her head. "Fine. You win."

I lifted my chest and shook my *chichis*. "I need your help for a date with Omar, so come on. Do your thing," I pointed at my miserable clothing options.

"Lil, did you just hear what you said? You just said you were going out on a date with *Omar*. I thought the guy you were dating tonight was named Alejandro? Hmm?" She pressed her lips together and shook her head slowly. "Telling. Very telling." She clicked her tongue, making her point clear.

"Please, just pick me out something to wear." I grumbled miserably.

She scowled and pulled out a T-shirt dress I'd bought at Target last summer. "I'm going to need some scissors." She held out her hand and fluttered her fingers.

"You're gonna cut up my dress?" I asked.

"Anything I do to this garment will be an improvement. Do you doubt my skills?" She looked at me as though I'd grown two heads.

I widened my eyes and backed up slowly with my hands out in front of me. "I'll get the scissors."

"That's what I thought you said." She winked, and I ran out of my room to the shared bathroom and grabbed the scissors Mama Kerri kept in there. While she was responsible for eight growing girls, she was constantly cutting our hair for us. Just one of our foster mother's many talents.

I brought back the scissors and watched in fascinated horror as Blessing didn't even flinch. She just went straight to town cutting vertical slits up each side of the dress to allow for maximum leg appeal. Then she cut a wide boat-neck type of opening across the entire top so that the dress would automatically hang off the shoulders. She continued cutting here and there, adding details I couldn't even believe she'd managed with just a pair of scissors, such as a bunch of narrow slits in the back that she somehow stretched into an accordion affect that ran down my spine to the very top of my *culo*.

"Strip," she said, and tossed me the dress.

I shoved off my clothes and stood naked as the day I was born while she foraged through my lingerie drawer and pulled out a matching strapless beige bra and panty set.

Once I'd put on the undergarments, I put the dress over my head, and it floated into place. She tugged here and there, adjusting the fabric until the top cut just across the fleshy top of my breasts. The slits in the side crawled up to mid-thigh but weren't too revealing. The dress was a bit slouchy as she plucked at the center, seeming irritated.

"You don't like?" I asked.

She stepped back looked at the outfit then went to my closet and pulled out a nude pair of sky-high heels.

"Put these on," she instructed.

I did as asked, then spun around in a circle.

"Your ass looks fiiiinnnne in that." She smacked said ass and watched my bubble butt bounce. "The slits are tight. My problem is the waist is too damn loose. You've got a bangin' body, Sprite. Let's show it off. Give those boys a show." Then she snapped her fingers and left the room in a hurry. "Be right back!"

I checked out my form in the large mirror that hung on the wall.

The teal fabric looked awesome against my light brown skin. A ton of lotion would make my skin shine like a star. I too plucked at the fabric at the waist that hung in a way that was kind of frumpy.

"Turn around," Blessing said. She entered with a gold and nude woven leather belt that had some dangling leather fringe at the ends. She tied it around my waist and then forced the top half of the dress to lay in a position that was far more flattening. "Perfect! Now we just need some bracelets. I say leave the neck open. Like an invitation." She waggled her brows and pursed her lips playfully.

I looked back in the mirror and the belt did the trick. I looked sexy and fashionable. "Omar won't know what hit him!" I smirked as Blessing covered her mouth and laughed so hard she had to sit down. "¡Mierda! I meant Alejandro! I did. I really did." I frowned and rubbed the back of my neck with my hand.

"Sure, you did, Sprite. You're gonna have to get that under control or you'll be saying the wrong name on your date tonight." She waggled her finger in an admonishing manner.

"Ugh. My life sucks." I groaned and sat on the bed next to her.

"Everyone's life sucks sometimes. It's part of living. If everything was peaches and cream all the time, we'd never know true joy and happiness. You remember that and you'll be just fine." She stood up, cupped both of my cheeks, leaned forward, and kissed my forehead. "Don't forget the shimmer and gold bangles. It will complete the look." She smiled and left me alone to finish getting ready.

"I meant, Alejandro," I mumbled to myself. "At least I think I did."

◎

When I came down the stairs to leave for my date, Omar was leaning near the door at the front entrance. His gaze slid from my high heels up and over my dress to my face, and then down in a slow gander, before looking back up again.

"Jesús mujer, estás impresionante," he said in an awe-filled rumble, which loosely translated to, "Jesus woman, you're stunning."

I licked my bottom lip and then bit down on it as I took in his hulking form wearing all black. Which on a daily basis wasn't unusual since he wore a lot of cargos and tight fitted tees or weather wicking type athletic shirts that plastered to his body like a second skin. This time for some reason he was in black slacks, a shimmery silver dress shirt and a black sports coat that had to be tailored to fit his form. It was that perfect.

"Why are you so dressed up?" I asked without thinking.

He squinted and smirked. "Maybe I have a date later."

I put my hand to my heart as the surprise of that response hit my chest and a tightening pressure gripped the tender muscle in what felt like a vice lock. I inhaled and exhaled slowly, attempting to get rid of the offensive response my body had to his reply.

"You're perfectly capable of seeing anyone you want. Why would I care?" I lifted my chest feeling pride at my quick retort.

"And therein lies the problem, *chica*. I *want* you to care, and you don't." He stomped over to me and took my hand. "Are you ready or what?"

I nodded numbly, feeling the intense *rightness* once again of our palms touching and our fingers interlacing. I closed my eyes and allowed him to lead me to the front door as I already had my clutch in my other hand.

The entire way into downtown Chicago, Omar kept flicking his gaze to my bare legs, especially when I'd recross them. He'd shake his head and grind his teeth, his jaw looking as hard as granite as he murmured something under his breath that I couldn't quite hear.

When we arrived at the restaurant, I moved to get out of the car, and he snapped at me.

"Wait! I take you in under my protection. I assess your safety." He growled the words between his teeth. "Then and only then, will I leave you to your...date." He sneered on the last word.

Uneasiness rolled through my form but instead of firing shots back like I normally would, I waited, breathed through my irritation, and nodded. The last thing I wanted was a scene, especially in front of a swanky restaurant. Also, the odds were good that Alejandro was probably waiting for me inside as that's what we'd planned. I couldn't let him pick me up at Kerrighan House because of the paparazzi and the intrigue surrounding me and my family, but I was committed to living my life the best I could even under the circumstances. And dating was a normal thing people did.

Omar exited the car, rebuttoned his suit jacket, and scanned the street before opening my door. Then he shut it, beeped the locks, and led me into the restaurant.

As we approached, a pretty blonde host lifted her head from a podium that held a reservation book.

"Welcome to Bavette's. Do you have a reservation?" she asked.

"I'm meeting a friend here, Alejandro Garcia."

The woman smiled and nodded. "Yes, he's arrived. I'm sorry there are only seating for two, was the party meant for three?" she queried politely.

"No, uh…"

"We'll find him, and I'll be on my way. *Gracias.*" Omar tugged me towards the entrance of the restaurant leading me with a hand at my waist.

The room was dark with mood lighting around each table, giving it a speakeasy-type feel. Red leather booths and warm rich wood made the space inviting and comfortable.

As I scanned the room, I noted a lone table with seating for two. An attractive Hispanic man tilted his head at seeing me, his frown apparent when he took in the brute leading me toward the table.

Alejandro stood. "Liliana?" he questioned.

We had to look like quite the picture. Me arriving with a well-dressed, good-looking man to a date with another well-dressed, good-looking man.

"Hi, Alejandro. Thank you for meeting me here. This is Omar." I hooked a thumb over my shoulder. "He's leaving now," I announced.

"Omar?" Alejandro questioned.

"I guard her body," Omar stated flatly.

"Um, okay. That's interesting?" Alejandro rubbed his hands together as if he were uncomfortable.

Who wouldn't be? I was uncomfortable meeting Alejandro with the brute standing over my shoulder.

"Not so interesting if you attempt to put hands on her body. Then I'd have to…"

"Enough!" I blurted, cutting off Omar's threat while noticing we now had everyone's attention in this section of the dining area. My cheeks heated to what I'm sure was a bright cherry red as I put my hands up and patted Omar's chest. "Thank you for ensuring my safety. As you can see, we're fine."

"I'll be waiting just outside for you to finish. Call when you're done." Omar scowled.

"What? No. Alejandro can take me home." I looked at my date who nodded. "See, he agreed."

Omar shook his head. "No can do, *mi lirio*. I protect you. I guard that beautiful body." His gaze scanned my frame once more. "And I like my job, *chica*. A lot." His pretty eyes shifted to my hair, my cheeks, and down to my lips before he licked his own. My heart pounded so hard in my chest I could barely breathe. And then he smirked, noticing my hot-guy stupor. "Text me," he said, and left me standing there stunned.

I smiled and turned to Alejandro. "I'm really sorry about that. He's a little protective."

"A little." He laughed and came to my chair and held it out so that I could sit.

I did so and then he helped me push it in before taking one of his own. The waiter who was likely watching the entire scene play-by-play approached within moments.

"Shall I take your drink order?"

Alejandro said, "Wine menu please," at the same time I blurted out, "Tequila, stat!"

My eyes widened when I realized what I'd said. "I mean, wine would be lovely." I gritted my teeth and tried to calm my racing heart, still smarting about Omar's behavior this evening.

The man had gotten under my skin tonight. Usually when a man did that, I kicked his ass from here to Timbuktu and then fell into bed with him.

For a minute the vision of Omar stripping off my dress, plumping my breasts, and kissing me silly swirled around my mind. I squeezed my legs together and opened my eyes to find Alejandro staring at me serenely. The man was attractive in that clean-cut, businessman on the town way that I'd not dated in the past. I liked my men a little rough around the edges, which is also why I have two failed serious relationships.

Men like Alejandro were the nice guys. The men you could trust with your heart. I could just tell from looking at the kindness pouring from the man in front of me that he'd be gentle. Sweet. Compassionate. Supportive. All the things a woman wanted in a mate.

Not an over-protective alpha male who clearly had a jealous nature, on top of being a mama's boy who dirty-talked his way into women's panties. All while looking at said woman as though she made the sun rise while wearing a symbol of his faith.

I needed a male who spent more time behind the computer than at the gym.

A man who didn't infuriate and challenge me at every turn.

"Liliana?" Alejandro broke me out of my revelry.

"I'm sorry. What did you say?"

"I said you look really pretty tonight," he reiterated, which in my head was a far cry from the *"Jesus woman, you're stunning,"* compliment Omar had given me earlier.

Liliana. Stop comparing. Alejandro and Omar are not in competition. You are on a date with Alejandro.

After my little pep talk, I smiled. "Thank you. You also look handsome," I offered because he did in fact look good. The man would not go long without female companionship. The only question after tonight…would that companion be me in the future?

There was only one way to find out.

Settling my spine, I sat straighter in my chair as the waiter brought over a bottle of expensive red wine.

"Wine?" Alejandro offered.

"Yes, please." I leaned forward and gave my full attention to my date, determined to give this experience a real chance. Even with the knowledge that the other man who carried way too much real estate in my head was waiting just outside.

Chapter
FOUR

Same day...
Just over four months until the bank heist.

OUR ENTREES HAD JUST BEEN SERVED, MINE A SIZZLING filet mignon with some type of bearnaise sauce atop what looked to be the fluffiest mashed potatoes ever. Thin baby carrots decorated one half of the small potato mountain in an artful display that was not only beautiful, but mouthwatering.

"Bon appetite," Alejandro said with a smile.

I cut into the perfectly cooked steak and plopped a bite into my mouth, humming as the juices and mixture of flavors burst on my tongue.

"Delicious!" I preened, surprised at how pleasant the evening had been so far.

Once Omar the Ogre disappeared, it was easier to focus on the handsome man before me. Alejandro had kind hazel eyes, unlike the striking deep brown ones Omar was blessed with, which made it hard to look away. Alejandro smiled often and his voice carried a harmonious timber that was soft, mesmerizing. Nothing like the fiery barbs and guttural growls I received daily from my bodyguard.

"So, may I ask why you need a bodyguard?" Alejandro spoke for the first time since our meals were delivered.

I pursed my lips. "Didn't Quinn tell you about what's going on? I mean, it's all over the news," I hedged, then ate a forkful of the potatoes.

Alejandro frowned. "I thought the danger surrounded the Senator, her sister, and that fashion model." He squinted and glanced out the window nearest us. "Michaels." He pointed his fork in my direction. "Addison Michaels."

I grinned. "They're both my sisters."

His brows rose. "Really? Different fathers or mothers, I presume. They look nothing like you." He frowned. "They look nothing like one another. The Senator is…"

"Blonde, blue eyed, and angelic looking. I know, I know. I've been hearing it all my life. Sonia is funny like that. She doesn't know her own beauty. And Simone is her blood relation. Addison and I, along with Blessing, Genesis, Charlie, and Tabby are foster sisters. We were raised with one another most of our lives by our foster mother Aurora Kerrighan who owns Kerrighan House."

He jerked his head back. "I'm sorry, I hadn't realized that you were related to the Senator in such a way. Quinn only told me had a mutual friend he'd like to introduce me to. I had no idea you were connected to all of this." He waved his hand in the air between us then reached out over the table and took mine in his.

"Lo siento, cariño. You must be terrified." He squeezed my hand. "And here you are. Out on a date with me. Such strength," he murmured, awe coating his tone.

I held his hand and squeezed it back, frowning at the lack of connection the touch proved but appreciating that his desire was to console me, not ask a million questions like I expected him to. Maybe this guy could be something. If I tried harder to make a connection, perhaps my body would get on board with more? I was just about to respond when the air behind me sizzled, prickingly the hairs on the back of my neck.

The sound of a man clearing his throat came from close behind me right before I felt a warmth at the nape of my neck. I closed my eyes as the sensation tore through my form like a sizzling bolt of electricity. I snapped my hand back from Alejandro and leaned toward the touch at my nape. I looked up and my gaze set on Omar's, seeing a swirling vortex of heat, passion, and *need*?

"We have to go. I'm sorry to interrupt you. There has been a development in the case." His voice was sharpened steel, cutting and decisive.

I frowned. "Are my sisters okay? Addy?" I stood up abruptly and my entire body started to shake, worry and fear making my heart pound. Those women meant everything to me. They were my family, the only things in the world I truly loved. After losing my parents at nine, I didn't think I would ever have that feeling of belonging again, but that all changed when I showed up at Kerrighan House. Almost twenty years later, our bond was deep. Maybe even deeper than blood because it was earned. Given over time through shared experiences, love, and most recently… loss.

Remembering putting Tabby to rest in the cold, hard, ground only a couple months ago was still devasting. I couldn't do it again. Lose another member of my family like I had my mother, father, and my soul sister Tabby.

He shook his head and cupped my neck at both sides, comforting me while keeping me focused. He leaned forward so we were eye-to-eye. "They are all fine. I'm taking you to them at Kerrighan House. We will meet the FBI there."

My heart relaxed a little and it was as if Omar and I were in our own little world. My focus entirely on his face, needing to see the truth in his words with my own eyes. The restaurant, everything else slipped away as I hung on every word.

"*Mi lirio*, I was asked to pull you and Blessing from your respective locations immediately and bring you back to the house." His words were lighter but still held that edge I didn't think he'd ever be able to soften.

"*¿Por qué?*" I asked why.

"I don't know," he stated flatly. He glanced to the side, and I followed his gaze to a stunned Alejandro who stood with a deep frown marring his once handsome face. Now he just looked frustrated.

I watched as Omar's jaw firmed and his lips gave the slightest hint of a smile.

Bastard.

He was enjoying this. Pulling me from a date he didn't want me to have in the first place. My cheeks heated as I put one hand to my hip the other, I swiped away his overtly familiar hold on my neck.

"If it wasn't serious, you could have waited," I attempted.

Omar shook his head. "I'm sorry, *chica*. Blessing was already delivered here by another member of our team who was closer to her location but had another assignment to get back to. She's in the car. I tried to give you more time, but we must go."

Right as he said that, his pocked buzzed. He pulled out his phone and his jaw turned to granite. "We go. Now." He hooked my elbow as if to pull me away without any further discussion.

I yanked hard enough to rattle my teeth. "What happened now?"

"The FBI will explain further," he said but his gaze swept the restaurant as though looking for any possible threat. "We need to get to Blessing. I do not like her waiting in the car."

Thinking about Blessing in the car all alone in the event someone was after us right this moment, I nodded and turned to my date. "I'm…I'm sorry. I'll call you?" I said with a note of sadness as well as defeat.

His face was set in a sour, pinched expression. "Take your time on that," he stated with zero emotion.

I closed my eyes and nodded. Another one bit the dust.

An anger so intense filtered through my veins making my blood boil as I spun on my heel and allowed Omar to take my hand.

The instant sizzle of recognition and rightness heated my palm, pissing me off even more.

When I was led into the back seat of the car, Blessing pulled me into a tight hug.

"What the hell is going on?" Blessing asked Omar.

He shook his head. "You get your information from the FBI," was his simple retort.

I sent laser beams at the back of his head. "What do you know that you're not telling us?" I demanded.

It didn't work. He shook his head and focused on the road. If he wouldn't tell us, but it was big enough to immediately bring all of the sisters back home at the drop of a hat, it had to be serious.

59

I leaned against Blessing as the city skyline disappeared behind us heading toward Oak Park where our home was.

As we pulled up there were fewer paparazzi than there had been the last two months, which made me think that whatever it was, it couldn't possibly be that serious. Through the front windshield I could see there were two additional vehicles lined up in front of the one we were in.

Owner of the security company Sylvester Holt alighted from the car directly in front of us and then he opened the back door from which Charlie, Genesis, and Rory exited. I noted Killian and Addison were exiting a Jeep in front of that, a huge animal barking from the back. Jonah and Ryan had parked across the street and ran to meet up with us, bracketing the worst of the paparazzi as Omar opened the door and Blessing got out. He offered his hand for me to exit the vehicle and I pushed it away. Too scared, annoyed, and freaked out to reach for that all too comforting touch.

I let all my upset rise to the surface. I felt like a ticking timebomb ready to explode. I stomped towards my sister Addy, lifted my hand, and pointed as I scowled.

"*Más vale que sea bueno, hermana,* or you are on my shit list!" I blurted, which translated to 'This better be good, sister,' then I hooked a thumb toward the man who stood behind me. "He pulled me out of a blind date! One I was actually enjoying." I barely refrained from stamping my foot against the hard concrete to make my point.

"I'm sorry, Lil, it couldn't be helped this time." She frowned deeply and I felt like *una cabrona.* An asshole. She didn't want to disrupt our lives any more than Simone did when the Backseat Strangler came after her.

I let my shoulders drop as my ire cooled down. Blessing

came up from behind me and locked arms with me as we followed Genesis toward the house. She held Rory protectively against her chest, keeping Rory's face out of the view of the cameras. Charlie followed at her back. All of the men—Jonah, Ryan, Killian, Holt, and Omar—surrounded us in a circle of protection until the entire group was able to enter Kerrighan House safely.

Sonia was already in the living room pacing, phone to her ear. Simone was sitting cross-legged playing a game on her phone, her dog Amber, calmly at her feet.

Each of my sisters made their way to a position on the couch as Mama Kerri entered with a tea kettle and enough cups to serve us all, setting the tray down on the big wooden oval coffee table. Next to the kettle was an enormous batch of fresh peanut butter cookies. Mama's philosophy had always been tea and cookies made everything better.

Killian noted something about bringing his dog inside as Sonia ended her call. Immediately after hanging up, she set those startling Caribbean-blue eyes directly on Ryan. "So, what in the world was so damn important that all of us had to race here immediately?" Sonia was using her Big-Sister-Now-Senator voice that made me proud. She was the hardest working woman I knew. Her mind worked a mile a minute and she always gave the most thoughtful advice. There was a good reason she'd been elected Senator. While pride filled me, Sonia's body language made it clear she'd be getting answers ASAP. This was thwarted by Killian bringing in his giant Rottweiler Brutus.

We each greeted the beautiful dog and watched while he and Amber got to know one another before they were taken out back by Agent Ryan Russell, Jonah's partner in the FBI.

Then Addy and the rest of us hugged warmly and settled in positions around the couch waiting to hear why we were all there.

Jonah stood up in front of the group. "I'm going to preface this by saying I apologize for the theatrics of pulling you out of work and social engagements." Jonah's gaze softened when it hit mine.

I nodded and waited but couldn't help but chance a glance at Omar. His lips twitched at the comment from Jonah, but he stayed silent and out of the way, leaning against the wall near the stairs in between the kitchen. Holt stood next to him. Both men extremely imposing with the large and in charge vibe oozing from their corner of the room.

"I received a call today from Addison. The security guard in their building was tased while they were walking Brutus. The other one doing rounds was stuck in the neck with a sedative and pulled into the bushes in the back of the building."

Several replies came at once.

"Oh no."

"Is he okay?"

"Was it the killer?"

"He's fine. Looks like the taser triggered a small heart attack or stroke because we found him unconscious. Again, he's doing well. I got confirmation of that fact on the ride over."

"Well at least that's good news," Mama Kerri said sweetly.

"It is. However, when Fitz and Addy headed back into the loft, dozens of images of all of you were taped on the door." Fitz was the name that Killian preferred his friends use.

"No! My children?" Mama Kerri gasped.

"Are you fucking serious?" Charlie cursed.

"I cannot believe this crap!" Simone grouched.

"Oh, hell no," Blessing added with extreme attitude.

Gen, Sonia, Addison, and I stayed silent as the reality of his statement filtered through. The man taking pictures. I looked at Omar whose intense gaze was on me. His lips curled into a snarl as though he wanted to leave immediately and go on a hunting expedition to find the threat and remove it.

Part of me liked his desire to protect me and my family as much as the liberated female within me wanted to rally against those feelings.

"There were many pictures of all of you. And Gen, I don't want to frighten you any more than you probably are, but there were individual pictures of Rory at her daycare, playing with toys outside."

That's when Blessing stood up from the couch. "Fuck that noise! This is not happening! No way. No how." Blessing's perfectly dark skin reddened at her cheeks, her chin, and down her neck. She was beyond angry. When she got like this, very little would pull her back from the ledge. As one of the family members with a legendary temper, I appreciated this side of her and would support it fully. Whatever it took to keep our family safe was the plan I was on board with. Even if it meant I'd have to deal with Omar for a lot longer.

Genesis reached out and tugged Blessing back into a seated position. "It's okay. Let's just hear what Jonah has to say."

Mama Kerri kept one hand at her mouth and the other over her heart. The reality that she didn't chastise us for cursing could only prove how deeply affected she was by the information.

Jonah sighed. "Every picture of Addison has a big red heart placed over her face as though the attacker is obsessed with her. This proves our theory that the ultimate target is

Addison. However, the fact that all of your pictures were taken makes it noticeably clear that this animal will go after any one of you to get to his prize."

I closed my eyes and inhaled slow and deep, trying desperately to be strong for the rest of my family... but I was scared. Scared right down to the tip of my toes that this psycho would get Addy or one of us and someone else would die. We'd lost Tabby just under three months ago. Three short months and another member of my family was being targeted.

When would it end? When could we live our lives in peace? Hadn't we all been through enough? We'd lost our given families at super young ages, become a new family that was built on love, trust, and loyalty and all of it was at risk... again.

Jonah continued to provide specifics about how each woman had been killed, the details making my stomach swirl with nausea. I pushed it down. Determined to be strong. This worked until Jonah explained that there was a message that was hidden within all of our pictures that was left on Killian's door to taunt Addy.

"What note?" Simone piped up.

"In the center of all the pictures was a note saying, *You can run but you can't hide,*" Jonah explained.

"*Jesús, María, y José.*" I gasped and put my hands together to pray. There was nothing left to do. This situation needed God. Only He could provide the FBI with the tools and skills to find this abomination. In the meantime, I also prayed that He would guide the eyes, hands, and hearts of the security team in order to help keep us all safe. Then I prayed for each and every one of the women who'd been killed and pleaded with our Father to protect my sisters. Last, I prayed to my parents, that they would help keep me strong through this unforeseen battle.

I focused back on the conversation at hand when my sister Addy stated, "Maybe I could offer myself up as bait?"

"Hell no!" Blessing cursed at the same time as Killian said, "Fuck, no!"

Addison jerked her hand from Killian's. "Why not? It's a good idea," she continued, and my fear doubled.

No, no, no. Please God do not let her offer herself as bait. Simone wanted to do that, and Tabby ended up dead and the two of them kidnapped.

My head started to throb as the ramification of what she'd suggested sank deep into my soul. I could lose her. Beautiful Addison. Sweet, kind, loving, and one of the best people in the world. This criminal could take her away from us all.

"Addy, baby, I know you want to help but…" Killian tried to reach out to my sister, but she yanked it back and stood, facing all of us on the couch.

"No! You guys have no idea how this feels. Wondering every single day when the other shoe is going to drop. When he'll get his window to kill another woman for the sole unfortunate reason that she resembles me? Or on the off chance that he decides to really get to me by kidnapping one of my sisters like the last guy did. Losing another one of my family members."

My heart cracked wide open, and sadness poured in. This was breaking my sister into a million pieces, and I physically ached for her.

"Chicklet, we understand how scary this is…" Mama Kerri interrupted but Addy wasn't having it.

"No! You. Do. Not. Yes, all of us lost Tabby. The only

one who understands is Simone." She stared at her until she pulled her face away from Sonia's hold, tears tracking down her cheeks. Simone had been through hell with Addy. Spent the better part of two months in therapy and climbing into bed with Addy at Kerrighan House in order to escape the fear of Addison's loss, to make sure she was still alive and breathing. None of us talked about Simone's behavior because we all knew it was part of her healing process. She'd randomly call me while I was at work even though she knew I was teaching and couldn't pick up the phone. If I didn't answer the first time, she'd blow up my phone for the next couple hours. When I would call back, she'd apologize profusely, but I knew that she wasn't yet well from her experience and it would take time for her to realize we were all safe and alive. And here we were, again. In danger.

"I get it," Simone whispered.

"And you told me you were willing to give yourself up, so I'd be safe. Isn't that right?" Addison's gaze was focused, daring her to say otherwise.

"Yes. I would have done anything to ensure all of you were safe," Simone admitted.

"Including giving yourself up as bait?" Addy pressed.

She nodded.

Addy flung out her arm and let it fall back to my side. "And there you go." She looked at every last one of us before stopping on Genesis. "And what if it was Rory? She's the most helpless. If I were a super twisted bad guy, which person would be the easiest to snatch? Hmm?"

Genesis couldn't hold back the tears as they fell down her cheeks silently.

Addy was not done. If the circumstances were different,

I'd be cheering her on for her ability to rally and confront us all. She was taking hold of her life and her future with a vengeance I'd not seen before. Pride swelled up my chest.

Jonah shifted to stand behind Addy where he put a hand to her shoulder. "Sweetheart, we get what's at stake. I'll think about it. Talk it over with Ryan and the Chief. See if they have any ideas or thoughts. If we run out of leads and they agree this plan has merit, we'll be in touch."

She spun around, her anger a living thing between them. "You do that. And soon. There is no time to waste. We've all been through enough. I want this over. I want to live my life again. I want to tell my man that I love him and not have to be whisked away to my mother's house to inform my sisters that they are all in mortal danger."

¡Dios mío! Addison had fallen in love! All of the anger, fear, anxiety, and stress poured out of the room as we all stared in shock at Addison. I held my hands up to my chest, a giant smile stretching so wide across my cheeks it almost hurt.

Golden happiness, pure and alive, filled the room.

Blessing went over to Addy with her arms out. "Baby girl, you're in love?" She pulled our sister into her arms, Addison's thick brown-reddish hair falling all over Blessing's shoulders.

"And all I want to do is bring my boyfriend to my mother's house and have dinner and let all of you rip on him all the time…like you do Jonah, but noooooooooo! We're in Hell. Again!" The upset took her once more, and the tears fell as she sobbed.

Blessing moved her into Mama Kerri's arms, where she plastered her face against her chest and her shoulders heaved with tortured cries.

"This has been a lot. For all of us, but more so on you and

Simone. You've been through the wringer, my sweet chicklet, but I can't help but say I'm happy that through it all you've found love," Mama cooed to our sister. "There is no better thing in the world than finding your soul mate. You know I had mine far too short but the love we had will last me a lifetime. I want that for all of my girls." Mama Kerri's gaze settled on me as she patted Addy's hair and then eased her into another pair of strong arms.

Killian's.

Mama came over to me and took my hand. "Come on, guys. Let's go check on Ryan and the dogs and figure out what we're going to do about dinner," she announced.

As we were about to pass by Omar and Holt, she stopped in front of them both. "Thank you for keeping my girls safe."

Holt nodded and rumbled, "My job, ma'am."

Omar focused on me. "It's my honor to watch over your daughter." His heated gaze ran all over my face as if to seek out my emotions after the difficult discussion we'd just had.

"Don't you mean my daughters, plural?" she reiterated with a quirk of her lips.

His gaze went back to her, he frowned, and then looked from her to me and then back. "I'm sorry? I do not understand. I take personal responsibility for Liliana's safety and well-being." He lifted his chest as though puffed with pride.

I rolled my eyes.

"And you've done a great job…" Mama continued.

"Mama," I gritted through my teeth in warning.

She patted my forearm. "Just a moment chicklet. I'm talking to the handsome young man. You have also been watching over Genesis and Charlie, no?"

His gaze widened and he cleared his throat before looking

at me, down at the floor and then back to her. *"Sí, señora,"* he noted at a lower tone than before.

Mama Kerri smiled wide, reached out, and traced her fingers over the gold cross that hung over the top of his shirt. "And you speak Spanish too. How lovely. Seems like you and my Liliana have much in common."

I groaned under my breath. Mama Kerri wanted all of us married and churning out *los bebés* as quickly as we could. Although she greatly seemed to enjoy raising a house full of girls that turned into women, she beamed brighter than the sun as Rory's grandmother, *la abuela*. That joy was unmatched.

"I am very fond of *su lirio* and agree that we have much in common." He smirked, his gaze lifting to mine while I glared and shook my head, unable to believe he was trying to win my mother to his side of thinking, especially now when everything was so crazy.

"Smitten with my girl. I like this. I see good things in the future." Mama hummed.

Omar grinned wide. *"Sí,* me too."

With that, I tugged on Mama Kerri's arm, prepared to drag her to the kitchen.

"Chicklet, what on Earth has you moving like your feet are on fire?" she noted with exasperation.

"Do not get any ideas about me and Omar, Mama. That man infuriates me!"

"Oh? Do tell?" Her cheeks were pink, and her blue-green eyes were shining with renewed excitement.

"I do not have any interest in the bodyguard." I slumped against the kitchen counter. "I'm not going to get into a relationship with Omar," I announced loudly so my sisters who were already in the kitchen as well as any male ears that may have been eavesdropping could hear.

"Wow. Such dramatics for a woman who is not interested in someone." Mama Kerri fluttered to the fridge and opened the door. "I guess time will tell, won't it?"

I clenched my teeth and looked at each one of my sisters who were pretending to mill about and not pay attention when I knew each and every one of them were. "Yes, time will tell," I stated sharply, heading to the backdoor so I could escape all the gossip. With a parting shot at the group that was laughing behind my back, I said, "Time will tell all of you that you are out of your minds!"

I'd show them *dramatics*, I thought on a grin, and slammed the door for good measure.

The sound of several different bouts of laughter bursting through the door did not help my mood.

Chapter
FIVE

Two weeks later…
Three and a half months until the bank heist.

L IVING WITH MY MOTHER AND SISTERS AFTER A DECADE OF NOT sharing the same space was the purest form of torture and a test of my sanity. Mostly because it seemed as if everyone slipped into their childhood roles. Sonia and Genesis were the oldest and used that few years' age difference in order to boss the rest of us around. Being naturally fiery, I was constantly going head-to-head with them. Usually starting first thing in the morning while the seven of us girls, not including Mama or little Rory, ran around the house like chickens with our heads cut off getting ready for the workday, fighting for the small upstairs bathroom.

Thankfully, since the pictures of Rory had been taken by the perpetrator, Genesis had taken her out of daycare and kept her within the safety of Mama Kerri, Aunt Delores, and the sisterhood. However, pictures of us were still being taken by the killer and left for Addison to find daily. Last week we'd celebrated Rory's 4th birthday which was a much-needed respite from the hell we were going through. Except, right on the heels of that happy time, the next day we received a photo of Addison sitting in one of our backyard chairs having her morning coffee, Rory snuggling in her lap.

The man who wanted my sister dead had gotten close. Too close.

That single image obliterated our small sphere of safety at Kerrighan House. Shit hit the fan.

Sonia was in contact with her protection detail and her team were in regular communication with the FBI team assigned the case alongside Jonah and Ryan.

Simone was a ball of nerves and tears.

Genesis was past worried and headed straight into terrified. Her daughter was the most important thing to not only her, but every last one of us. We'd gladly take any pain, any hurt, to ensure little Rory was protected.

Charlie started carrying weapons to protect herself. A dagger she hooked on her jeans, visible at all times. She swore she wouldn't ever get caught unaware, even though we each had a personal bodyguard who never left our sides if we weren't at work protected by security, or safely tucked inside Kerrighan House where Jonah, Ryan, and Killian were now sleeping alongside all the rest of us.

Blessing threatened to contact her father who was a member of the South Side Players gang. The entire reason she'd been put into foster care was because her mother was murdered in gang retaliation against her father. From what I understood, Blessing still had a strained relationship with her father but wouldn't talk to any of us about it, other than Mama Kerri. I figured if Mama Kerri was keeping an eye on that situation, it was in my best interest not to get involved.

Basically, the situation with the copycat killer or whatever he was, had hit peak temperature. Now Addison was going to offer herself up as bait in order to catch a madman. The plan was for Addy to dress in a slinky getup and pretend to get drunk while out dancing with her friends. Those friends would actually be undercover female FBI agents, and there would be a team of additional agents watching. They'd be ready to attack if she was approached, a kidnapping was attempted, or anything else that would make a normal woman's teeth chatter in fear.

Not Addy. No, my sister decided she was going to kick ass at this bait thing and catch a serial killer. All of this without any of us at her side. I bristled, angry that there was nothing I could do to help other than take my turn watching Rory today, keeping her and myself out of the line of danger. Genesis had to work while my school had the day off. The administration were meeting for the end of the year planning as there was only a month left of school.

While I pulled my hair up into a ponytail, my niece raced into my room.

"*¡Tia Lily!*" She screeched her face sporting a huge smile as she clamped her arms around my legs and pressed her face to my belly. "Where we goin' today?" she asked while bouncing against my body.

I grinned and cupped her cheeks, dipping down to kiss her forehead. "How about if you guess where we're going when I tell you hints in Spanish, and I'll add ice cream to the plan?"

"*¡Si, si, si!* I'm good at Spanish," she boasted.

I laughed and gestured for her to sit down on my bed while I finished my hair. I encircled my ponytail with one of those bun tools and spun my hair around it, shifting the hair to cover up the sponge circle, and tucking bobby pins in around the swirl. The overall affect was a perfect, large bun at the crown of my head. Think JLo bun. Sleek and sexy while still seeming a little innocent.

"Wow, will you do my hair too?" She fluffed her naturally curly black hair.

"You want the same as Auntie, ¿cielo?"

She nodded avidly, pulled her legs up on the bed and sat cross-legged.

I finished my bun and then grabbed a smaller bun tool and had her turn around on the bed so that I could do her hair while standing. "Okay, the place we are going has muchos árboles."

"Trees!" She hollered as though I wasn't right behind her doing her hair.

"Many trees. Muy bien."

"Good!" She translated my compliment, and I chuckled.

"The place we're going has los osos," I pronounced it slowly.

"Bears!" She shimmied on the bed as I pulled her hair into a ponytail.

"¡Sí! You are excellent at Spanish. Do you know where we're going yet?"

"Trees and bears?" She frowned and lifted her head, so she was looking at me upside down with those unusually colored eyes. They were a mixture of every facet of gold I'd ever seen. Genesis referred to them as amber. Whatever they were, the child was by far the most beautiful I'd ever seen. Then again, I was absolutely biased. "The woods?" Those pretty eyes widened.

I shook my head with a laugh. "Nope! You need more hints," I eased her head back down so I could add the bun making a hair circle. "The place we are going also has tigres, delfines, y el león."

"Tigers, I don't know that middle one, and lions!" She tapped on her fingers. "I know what it is!"

"Be still, cielo, or I'll mess up your pretty hair."

Her small form went stock still as I finished covering the bun maker and pinning her hair in place. When I was done, I spritzed her hair with product making sure the flyaways right at her hairline were slicked down much like my own.

She spun around on the bed, stood up, and wrapped her arms around my neck. "We're going to the zoo!" Her voice was filled with excitement as she jumped up and down on the bed.

I laughed, hooked her around the waist, and swung her around. "*Sí, mi niña bonita*. How does that sound?" I asked setting her back down.

"Awesome!" She shouted so loud I backed up a couple steps.

I grabbed my heart necklace with my parents' pictures in it and latched it around my neck.

"Ooh, I want jewels!" She pointed to my necklace with the most sweet and innocent expression of awe on her face. I swear I'd give that girl the world on a silver platter. All she had to do was ask nicely and keep being so wonderfully sweet and loving.

I grabbed one of my pieces of costume jewelry that wasn't expensive. It had big golden circles that I often wore with my gold hoops. It hung in two strands, one shorter than the other. Her eyes bulged as I brought the necklace to her chest and latched it at the neck.

She caressed the necklace as though it were pure gold and she'd been graced with a fortune. "I'm gonna need my queen crown!" She gulped and then dashed out of the room. The second I put on my heeled suede ankle boots, she was back handing me the crown to add to her outfit. I pinned the crown that Blessing had spoiled her with on her birthday.

"Let's get going, *mi niña*!" I spun her around and patted her on the booty to get moving.

As we passed Blessing in the hall, she looked at my hair and outfit then my niece's matching look with the added crown. "Going regal today, your majesty?"

"I'm the Queen," Rory claimed immediately.

"You sure are, girl. Don't ever forget it." She tapped Rory's chin and blew her a kiss. Rory pretended to catch it and smack it on her cheek with a giggle.

"Be safe with yo' man, out there in the open, yeah?" Blessing warned.

I groaned. "He is not my man."

"He will be, mark my words, Sprite. One day, you will be on that man's arm and loving every second of it," she said as she fiddled with her hair in the mirror.

"*¡Cállate!* I highly doubt that!" I fired back, irritated they wouldn't let the Omar thing go. Every last one of them were on my back about us hooking up.

"Um! That's a bad word, Auntie!" Rory pointed at me accusingly.

"I shouldn't have taught you Spanish!" I narrowed my gaze playfully and swiftly tickled her sides. "You're too smart!"

She giggled wildly. "That's what Momma says!" She finished with a cheesy grin that made me love her even more.

"Have fun!" Blessing called out as I led my niece down the stairs to where I knew Omar was waiting. The man was never late. Not even a minute. Every day he waited on me to finish getting ready before he drove me to work or wherever it was I needed to go. My poor Chevy hadn't had any action in weeks other than one of the guys turning it on and driving it for me so that my baby didn't get all gunked up or whatever it was that happened to vehicles that sat too long without being driven.

We entered the kitchen and Genesis was chatting with Mama Kerri and Omar who held a cup of coffee in his hand. The giant yellow mug looked tiny in his big paw.

"Momma! *Tía* Lily is taking me to the zoo!" she cried out and bum-rushed her mother.

She lifted her daughter and put her on the counter. "And I see you are ready for it. Crown, jewels, and beautiful hair." She nuzzled her daughter's cheek.

"I'm pretty like *tía* Lily."

Genesis gaze landed on me softly. "Yes, you absolutely are as pretty as your auntie. Omar, do you think the zoo is a safe location?" she asked.

He nodded. "I do. Very public, a lot of people around. And I will be vigilant with *mi lirio y tu hija.*"

I rolled my eyes and groaned under my breath. "Can we go already?"

Genesis said goodbye to her daughter as I hugged Mama Kerri and then switched places with Gen.

Omar led us over to the front door where he paused with his hand on top of Rory's head then he crouched low to be at her level.

"Ms. Rory, I'm going to be watching out for you and your *tía* today at the zoo. You cannot run away from me or your *tía*. It is very important. We are trusting you to be a very good girl. Can you promise to stay with me and your *tía* at all times?"

Her eyes widened as she nodded. "I will be good, *tío* Omar," she said, calling him *Uncle* Omar. I ground down on my teeth but didn't say a word.

"May I hold you while we walk through the cameras?"

She nodded and he scooped her up, put her on his hip, and

then opened the door. Within seconds he had his free hand in mine and was leading us to the blacked-out SUV.

"Look, look, look Auntie!" Rory pointed at the elephant munching on a watermelon in the distance. "He eats watermelon! That's so funny!" She laughed boisterously.

I stood at her back and Omar stood at mine. If you looked at the three of us, you'd think we were a small family. A married couple taking their daughter to the zoo. I pushed away the sweet vision because it was not meant to be and I shouldn't get any ideas.

Omar's hand curled around my hip as he pressed his front to my back and his chin to my shoulder. "I'm enjoying this day, *chica*. Your niece is *preciosa. Mi madre* will love meeting her."

I turned my head and bumped his body, leaning against the entirety of his tightly packed muscles from chest to knees. "Don't say things like that. You'll put ideas in her head."

He hummed against my neck, and it sent a river of pleasurable tingles through my system. "I have many ideas about you and me in my head, *mi lirio,* but none of them are acceptable for little ears."

I gasped and pushed back so that he had to back up. "Seriously? You're incorrigible."

Omar smiled wide, which made him ridiculously handsome.

"And stop smiling like that at me!" I snapped, not exactly sure why I was so pissed all of a sudden. The man brought out such a feisty side of me. Not that it was hard, I mean I'm known for being the spirited one at Kerrighan House, but this man had my hackles up and my engine revving at top speed.

That time he smirked. "Why do you fight me?"

I huffed and grabbed Rory's hand leading her to the giraffe exhibit.

"Do you remember what these are called in Spanish, *¿cielo?*" I called her sweetheart because she absolutely was a sweet little girl.

Rory pursed her lips and put her finger to her chin. Her crown was tilted but she looked so dang cute I left it sideways.

"Rah-fah?" she enunciated.

"Almost, baby. It's hee-rah-fah. *Jirafa,*" I clarified.

Rory repeated it, and I clapped for her as she stood on the bottom metal rung of the enclosure and stared into the exhibit.

"I don't fight you," I tossed over my shoulder in answer to Omar's last question. "I respond to your ridiculous innuendos and off-handed remarks."

"It's not innuendo, Liliana. I fully plan on making you mine. Whatever it takes, woman. And I'm a patient man." He stood about five feet away from Rory and leaned a hip on the metal railing and scanned the crowd before his gaze settled on mine once more. One thing I could say about Omar, he was damn good at his job. He hadn't let anyone get close to us, nor had either one of us been out of his sight for even a minute.

"I don't get it. Why?" I lowered my voice and stepped closer so that Rory couldn't hear, but we were still close to her at all times. "I tell you I'm not interested, and you push harder. Most men would have given up already."

He pursed his lips. "I'm not most men, *chica.*"

No, he was not.

He was insanely good-looking, hard-working, with the prettiest brown eyes I could stare into for hours and not get tired. Not to mention that body, my goodness. I dreamt of touching those abdominal ridges at night. Running my tongue over the square shape of each pec, digging my fingers into the thick muscle at his back. All of these things were incredible, but with the good there was always bad. Which was what I intended to focus on.

"Yeah, you're bossy, hard-headed, irritating, pushy, over-confident, and a know-it-all who likes to press my buttons!" My ire started to rise out of nowhere like it usually did when in Omar's presence.

That sinful smile of his came out again.

"I'm also faithful, respectful, appreciate what a good woman can bring to my life, secure financially, fit as a fiddle, a family man, and I'd never lay a hand on a woman even under the threat of death," he stated.

I swallowed at the dry, scratchy feeling that crept into my throat. The man would be my undoing. I just knew it. I was going to fall into the same pattern as I did with the last two men who promised to be good men but turned out to be losers.

"Look, I don't mean to be harsh, but I've been told that story before. Twice in fact and it wasn't a good tale then. It's not something I'm going to fall for a third time." I let out a long, tired sigh.

He pushed off the railing, looked around, made sure Rory was in his line of sight, and then cupped my cheek. "I told you I'm not most men. When I have something special, I cherish it. I don't ruin it by looking for other shiny things. I hold on to what I have, protect it, love it, and keep it safe. That's the kind of man I am. The kind of man you can count on. Give me a chance, and you'll find out." He glanced at Rory who was busy talking to another little girl standing on the railing next to her.

Omar leaned closer to my face, his warm breath smelled of coffee and mint. A delectable pairing for sure.

He ran his thumb over the plump part of my bottom lip. "What I wouldn't give to show you physically how I worship things that are precious to me."

"Omar," I gasped, arousal swirling through my veins at his touch and nearness.

He leaned forward and took my mouth in the softest featherlight kiss. I could barely feel his touch as I closed my eyes. His free hand curled around my waist and pressed me against his strong form. He sucked my bottom lip into his mouth, and I whimpered. The sound must have broken him from the sizzling heat and heady air surrounding us because before we could take it further, he pushed back, holding me at arm's length. His eyes went straight to Rory to check on her and then he closed them for a brief second as though in relief.

"You move me to do things I wouldn't normally do, *Liliana*. We need time. The two of us. Alone. When I'm not working and there is no present threat."

I shook off the kiss haze that had settled over me and put my fingers to my lips, feeling his kiss a second time.

"Um, yeah." I went over to Rory. "Want to go check out the water animals?" I asked her.

"*¡Tortugas!*" She hollered turtles.

I laughed and took hold of her hand. Omar surprised me by going to her other side and reaching out. She looked up at him, smiled, and took his hand.

"I like you, *tío* Omar." She swung their arms happily.

He grinned huge at her, then looked at me with a wink. "I like you too, Rory."

"Do you like *tortugas*?" she added.

"Who doesn't like *tortugas*?"

"I know, right?" she said with awe in her tone. "They're so cool. Did you know they carry their house everywhere they go!"

He chuckled. "They must be very strong."

Rory nodded with enthusiasm.

While they chatted, I let my mind wander. And the more I watched him and my niece interact the more I got sucked into the net that was Omar Alvarado. The man was beyond charming, and he seemed to like kids as much as I did.

I was so screwed.

Maybe I should just jump in with both feet and no life vest? Let it all go. Give this connection between us a real chance?

God, what should I do? I prayed silently.

My cell phone buzzed in my back pocket, and I pulled it out to check the display. It was a text. From Mama Kerri.

Hope you guys are having a good time. Please check in.

Mama Kerri. That's it. I needed to talk it through with Mama Kerri when no one else was around and I could tell her all my fears and concerns about jumping into a relationship again with a man like Omar. She may have wanted grandbabies and for all of us to find happiness with mates of our own, but more than that, she didn't want her girls doing anything that made them feel uncomfortable or uncertain.

Right now, I had no idea what to think, say, or do.

I needed my mother.

Chapter
SIX

The next day...
Three and a half months until the bank heist.

THE NEXT DAY WAS THE SECOND PLANNED STING OPERATION with my soul sister and the FBI. Addy was putting herself up as bait at the club Simone used to work at called Tracks, located in downtown Chicago. The rest of us sisters were nervous wrecks waiting back at Kerrighan House.

I decided the best way to keep my mind off Addison and the peril surrounding all of us was to stay home with my family and cook up a big Mexican meal. Much to my annoyance, Omar and another security guard from Holt Security were manning the house while Jonah and Ryan were on the sting operation. Killian would not stay back another night while his woman was in potential danger. That meant he was hiding out somewhere in the club watching all the drama unfold.

All of us sisters would have gone to the club and played the part with Addy, but the FBI emphatically denied that request. In the end it made sense because with all of us there, not only were there more potential targets, but it would also be harder for them to keep an eye on Addison, who was the primary target. And the ultimate goal was for the serial killer to go after her so the FBI could nab him.

I groaned as I watched Omar through the kitchen window

walk the backyard perimeter, prodding the heavy foliage, looking for scary guys with cameras, I assumed.

Mama Kerri came up from behind and wrapped her arms around me, snuggling her chin against my neck. "How's my chicklet doing?"

I sighed deeply, allowing her energy to wrap around me like a warm blanket. Her essence always brought peace and serenity, especially during a time of such great uncertainty.

"Frustrated. Worried. Scared. You name it, Mama, I'm feeling it."

She hummed against my cheek and kissed my temple. "We are all worried about Addison, but Jonah, Ryan and Killian would die before they let anything happen to her. We have to trust them." She backed away and went to the stove where I was simmering the carnitas, refried beans, and rice.

"Smells delicious as always. Now tell me what's on your mind that's not related to Addison, hmm? Perhaps the fella you're watching like a hawk outside in the yard?"

I spun around and pursed my lips while she simply smiled and went to the stove to stir the beans that were heating, before I mashed them into the perfect texture.

She wiggled the fingers of one hand in a gimmie gesture. "Tell Mama what's got you twisted up inside?"

I sighed and leaned against the counter with my arms crossed over my chest.

"Well, Omar is actively pursuing me in a romantic way," I admitted.

She nodded. "Mm hmm. And?"

"And I'm not sure that I should give in to his advances. He's very forward much like José and Anthony were. I've already been down that road with a Mexican-American macho man. Twice, as you know. Jose expected me to move in, clean his house, have his babies, and dote on him like a maid, as you may recall."

Mama scrunched up her nose. "I do. I clearly remember thanking God the day you kicked him to the curb."

"And Anthony had a woman on the side. He was actively in a relationship with both of us and I'd met his *family*! He thought because he'd brought me around them that I was ultimately 'the one' but he had to be sure. And Omar already talks about bringing me to meet his mother and we're not even dating!"

Mama Kerri's brows rose. "Really? That is rather soon."

"I know! I mean, we would need to go on a proper date and be in a relationship before I'd be willing to meet any of his family members."

She nodded. "That makes good sense. But what you're not saying is how I can hear it in your voice that you *want* to do those things with Omar. Go out on a date, meet his mother. Never once have you said you're uninterested in the man."

I frowned. "Well, I mean, it's not that I'm not interested or that I am interested. I don't even know what I am. It's confusing, Mama."

"I know, chicklet. Matters of the heart always are." She stirred the rice as I picked up the masher for the beans and got to mashing.

"Has Omar asked you out?" she asked.

"*Si*..."

"And you've said no, I take it?"

I shrugged one shoulder. "*Si*."

"Are you not attracted to him?" She smiled in that knowing way.

"Mama, you'd have to be dead not to be attracted to Omar." I cocked an eyebrow. "That man is beautiful from his black combat boots to his slick hair."

She chuckled. "This is true. All those muscles. And here I thought your sisters' men were fit, but your Omar takes the cake, doesn't he?"

Immediately my mind went to the way Omar's shirts hugged his muscular form as though they were a second skin. "He definitely takes care of his body. *Muy caliente.*" I waved at my suddenly heated face. "And the brief kisses he's given me..."

"Whoa, whoa, whoa. You've said nothing about kissing? You've kissed him?" She held the rice spoon aloft so that rice was falling off and splatting into the pan below.

I adjusted her hand that held the spoon, and she shook off her surprise, jumping back into action stirring the rice.

"*¡Sí!* And keep it quiet. I don't want the others to know, or they'll never let me live it down. And they weren't exactly full kisses. More like a couple pecks than anything else. Still, they were pretty nice, and I wouldn't be against more."

She nodded. "Do you want my advice, sweetheart?"

"*Sí*, I do. I'm so confused, and I don't know what to do."

Mama Kerri turned the burners to super low and then we both put down our cooking utensils. Then she took my hands within both of hers.

"Liliana, you have so much love to give this world. I would hate to see you ignore a man that you have chemistry with, simply because you've been hurt before. Omar is not José nor Anthony. Will he hurt you? I hope not, chicklet. But love is always a gamble. You have to take the good with the bad and learn from those lessons. Don't use them to barricade your heart or you'll be alone forever." She lifted her hand and cupped my cheek. "I do not want that life for you, Liliana. You deserve a man who will love and cherish you the way my husband did before he passed." Her eyes filled with tears. They always did when she spoke of her lost love.

"I want what you had, Mama. I really do. But I'm scared." My voice cracked at the admission.

"If you think Omar might have this kind of potential in your life, you owe it to yourself to give it a shot. Don't punish him for the sins of others. That's not right, and not how I raised you, chicklet."

"So, you're saying I should go on a date with him?" I hedged, my heart beating hard in my chest.

She cocked her head to the side and patted my cheek lovingly. "I'm saying you need to follow your heart and not let fear get in the way of something that might be amazing. You'll regret it if you do."

"*Gracias, mamá. Te amo.*" I thanked her and told her that I loved her.

"I love you too, chicklet. Do you feel better?" She rubbed a comforting hand up and down my back, soothing me from the swirling confusing thoughts running rampant in my mind.

I nodded. "I do. I'm going to tell Omar tomorrow that I'll go out with him." I lifted my chin and stood up straighter. Once I've made a decision, I don't go back on it. If there was something between Omar and me that could be real, I owed it to myself to push old fears aside and live in the present.

She smiled wide. "I'm proud of you."

I grinned. "I'm proud of me too! Now let's feed *la familia!*"

Our world imploded once again the next night. Not only did Addison end up in what amounted to a bar fight, breaking her wrist in the process, but the serial killer ended up being an individual who worked at the hospital. Both Killian and Sylvester Holt were drugged, but ultimately Jonah and Ryan were true to their words. The FBI took down the killer as he was trying to kidnap Addison from the hospital. Now it was time for the healing process to start once again.

After Addison was released from the hospital and safely back at her man's loft, the rest of us were finally able to go back to our homes.

I watched Omar's profile as he maneuvered through the streets of my neighborhood. His jaw was pronounced and strong, a light dusting of scruff had appeared over the past twenty-four hours. The man hadn't stopped or slept. I knew he had to be tired keeping track of all of us sisters, taking us to the hospital to see Addy and then finally to Kerrighan House. I had planned on getting an Uber to take me back to my apartment, but he wouldn't have it. He said I was his responsibility until I was safely behind closed doors. This ended up being a relief because the presence of the paparazzi was a thousand times larger when we returned from the hospital. Picture after picture of our tired, teary faces had been taken once word got out.

I'd given up caring what the public saw when they took my photograph. The entire situation from Simone to Addy had been going on for what felt like months on end. I was exhausted. Drained emotionally, physically, and spiritually. I needed my bed. A huge breakfast in the morning and God. First place I planned to go tomorrow was my church. Not only did I want to connect with God, but I also needed fellowship.

Needed to feel God's presence running through my veins as I sat in one of His houses. There was no feeling like it. Being in a place where everyone felt the holy spirt at the same time was beyond moving. It was soul-filling.

"You know, you really didn't have to take me home. I could have taken Mama Kerri's car and had one of the girls follow me."

Omar's jaw was clenched when he grumbled low under his breath. "Told you, *Liliana*. You are my charge. And after all that has happened, can you just humor me. Give me this one thing. I need to see you safely in your home. I need it." His nostrils flared as though he were feeling something more than what he was saying.

I nodded. "Okay. Thank you, Omar. Really. Thank you for taking care of me through this..." I sighed. "I don't even know what to call it. Situation. Tragedy. Horror. You name it, whatever it is, you were there for me and kept me safe." I reached out my hand and curled it around his forearm. "I mean it. Thank you."

"All I want is to keep you safe, Liliana." His words were a dagger to the heart, dipped in such sincerity my eyes filled with unshed tears.

I licked my lips and shifted my gaze from his searingly pretty eyes. I couldn't continue to look into them without crying. My emotions were raw jagged edges and I was splitting at the seams. The last thing I needed was a full emotional breakdown in front of a man like Omar. I wanted this man to see me as strong, capable, independent woman. Not a damsel in distress who needed to be saved.

Omar rubbed the back of his neck. "This situation has been hard on all of you. Hell, chica, it's been rough on the security team too. Not knowing when *el cabrón* was going to strike. Every member of the team started to doubt that we'd be able to protect you."

My spine straightened, the hairs on my arm prickling as I turned in my seat. "Really? You all seemed so confident with those take no shit attitudes."

He chuckled dryly. "*Sí, mi lirio*. Except we are all human. As the days dragged on and more people died, more pictures kept arriving…" He shook his head and sighed long and hard as though he were releasing a bucketload of stress he'd been holding in. "Let's just say we were worried."

I reached for his hand and squeezed it tight. "Well, none of you showed it. We have that to thank you for too because if you big guys had showed your fear and concern, the rest of us would have been a mess."

He lifted our clasped hands and pressed the back of mine to his cheek where he rubbed his scruff against it. A shiver of excitement raced down my arm and spine at the action.

I swallowed the sudden dryness in my throat and realized that we were at my building. "Um, we're here."

He nodded, turned off the car and there we both sat for a full minute not saying anything, just letting the quiet of the vehicle penetrate the air between us as it started to get thick and heady.

Omar curved his shoulders to the side, and I turned to match his position. He reached out and palmed the back of my neck where he used his leverage to bring me closer to him. When we were only half a foot apart, he rested his forehead to mine.

"I'm grateful to God and the FBI that you and your family are safe, Liliana."

I licked my lips and bit down on the bottom one.

"Once things are settled and you've had some time to get back to your normal, I want to take you out. On a date. And I want you to say yes. You can no longer deny the chemistry between us. I know you feel it." His breath was warm against my face as we stayed pressed together.

"I do feel it," I finally admitted.

"Good. I'm going to call you in the next week or so. Give you some time with your family first. Your sisters are going to need you during this healing process. Then, all bets are off."

I giggled like a silly girl at his demand-slash-warning, when in reality I was just an oversensitized adult woman who had been put through the wringer these past weeks and had no more power left in her to fight his advances. Besides, I'd already decided to give him a shot. He wasn't lying. I felt the chemistry, the attraction, the relentless desire that poured between us. I'd just been pushing men away for so long it became my go-to, my safety net for protecting myself and my heart.

"I'll answer your call," I whispered.

He grinned, eased back, and stared into my eyes. Time stopped. The air in the car buzzed but everything else just slipped away. Inch by inch, his face got closer until he kissed me. Not the little pecks we'd had twice before but an out and out, back to the seat, hands in my hair, wild kiss that went from simmering to scalding hot in seconds. His tongue demanded entry with a slick swipe against my kiss-swollen lips. I opened instantly, tasting him fully on a heartfelt moan.

He tasted of salt and sin, like a margarita on ice with the perfect splash of lime. He growled as he tipped his head to the side and drank deep. I couldn't get enough. My heart pounded, my mind swirled, as I envisioned us taking this kiss to a place far more private than his car. He sucked on my bottom lip as I tongued his top one. We switched, me going for his lush bottom lip as he attacked my top. Our tongues danced, sucking, taking, grinding against one another until neither of us could breathe. I pulled back on a mighty gasp of air and he did the same, only he pulled my head close and rested our foreheads together once more.

"*Liliana*, you'll be my undoing. If you kiss like that, I can only imagine what taking you to my bed will be like," he said, tunneling his fingers through my hair and holding me in place.

I took in a few deep breaths as his words penetrated my brain. Instead of lashing out at his macho man response, I fell into an uncontrollable laughter. It started in my chest and spread out through my entire body until I was bursting with intense belly laughter that had tears of joy leaking down my cheeks.

He shook his head and grinned. "Tell her I'm going to take her to bed one day, and she laughs like the hyena *la niña* Rory loved at the Zoo. This could give a man a major complex, *chica*."

I smiled wide and tried to pull myself together, wiping my eyes with the backs of my fingers. "*Lo siento*, I swear. I don't know what's come over me. I'm just tired. Bone tired."

He cupped my face and wiped away some of the tears still falling down my cheeks. At this point they could have been from laughter, or stress. Whatever the reason, it was nice to have a man be so tender and caring with me. I'd not had that type of concern in so long I'd forgotten how beautiful it could be.

"Let's get you back into your home." He leaned forward and kissed the apple of my cheek before backing away and getting out of the car. He came around to my door and opened it. Then he went to the back of the SUV to where my two rolling suitcases were and pulled them out.

He followed me to my apartment and waited while I got my key out then surprisingly, he followed me in, setting the two cases by the door.

"Stay here, let me take a look around."

I frowned. "But the threat is gone."

He tilted his head to the side and stared at me. "Let me do this. It will make me feel better leaving you alone."

I shrugged. "Okay."

He didn't waste time, quickly checking the balcony, making sure it was locked, then the small kitchen and tiny coat-closet-sized pantry. With assured strides he went down the short hallway, checked the bathroom, and then I assumed my bedroom. I couldn't see what he was doing from where I was standing near the front door.

Within moments he came back and nodded. "It's clear."

I grinned. "I figured it would be."

"You've got my number programmed into your phone. Call me for any reason. Day or night. You feel scared, call me. You get a weird feeling, call me. You're uncomfortable being alone, call me. Got it, *chica*?"

That had me groaning in irritation, but I pushed down my need to fight back at his caveman-type approach. He sounded as nervous to leave me as I was to have him leave but we all needed to get back to some semblance of normalcy. Whatever that looked like. And it started with me being in my home alone.

"I'll be fine. Thank you again for keeping me safe and driving me home."

He nodded and then went to the door. "Lock this behind me. Both locks at all times."

Now he was starting to piss me off. I clenched my teeth. "Got it. Now go. I'm good. I can take care of myself like I did before you came along."

His gaze traveled my body from my feet, up over my jeans and simple tee to my face. "I know you can, Liliana. I just want you to realize that you don't have to take care of yourself alone anymore. Not when I'm around."

I pushed at his rock-hard chest, easing him out the door. "Go, before I get mad."

He grinned and his gorgeous brown eyes twinkled. "I like your fire, Liliana. I don't mind being burned."

I rolled my eyes and nudged the door shut.

"I'll be calling in a week." His voice was a muffled boom through the wood of my front door.

"We'll see if I answer!" I hollered.

"Lock the door!" he yelled back.

Damn that man could not help himself. I turned both locks and then went to my balcony to watch him walk away.

My lips still felt hot from the incredible kiss in the car as I watched him fold into his SUV, look up at my apartment, and wave. I smiled and waved back.

Maybe this was the start of something beautiful between me and Omar.

Time would tell.

Chapter
SEVEN

A week later...
Just over three months until the bank heist.

"I CANNOT BELIEVE YOU DRAGGED ME *HERE* OF ALL PLACES!" Charlie hissed under breath. "The last time I was in a church was..." She frowned as we got out of the car, then her gaze cut to mine. "Was when I was thirteen and you made all of us come for your 12th birthday."

"And we had fun!" I reminded her as I closed the door of my blue baby.

"Fun is rocking out at a concert, going to a bar, dancing the night away, getting shit-faced with your friends, and waking up the next day without a hangover so you can do it all over again the next night. Not sitting in a pew being preached to about a man who walked the earth a couple thousand years ago! Then going up in front of the congregation and getting a shitty-tasting cracker to get blessed by an old dude in robes. All of this before entering a scary little box, much like a *closet*, I might add, something I've never spent a day in, and telling a perfect stranger your sins so that you can score your 'get-out-of-sins-free' card by whispering over some beads and praying to the head honcho." She pointed to the sky.

Charlie crossed her arms over her chest and leaned against

my Chevy. "Seriously, Sprite, this is cruel and unusual punishment, even from you."

I shrugged. "You lost the bet. This was my reward."

"A reward is me taking you out to lunch. Buying you a new pair of heels. A donut, for crying out loud." She raised her hands into fists in the air and shook them. "A fucking donut is a reward. Making your bisexual sister go to church as your reward blows, Lil." She let her arms drop down to her sides. She wore a simple dress and sandals which I thought was really cool of her. Charlie was the type of girl who wore mostly denim on her bottom half by way of jeans and jean shorts. The only dresses I've seen her wear were to the club, and those showed more of her body than they concealed. This was a summery simple sheath dress she must have got from Blessing.

"You said *anything* I wanted within reason and cost. Attending church doesn't cost you a single penny and only takes an hour or so of your time. And you look beautiful. Very respectful, *hermana. Gracias.*"

She lifted half her lip into a snarl. "Well, I wasn't about to embarrass you in your favorite place." She finished with a salty roll of her eyes.

I looped my arm with hers, my tall wedge heels making me closer to her natural height since she wore flat sandals.

"I appreciate you coming with me. I was too tired to go last Sunday after everything that happened, and I did pop in for confession on Wednesday but for some reason I didn't want to be alone today. It really does mean a lot that you're here."

She let out a long, drawn-out groan, and patted my hand. "Fine, I'll be the big sister and give it my attention."

I smiled wide and nudged her shoulders. "Thank you,

Charlie bear," I teased, calling her one of the many nicknames I used to call her when we were young girls.

"I just know I'm going to regret this." She sighed as we walked up to Old St. Patrick's Church. The green spire on top always stole my breath as did the Romanesque architecture.

"The red crosses on the doors are really cool," Charlie noted a little begrudgingly.

"They are Celtic crosses. This church is actually the oldest in Chicago. It predates the Great Chicago Fire of 1871 and the main church building actually survived it. The parishioners come from all walks of life, but they have a heavy Irish influence."

"All right, that's pretty interesting. Let's go inside and see what else they've got going on." She moseyed toward the front steps at a faster clip than my short legs could move.

As we entered, I was immediately bombarded by the change in the air. The sensation of peace filled my pores with every step we took inside. This was definitely what I needed after everything that had happened last week.

"Wow, this is badass!" Charlie gushed as we stood on the marble floor at one of the entrances.

I looked around the cavernous space as though it were my first time seeing it. There were beautiful walnut-colored pews that lined up in rows all the way to the front altar. But what I think was moving her was the incredible art along with the stencil-cut wooden shapes running horizontally across the ceiling. There were arches and hearts cut into the wooden structures with edges and shapes as fine as a baker might shape dough with cookie cutters. Forest green, mustard yellow, and pinkish terracotta were colors that were liberally used in the artwork gracing the ceilings and walls. Not to mention the intricate stained glass windows that ran the sides of the worship hall.

While she gawked, I led her to a position in the middle of the church closer to the aisle. I didn't want to be in front or back, but I did like to see the priest as he gave his sermon.

We sat down and Charlie immediately grabbed a bible in front of her seat that was tucked in the holders behind each pew. "They give you free bibles?"

I chuckled. "Those are for parishioners to use if they didn't bring one of their own." I showed her my worn-out bible, the same Mama Kerri had given me on my 10th birthday, not long after moving into Kerrighan House. She respected my desire to attend church as my biological parents had every week and while I was too young to attend alone, either she or Aunt Delores would accompany me to service. Then when I was a teenager, she'd drop me off in front of the building, run her Sunday errands, and would then come back to pick me up. I knew she believed in God, but I also knew she didn't feel compelled to do her worship in a church. She felt comfortable privately worshiping God in her own way. Me, I needed the fellowship to refuel my connection to God throughout the rest of the week. It's just the way I was wired.

"Huh, makes sense if they want a person to follow along." She cycled through the gold-trimmed pages. "Not that I'd understand how to navigate the damn thing anyway."

"Look at the tabs on the side when its closed. See the three little letters?" She tipped the book to the side at my instruction. "Now you look for the abbreviation when the priest calls out the name and verse."

She scanned the tabs and ran a blue-tipped fingernail down them. "They're not in order? Look at this. The first three abbreviations say GEN, EXO, LEV but then this tab way back here says NEH, EST, JOB. How the hell can you figure it out if it isn't in alphabetical order?"

"Charlie, shhhh no cursing in church," I warned at a whisper. People were starting to fill in, greet one another, and find their spots.

"Sorry, shit…I mean shoot!" She snort-laughed and covered her mouth.

I held down my own laughter but bumped her shoulder. "I'll make sure you get to the right part. The priest will call out the name, chapter, and then the verse. So, say you want to find Psalms 9:10." I pointed to the PSA. "You turn to Psalms first. Then you go to the chapter number 9, then the verse which is 10. They also have screens up there to help guide you." I pointed to a screen that was out of the way but clearly visible to the parishioners.

"Oooh it's like detective work. Where in the world is Carmen San Diego!" She sang, referencing the computer game we all played in beginning computer class back in high school as she located chapter 9. "Got the 9, woot-woot!"

"Now find verse 10, and read it to me."

Charlie wiggled her upper body as though she were chair dancing when she got to the right verse with the tip of her finger. "Here!" she blurted, not realizing how much her voice carried in such a large open space that wasn't quite filled yet. "Psalm 9, verse 10 baby! Booyah!" She pointed to the page several times.

I couldn't help but laugh at her outburst. I waved my hand at the two mature ladies in the pew in front of us who promptly both turned around to assess the noise.

"New to church. Teaching her how to find the bible passages," I explained.

"Oh, that's excellent, dear. You're a good friend," one of the women noted.

"Sorry, Lil. I got excited," she whispered.

"Being excited in church is a good thing. Now that you found the passage, what does it say?" I prompted her.

Charlie put her finger under each word and read the passage I literally pulled out of the sky for her to find. *"Those who know your name will trust in you, for you, Lord, have never forsaken those who seek you."*

Damn. If God didn't send just the right passage for the moment.

"To me it means that if you know the Lord, or truly want to know him in your heart of hearts, he will never forsake you. Basically, he'll always be there for you."

"You know I believe in a higher power. Right, Lil?" She dipped her head and whispered. "I'm not here just because I know you love it and I lost a bet. I'm here because I too have faith in something far larger than us, and after the hell we've been through, coming somewhere you feel safe makes me feel safe too."

I smiled wide and nudged her again. "I knew you liked going to church last time. You can't fool me."

She snickered and sat up straight, her gaze going to something across the room. Her eyes narrowed into slits as her lips flattened into a white, thin line. I followed her gaze and my heart stopped beating and my stomach dropped.

"Didn't you say that Omar asked you out and that you were waiting on his call this week to set up a time?" Her words held a hint of acid in them.

I followed where she was shooting daggers across the room and swallowed against the cotton coating my throat at what I saw. "Uh huh," I finally answered.

"Then what the fu...frack is he doing with his arm around the waist of a woman." She lifted her chin toward that side of the church.

Across the room in the second set of pews, about three back from the front of the church, Omar stood in a pristine black suit with a white dress shirt and a tie. His arm was loosely around the waist of a woman wearing a skin-tight, rose-colored dress. I could only see the woman from the back but at this distance, and standing next to Omar, she was only a few inches shorter with long, black, pin-straight hair that went down to her very curvaceous booty.

"I don't...I don't know." My voice trembled in shock.

"Maybe it's his sister, friend, cousin?" She offered other alternatives.

Then we both watched in horror as Omar nuzzled the woman's cheek with his nose playfully. The room started to become hazy as both Charlie and I had our eyes glued to the man I was supposed to start dating as of this week. He'd even sent me a text on Wednesday to remind me I had four days left until he intended to ask me out. I thought it was cute. Sweet even.

His hand moved up to the woman's bicep and he rubbed her shoulders, squeezing her to his side as though sharing an exciting moment with her and whoever they were talking to.

The woman turned sideways to set down her purse and both Charlie and I gasped out loud and smashed our backs against the hard wood surface of the pew.

A huge pregnant belly greeted us. I turned my head with

my hands over my mouth, shame and pure embarrassment heating my cheeks. Charlie's mouth was open, her eyes bugging out of her head.

It only got worse from there.

Omar proceeded to hunch over, and rub said woman's belly. Then he brought his face close to it where he pressed his forehead, the same way he'd done to me only a week ago, before he kissed me hot and heavy in the car. I could see he was saying something against the woman's belly, just like a proud papa would with his pregnant partner.

"¡Dios mío! ¡Dios mío! ¡Dios mío!." Oh my God, I chanted just under my breath. "Please God deliver me. I don't know how this could be happening."

"Oh, I fucking know." Charlie stood up, dropped the bible onto the pew, and pulled her hair back into a ponytail. "I've got this," she snarled, and I barely was able to get ahold of her before she stormed over there.

"No, no, no. Hell, no! He does not get to string my sister along when he has a wife and baby on the way. Fuck that!" Her voice rose loud enough to disturb the women in front of us.

"My goodness, your language! So inappropriate, young lady," one of the old women chastised.

Charlie glared at the ladies. "You think me cursing is inappropriate? I'm about to whoop some a…" I barely got my hand over her mouth before she caused any more disruption to the rest of the congregation.

Twirling Charlie around, I put my hands to both of her cheeks. Her pale skin was a bright rosy hue that made her freckles stand out. Her green eyes were blazing white hot fire and her mouth was in a scowl so deep it bordered on ugly. Angry Charlie was not to be reckoned with.

"Let. Me. Go!" She snarled through her teeth.

I shook my head. "Come. Now." I tugged her hand and used all the force I could muster in my body as my heart was ripping into pieces at what just transpired.

My mind was spinning as I barely maneuvered Charlie outside and onto the sidewalk before she spun around and yanked her arm out of my hold.

"Fuck this noise! I'm going to kick his motherfuckin' ass in front of God and everybody! And you know what?" She put both her hands to her waist and bent over to get into my face and make her point more clear. "God himself would probably thank me! What an asshole!"

I took two full breaths and looked at my pretty sandals as I shook my head. "He's not worth it, Charlie. I had a feeling he'd turn out like the last two. And lo and behold, he did. Honestly, I'm no longer surprised."

Humiliation poured through my veins as the realization that once again, I was being played by a man. I was so damned tired of being taken for a fool.

Charlie paced the sidewalk, stomping one way for about fifteen feet, and then repeating it in the opposite direction. "This is bullshit. He deserves to be called out right in front of his pregnant woman. Let her know what type of man knocked her up. It would serve him right," she seethed.

I shook my head and reached for her wrist. "Charlie, it wouldn't be right. He didn't make me any promises and maybe I thought there was more to what we had than there was? Omar came around during a crazy time in my life." I looked up at the blue sky as big puffy white clouds floated by. I let out a pained sigh. "Honestly, I don't know what to think anymore. Let's just get out of here. I can't go back in there now anyway."

I can't ever go back to my church. Especially if he planned to take his pregnant woman there with him. That was definitely not something I could willing subject myself to every Sunday, over and over. No thank you.

"I'm so pissed. Why aren't you pissed?" Charlie grouched. "Usually something like this would set you on fire! Bring out the *loca* in you." She put her hands to her hips. "Why are you letting him off easy? He deserves to be burned at the stake for the shit he pulled."

"Burned at the stake?" I huffed. "What are we? Back in the 1600s?"

"At the very least his ass should be called out. He *kissed* you, three times. Three. He made endless advances. Consistently told you how he was going to win you over and take you home to his mama! Who the hell does that kind of sick, twisted shit when he has a preggo at home? Man, now I hate men again. Blech! Only women for me for the next long while." She slumped over and frowned.

"Women are catty too," I reminded her sadly because that's all I had in me now. Sadness. Seeing him with a pregnant woman put out my fire. I was nothing but crusty dried ash.

"Ugh," she grumbled and then took my hand and started walking down the street.

"Where are we going?" I quick-stepped so I didn't fall behind.

"To get drunk. Hammered. Then maybe we'll find you a new hottie to ease your sorrows."

I shook my head. "Yes to the booze. No to the men. I

don't even want to look at a man for at least another year. I'm so over it."

"Here, here. Fuck men!" She raised her hand in the air as though she were a mighty warrior.

One drink turned into two which turned into one shot of tequila after another. The best part, Simone, Sonia, Genesis, Blessing and even Addison showed up in sister solidarity. Killian, his friend Atticus, and Jonah also came but kept to themselves at the other end of the bar. Always within sight of us. With the paparazzi chasing us around, not to mention the talks about Sonia possibly running for President of the United States, we had to be vigilant.

Mark, the awesome bartender who'd been serving us the past two hours, lined up seven more shots of Patrón and filled them to the tippy top before presenting them in front of each of us. Jonah, Killian, and Atticus were sipping their beers since they promised to drive us all home.

I focused my attention on Atticus, Killian's brother-in-arms. They were laughing heartily and looked mighty sexy doing it. The guy was huge, much like Omar, but taller and even broader. That thick black hair and startling clear gray-blue eyes could be a woman's undoing. Once they took a gander at his body, it would be over. Worshiping at his feet would occur.

In my drunken haze I stared at the man trying to decide if I wanted to make a move and take him home with me. It had been a long time since I'd had a man in my bed, and Atticus was rough around the edges and sinfully good looking. He

105

might have been just the thing I needed to get past this stupid heartbreak over a man I wasn't even officially seeing.

"Whatcha thinking about?" Simone asked me drunkenly.

"Having sex with Atticus," I answered honestly.

Her mouth dropped open and turned into a huge smile. "Naughty, naughty. You thinking, the best way to get over one guy… is to get under another?"

Charlie put her face directly over Simone's shoulder from behind. "I approve. Atticus is yummy. I would lick him like a lollipop, he's so hot!" She gushed, also slurring a bit.

"Who's hot?" Genesis asked as she strutted back to our stools with Blessing at her side. They'd ventured to the bathroom together. Because safety in numbers. Especially in bars.

"Atticus." I pointed to the man candy at least ten seats from where I was barely keeping my ass on the stool.

Genesis glanced over her shoulder. "Definitely hot but…" She shrugged her shoulders. "Do you really think that's a good idea? I mean, we're here to help you get past the man that should not be named…"

I scrunched up my face.

Blessing crossed her arms over her chest. "Usually, I'd say to go for it, but not right now. We're all too emotional and adding sex into the mix when you're already messed up in the head isn't usually the wisest plan."

Charlie made a stink face. "Have you been talking to Mama Kerri? You sound just like her, ya party pooper!" Charlie pointed a finger accusingly.

Blessing chuckled and then pretended to bite at the finger which made Charlie fall into a bout of hilarious giggles.

Sonia ran her hand down my back from where she sat to my left, the other girls on our right. "Hate to say it, but

Blessing is right. You need time, Lil. We all do. The past few months have more than sucked."

I nodded, thinking back to Simone and her scary situation, then Addison's. Through it all, we lost a sister. Tabitha. We almost lost Addy and Simone. We'd been through so much in the past six months.

"I say we drink!" Charlie shouted, picking up her shot and spilling a little in her exuberance. Eventually she got her shot aloft in front of her. Her tongue was sticking out the side of her mouth and she squinted as she steadied her glass.

"What should we drink to?" I asked, my belly already filled with alcohol. Pretty soon we were going to need to add some food to the tequila bowl that was my stomach.

"Ho's before bro's!" Blessing suggested.

"Sisters before Misters!" Genesis added with a cute little hiccup.

"Chicks before dicks!" Charlie cackled.

"Bellas before fellas!" Sonia lifted her shot in a salute.

"Besties before testes!" Simone blurted, as we all laughed at her contribution. "Hey, I tried! You guys took the best ones!"

"*Salud!*" I clinked my shot glass with theirs. Some spilled on the floor, but we were far too gone to care as we slammed our shots back.

"*¡Las quiero tanto!* I love you so much," I repeated in English. I set down the glass and put my arms out wide. "I'm so lucky to have amazing sisters."

"Group hug!" Charlie squealed and I was surrounded by the love and strength of the women I called my sisters.

I'd beat this heartbreak through *love* not sadness.

And maybe more tequila.

"Another round!" I hollered as my sisters cheered me on.

Chapter
EIGHT

Present day...
The day of the bank heist.

"YOU WILL BE MINE ONE DAY, LILIANA. STOP FIGHTING it and enjoy what's burning just under the surface between us." His words were direct, straight to the point, and filled with desire. A desire I wanted nothing more than to succumb to. But it wouldn't work. I wasn't the woman he wanted. I'd never bow down to him. Never serve in a stereotypical role that I was certain he was used to. And I'd never be the other woman again. Ever. I didn't care how many times he texted, called, left voicemails, or dropped by my house unannounced over the past three months. I can't unsee what I did in that church.

I was able to avoid him all those times, and I'd continue to do so in the future. Eventually he'd realize that I was no longer interested in a romantic relationship. Even though my body didn't agree. Traitor. Arousal was already churning in my gut at the physical sight of him. I soaked in what I could and promptly shook it off. My resolve back intact. "I'm not the woman for you," I whispered, knowing it was the God's honest truth.

"You're exactly the woman for me. And I'm going to stop at nothing until you feel it too." He whispered, and my resolve quivered but it wasn't easy to forget what I saw three months ago. It was too important. I needed to set the truth free. Tell him exactly what I saw that day that destroyed any hope for more between us.

I closed my eyes and was just about to rebuff him when a series of gunshots rang out.

Both of us twisted around, Omar hooking his arm around my form and pushing me behind his back so his body served as a shield.

I peeked around his massive frame and saw four masked men at the entrance to the building with ginormous guns. Bigger than anything I'd ever seen in real life.

People screamed in terror. Chills raced down my spine and out every nerve ending as the reality of what was happening filtered through my brain.

The bank was being robbed.

I looked at the floor near the entrance to the bank where the men had entered and were currently fanning out. A large white man in a security uniform with blood soaking the front of his chest was down, bleeding out on the white marble floor. He wasn't breathing.

"Nobody move! Everyone, face to the ground. NOW! Or you die just like him," one of the masked men commanded in a no-nonsense tone.

Omar and I fell to the ground and plastered our bellies to the cold marble floor. Fear pumped through my veins hot and heavy as the hairs on the back of my neck rose.

"It's going to be okay, just stay still and be quiet," Omar whispered.

As quick as a flash he slid the bag of what I figured was money across the floor and directly under a table. Maybe the bad guys would find it. Maybe we'd be dead and would never find out.

"You, you, you." One of the men hollered to three cashiers standing behind a glass barrier with their hands up. "Touch an alarm and you all die along with everyone here."

Three sets of faces turned pale, devoid of color as one by one they nodded at the masked man.

Another gunman was rounding up patrons of the bank and pressing them against the wall where you waited for a cashier. Before I knew what was happening, I was being hauled up by my elbows from behind, my back arching painfully.

I screamed at the top of my lungs as I was yanked uncomfortably to a standing position, held to a stranger's front for only a split second before Omar reacted in a series of combat moves I'd only ever seen in an action movie.

The gunman was down on the ground, his face spewing blood across the white marble tile in a macabre display one might see only in a boxing ring. His gun clattered to the floor and skidded a distance too far for either of us to reach.

"Don't. Touch. Her." Omar hissed through his teeth, his booted foot pressing on the gunman's neck. Unfortunately, it was a single gunman he unarmed not all four. Before he could react to anything more, there was a new threat behind him dressed from head to toe in black, face covered, holding the barrel of his weapon flush against Omar's head.

"Back off or I splatter your brains all over your girlfriend." He spoke in a calm, emotionless tone that I believed was the absolute truth. This man had no bones about taking a life and probably had countless times before.

"Omar, please." My voice shook.

I watched Omar grit his teeth and lift his hands while

taking his foot off the other man. That man jumped up and smashed his fist into Omar's face as I screamed.

Omar took the hit and shook it off like a pro, not showing an ounce of response even though that sucker punch had to hurt.

The man behind Omar shoved at his head and his back with the tip of the gun. "Get against the wall now!" he demanded.

I reached for Omar's hand and interlaced our fingers as we were shoved toward the other customers and pushed roughly to the floor, my knees hitting the marble painfully. Omar tried to grab me and soften the blow, but it was too late. I scrambled forward and pressed my back to the wooden counter. Omar wedged himself half in front of me with an arm around my hips holding me close to his side.

The gunman that Omar had taken to the ground held his weapon on the frightened customers, his blue gaze a fiery brand on me and Omar as if ready to dole out retribution for Omar taking him down.

"Get the cash and let's go!" one of the men yelled.

Sirens were ringing in the distance, but the crew didn't seem to be fazed. Gunmen continued forcing crying cashiers to fill their bags with the money in their drawers. Another gunman ordered entry into the vault. I continued to listen intently, hope filling my veins as the sound of sirens got closer. Salvation only minutes away.

I watched in horror as cop car after cop car flew down the road, sirens screaming as they blazed a trail right by the bank, clearly on a different hunt. My shoulders slumped and desperation sank deep into my heart. The jerk gunman in front of us started to laugh maniacally. Omar wrapped both his arms around me, and I pressed my cheek to his chest, letting the rhythm of his heartbeat soothe the ragged edges of fear just enough to keep the tears at bay.

Which is when another gunshot rang out loud enough to pierce my ear drums and set my teeth chattering. Screams bounced off the walls as the pungent smell of iron filled the air.

Another body dropped to the floor.

I jerked in Omar's arms, but he held me tight. "Shhh, *mi lirio*, it's going to be okay. I've got you now. Listen to my voice," he whispered against my hair, his hand running up and down my back.

"Another one?" A man yelled angrily from where we heard the second gunshot. "You were supposed to take the guard hostage, not kill him. Now the bank manager? Are you fucking insane?" he roared.

I trembled within Omar's arms as the other bank customers huddled together in twos and threes. Some were crying, others were cowering, and one person was tucked into a ball rocking back and forth with her head against her knees praying.

"Fuck! You ruined everything!" one of the men said.

"I did you all a favor. You're welcome!" was the sarcastic angry reply from one of the men behind us. I assumed it was the man who'd killed both the guard and apparently now the bank manager.

Dead.

Two people were dead.

"Just pack up what you can, and let's get the hell out of here," the gun-toting man in front of us stated with a lift of his masked chin.

"You've signed our death warrants. This is no longer a robbery. It's murder. The cops will stop at nothing to find us now," another masked man complained.

"Not if we kill all the hostages. The cops are at the other two banks manning the false alarms we set and no one here can identify us," one of the gunmen touted.

His words swirled through my fright and fear and I was able to put two and two together making an important connection. *So that's why we saw them race by without stopping to save the day.* Dread slithered deeper into my veins as I realized how dire the situation had become. I held on to Omar tighter, digging my fingernails into the muscles of his back through his shirt.

"I won't have anyone else's death on my conscience. This was never supposed to happen. You're a loose cannon and can't be trusted. I knew we shouldn't have brought you on!" one of the men hollered heatedly.

Maybe he was the ringleader, maybe just part of the team, but he definitely sounded upset that the other guy shot and killed two people. That had to mean there was decency in at least one of them.

How the heck were we going to get out of this alive?

The next ten minutes were the most frightening of my life as the hostages were led in pairs to a back room. Omar and I stood when the gunman touched my shoulder with the tip of his gun.

"Please," I croaked, cowering closer to Omar.

"Move, bitch!" The gunman pressed the gun straight between my shoulder blades.

I cried out and stumbled forward.

Omar stupidly shoved the guy to the side as he tucked me to his form, shielding me as much as possible.

"You have a death wish, bro? I already want you dead. Your bravado bullshit isn't helping."

"Just following orders," Omar stated flatly as we followed the other customers in front of us who were now lined up single file.

Once the first set of customers got to the vault, a woman in her fifties screamed, throwing up her hands and turning around as she fell into body-wracking sobs. The man just behind her grabbed hold of her and held her close as they made a strange arc around something.

I didn't have to wait long to find out what had her so upset.

When we turned the corner, the rest of us were greeted by the grisly image of what I assumed was the bank manager. An older gentleman with crisp white hair wearing a suit. There was a bullet hole in the center of his forehead, his blue eyes still open.

I whimpered as the sour taste and salivation that proceeded vomiting filled my mouth.

"Breathe, *mi lirio*. Breathe slowly. Look away, close your eyes. I'll lead you. Trust me." Omar had his hands at both of my biceps. His front was pressed to my back.

I swallowed down the foul taste and closed my eyes, taking in a huge breath of air through my nose and letting it out my mouth.

Omar, as promised, led me around the poor man's body until we reached our destination.

"You can open your eyes now," Omar said softly against my ear.

I did and noted the rest of the customers were cowering in a line, huddled against a wall of tall gray file cabinets.

"Stay in here and shut the fuck up!" one of the masked men said and then went over to the desk and ripped the phone right out of the wall. Then he cleared the desk of the computer and smashed the monitor with his booted foot.

Omar led me to the far left-hand side where he once again placed his body as a shield in front of mine. I didn't have time to really think about the ramifications of that decision, especially if he had a woman with a baby on the way. Heck, that woman back at the church was so far along in her pregnancy the child may have already been born.

My heart sank as the thought burned violently in my chest. If anyone needed to be protected, it was a new father, not the woman he planned to date on the side.

I ground down on my teeth as I watched the gunman lift up the small trash can and dump its contents on the floor. He held out the can and placed it on top of the desk.

"One at a time, I want you to drop your wallets and cellphone in the can. Don't even try anything or you'll be dead before you can even dial the nine in 9-1-1." He waved his gun at the man farthest to the right. "You, put your wallet and phone in the can. Now!" He boomed.

An older gentleman who was maybe in his seventies jerked to attention. He wore a navy suit, white shirt, and a red tie. *Very American*, I thought numbly. He nodded and his hands trembled a bit before he slowly put one hand into his suit coat, the other still up, and slowly withdrew it holding his phone. He tossed it in the basket.

"My wallet is in my pocket. I'm going to reach for it," he told the masked man.

The gunman nodded. "Hurry up," he growled.

The gentleman used one hand to secure his wallet and tossed it in the bin then lifted both hands in a gesture of surrender and backed away from the desk until he hit the file cabinets.

This went on for a while. Each person in line going one by one until it was the tenth person in line's turn to go. A twitchy young man who was maybe in his mid-twenties, wearing a baseball cap and T-shirt with an American flag emblazoned on the front. He slowly reached into his front jeans pocket for his wallet at the same time his other arm cocked behind his back.

Omar tightened his hold around me and shoved me into the corner. I peeked over his shoulder and watched in abject horror just as the young guy lifted a handgun from behind his back and fired off a single shot. That's all he got off. It wasn't enough. Before he could shoot again, the gunman riddled him with a series of automatic bullets right in his chest. His body jerked grotesquely as blood splattered the people closest to him, the floor, and the space around his form.

Screams of terror filled the room as I pressed my body to the corner. Tears poured down my cheeks in sorrow-filled rivers. There was no being strong anymore. This was life and death being doled out right before my eyes.

The gunman lifted his gun, the tip pointing at the ceiling. His other hand pressing against his neck where the bullet must have grazed him. Blood oozed through his fingers as he bellowed. "Fucking idiot! Any more of you want to try something stupid and die now? It sure as hell would make things easier. Fuck!" He continued to curse as blood trailed down his neck soaking his black shirt.

I shook where I huddled against the corner and Omar's back. He didn't so much as move a muscle. Standing strong as my shield.

Another man with a gun raced into the room and looked down at the dead man then at the other guy holding his neck wound.

"What the fuck happened!" he barked.

"He had a gun." He pointed to the gun still gripped in the dead young man's hand.

The other gunman snatched the gun away. "We have to go. Now. The cops are on their way. Something tripped them. We think it was the people waiting outside the bank to get in."

My heart started to pound as hope filled my veins. Maybe we would make it out alive.

"What do we do with these people? They know our voices and my blood is everywhere! DNA, man." He groaned as though in extreme pain.

The other gunman shook his head. "I don't know. I'll ask the Primary," he said before he disappeared behind the door.

"Put your goddamn wallets and phones in the basket! All of you, now!" the wounded gunman demanded.

The rest of the hostages pulled out their phones and tossed them and their wallets into the bin. I didn't have anything on me as my purse had been sitting out in the open in the lobby since they first arrived.

The gunman pointed to me with his gun. "You there." He lifted his chin. "Put. Your. Shit. In. The. Basket."

"Leave her alone, man," Omar warned standing more fully in front of me.

The gunman huffed. "You think this is a game? Three dead not enough for you, huh, ya fuckin' jagoff?"

Omar didn't say a word. He stayed perfectly calm.

"Do I need tell you again, princess?" he warned, putting the gun right in front of Omar's face, the tip only two feet away from his face.

"I'm sorry. My bag is in the lobby. My wallet and phone are there too," I said on a rush gulping down air as I did so.

"Come here." He waved the gun at me.

"I said leave her alone, man. She has nothing to do with this. Whatever you need, you get from me." Omar's tone brooked no argument, but the fact remained, he had no leverage whatsoever. No weapon. No phone. Nothing.

The gunman laughed dryly and stepped so close that the tip of the gun pressed to Omar's forehead. "Try me, and we'll see how fast I can pull the trigger. You'll die before your body even hits the floor, right in front of your little woman."

I could hear Omar growling as dread sizzled through the entire room.

I shoved Omar to the side the best I could. "I'm here, right here. Please don't hurt him," I said with my hands up, palms out, facing the gunman.

He reached out with his free hand and encircled my bicep, squeezing my arm painfully as he yanked me to his side so forcefully my shoulder popped out of place. Pain the likes I've never felt before bloomed throughout my body.

I screeched as the blistering heat surrounded my shoulder and my arm fell limply, dangling out of the socket at my side.

"Motherfucker," Omar growled, stepping forward, but

the gunman was faster, bringing up his weapon and shooting, catching Omar in the upper shoulder. His body jerked wildly to the side, hitting the wall with the force of the bullet. Blood soaked the white wall behind him as he slid down, then tried to get up.

"That was a fuckin' warning. Anyone else want to play hero today?" he asked the horrified hostages cowering against the wall and one another.

"Stay down, Omar! Please, please just stay down," I cried, tears falling down my cheeks while my nose ran, and I cradled my limp arm as best I could to my abdomen.

The gunman tilted his head and backed up. My arm was still in his hold as he forced me to back up with him.

I moaned as stars started to blink at the edges of my vision. Pretty soon I was going to pass out. I was in excruciating pain.

"You'll never get away with this," Omar sneered while he held a hand over the gunshot wound.

"Watch me!" the gunman boasted, and backed out of the room, taking me with him. He used a booted foot to slam the wooden door shut.

"Stay alive!" I heard Omar shout from behind the door.

I sure as heck hoped I could.

The gunman grunted as blood continued to pour down his tall frame while he maneuvered a heavy side table in front of the door, hissing in pain as he did so. I stood off the side and looked around the empty bank for a possible exit. From this location, I couldn't see out the front, but I could see the body of the bank manager and the dead guard who'd been dragged to the far side of the lobby. The blood streaks from the guard's chest wound painted the floor a gruesome red where he'd been set aside like yesterday's newspaper, not like a human being who probably had a family and a ton of people who loved him who would soon mourn his loss.

Before I could function properly, I was shoved forward, my steps faltering as I teetered on my heels. "Move your feet, princess," the gunman said, shoving me in front of him. The three other masked men were hauling giant canvas totes of what I assumed was money over their shoulders and taking them down a small hallway. I figured that hallway led to the back of the bank.

When there was only one guy in front of us hauling bags up his shoulder, he growled at the guy behind me. "What the fuck are you doing with her?" he asked, looking me up and down.

"Insurance," the bad guy behind me grunted.

"Fuck! Add kidnapping to the list of charges? The Primary is going to be pissed! I can't believe you did this shit, man. You were supposed to play it cool. Go with the flow. Now we have how many dead bodies, a room full of hostages, and a woman you plan to kidnap? No way. No fucking way! None of this was supposed to happen. God!" He grumbled through his teeth.

The gunman behind me shoved at my back and I was barely able to keep upright. "Pick up one of those bags, princess." He gestured to one of the stuffed bags sitting just outside the vault about ten feet in front of us. The other two masked men were steadily grabbing loaded sacks and taking them back down the hallway two at a time.

"You pulled my a-arm o-out of it's ssss-sss-socket." My teeth chattered as wave after wave of freezing cold slithered over my skin and clawed deep into my muscle and bones. I thought I was going into shock.

"Jesus, man, you're in so much trouble," the other man griped.

The evil masked man holding the gun on me pulled something out of his cargo pants pocket that looked like a zip tie. Then without warning he grabbed both of my wrists and yanked them behind my back.

White-hot, searing pain encompassed my entire body. I screamed at the top of my lungs before the sound of a train horn blared in my ears, my vision went pitch black, and I lost consciousness.

Chapter
NINE

THE ROCKING SENSATION HAD MY STOMACH CHURNING AS I blinked open my tear-encrusted eyes. My cheek was pressed to a hard, wood floor that was cool against my skin. Across from where I was huddled on my side, there was a wall with a wooden door and a white knob.

I tried to move my arms and pain tore through my dislocated shoulder. For long moments I breathed through the pain, praying I wouldn't pass out again. Once I got it under control, I swallowed down the bile threatening to exit my throat and wiggled against the floor until I could scrunch my knees closer to my chest.

More agony blasted through me as I stretched my bonds as much as I could to wedge up my knees one leg at a time. When I started to see stars again, I stopped and rested my sweaty forehead to the floor and simply breathed for a few beats.

I needed to get out of there.

Once I could see past the pain coming from my shoulder, I used my core strength to lift my upper body until I was resting back on my calves.

I bit back the fiery pain shredding its claws over me as I closed my eyes and breathed.

One breath in for four, then out for four.

Two breaths in.

Three.

Four.

By the time I got to five, I could manage the pain a little better. The entire arm was going numb, and I hissed as I attempted to wiggle my fingers. At least I was finally in a position to look around the room they'd caged me in.

It was strange.

Like a well-decorated hotel room, but in a nautical theme. The comforter was white with golden anchors stitched into the decorative pillows. The floor was a rich oak as was the entire wall behind the bed. There were two nightstands, one on each side of the queen-size bed and a window above the bed with curtains covering it. I could still see daylight shimmering through the dark gold curtains, so I knew I hadn't been out for too long. There was another door open kitty-corner to me. I could see white tile, a toilet, and a vanity from where I kneeled.

I took a big breath, calming my nerves, and then fell to one hip and shimmied a leg up and into a 90-degree angle, then pushed off, leveraging my weight in order to come to a standing position. The room wavered and swayed as I blinked against the blurry edges surrounding my vision. I ground down on my teeth to ward off the agony threatening to make me pass out, and instead, took deep breaths until I could see clearly.

"You can do this, Liliana. Just be quiet," I reminded myself on a shallow whisper of air.

Step by step I padded to the single closed door on bare feet. I no longer had on my shoes. Where they went, I hadn't a clue.

I turned around and used my good hand to try the door-knob. Of course, it was locked.

"Damn it!" I murmured angrily.

Next, I turned around and pressed my ear to the door in an attempt to hear something. I could hear voices in the distance, but I had no way of knowing how close or far they were. And I wasn't sure if I wanted to bring attention to myself.

Evaluating my options, I glanced around the room again, looking for anything I could use to cut the ties off my wrists. There was a wardrobe on the other free wall, the set of end tables with no drawers, and the bathroom.

Maybe the bathroom has grooming scissors?

I moved as quickly as I could while still being silent and entered the bathroom. Briefly I caught my reflection in the mirror. Wild brown curls all ratty and squashed against once side where I'd been left on the floor. My eyes, normally a choc-olate brown, were almost an inky glazed black, my pupils so wide, it was obvious I was scared straight. I took in my right shoulder that hung awkwardly at a weird angle. The most surprising was the blood splatter that ran down the front of my shirt. It wasn't there before I blacked out.

Blood? I thought, confused, trying to put the pieces together.

I catalogued all my pain. It centered primarily on the right shoulder and my tied wrists which I'd rubbed raw already.

My thoughts flashed back to the guy who tied me up and killed that young man right before our eyes. That young guy had shot the gunman in the neck.

He probably put me over his shoulder when I passed out, his blood transferring to my shirt. Good! I snarled at my image. At least I had his DNA all over me if the worst happened.

God, please don't let the worst happen. I prayed silently.

Please, God, help Omar and all those other people. I continued praying as I scanned the vanity. Spinning around, I curled the fingers of my good hand around the edge of the drawer and walked forward. It opened as I moved.

I turned around and checked the contents. Unused toothbrushes, toothpaste, and floss still in the package greeted me. I dipped down to see in the back and noted washcloths and nothing else.

"Come on," I whispered going to the next drawer and repeating the process. A hairbrush, hand mirror, and hand towels littered the rectangular space until something shiny and metal caught my attention.

Nail clippers.

"*¡Gracias, Dios!*" I bounced on the balls of my feet in a mini touchdown dance while thanking God. Not sparing another second, I wedged my body to the side of the open drawer and bent back over it as much as I could to bring my hands closer to the inside of the drawer.

With the tips of my fingers, I brushed the clippers back and forth around the drawer trying to grasp them.

My arms screamed as I winced against the sharp bite of the drawer digging into my lower back. My wrists were no longer raw but bleeding. The zip tie had broken the skin around my wrists and blood dripped down my hands.

Good. More evidence I was here.

Pushing past the extreme pain and exhaustion threatening to overwhelm me once more, I prayed to my parents up above.

"*Mamá y Papá, por favor ayúdenme.* Help me, please," I

repeated to my parents in Heaven. If anyone could help me, it would be them and God. Even if it was only to give me strength to keep trying. To never stop until I was free.

Over and over I tried, moving through the agony and welcoming the pain into my body as I reached, stretched, and bent over the drawer. There would be no giving up. Period. I'd never stop trying to survive.

Eventually I was able to push the nail clippers up against the hand towels and finally got them to a standing position where one end leaned against a towel. I curled my fingers around the metal as tears of relief filled my eyes.

I leaned my booty against the vanity and wiggled and stretched my numb fingers around the clippers until I was finally able to flick them open. It felt like hours maneuvering over the metal tool in order to get the handle opened and turned around so it could clip.

Once I succeeded, I sobbed with joy and promptly snapped my mouth closed as the tears continued to fall.

"Okay, Liliana, now cut yourself free," I said under my breath.

The first attempt was a huge failure. I got the clipper in place and clamped down with all my might, but it wasn't on the plastic. Instead, the clipper bit sharply into the skin of my wrist that was near the zip tie. I almost cried out. *Almost.* My body heaved as bile raced up my throat in reaction to the severe jolt of agony.

No! No! No! Not now. Be strong, Liliana. Strong. You can do this.

I pressed my lips together so hard at that stark burst of pain that whimpers escaped softly unchecked as I tried to brave the pain and breathe through it.

I could hear my heartbeat as I waited to see if my captors heard me.

For three breaths I waited. Listened intently and curled my hands around my tool as though my life depended on it. For it very well could. It wouldn't do for them to catch me with the clippers either.

Nothing happened.

They hadn't heard.

Doubling my efforts, I wiggled my fingers and twisted and turned until I could see over my shoulder and through my reflection in the mirror that I finally had the clippers right over one of the ties. I snapped the tie, and my arms sprang free.

I fell to my knees right there on the bathroom floor as an anguish so torturous poured like hot lava over my upper body.

Tears fell and my body convulsed in a physical response to the shock of pure bolts of lightning racing down each arm to my numb fingers making them sizzling bits of fiery flesh. I barely held myself up with my good arm, palm flat to the tile bathroom floor as I held strong through the torturous explosion of renewed pain.

Don't pass out. Don't pass out. Don't pass out, I chanted internally.

When the worst of it finally passed, I got myself together and stood. I wanted desperately to take a drink of water, but I didn't want them to hear the sound if they were close to the room.

The rocking sensation continued to make me woozy and unbalanced as I realized there was a plate-sized circular window near the small shower. Blue water greeted my gaze as I walked closer and looked out what I now knew was a portal.

The Chicago skyline was off in the distance but not too far to swim if a person was desperate. Which I was.

They had me on a boat.

From a bank to a boat? Why? And why the hell were we on Lake Michigan?

Shaking my head at the oddity, because it didn't matter in the grand scheme of things why they did this. The point was to get the hell out of here. To escape.

With my goal locked in my mind, I dashed out of the bathroom and got on top of the bed. It bounced along with the rocking. I had to stretch my legs out wide to balance myself. Then I carefully pushed back the curtains and saw nothing but water and the skyline way off into the distance. There were tons of boats not too far from here. If I could get out and into the water, maybe, just maybe, I could swim close to one of them and scream for help.

If I didn't die drowning.

Needing to take the risk, I unlatched the lock and opened the window as quietly as I could manage with one good hand. When it was open, I listened to see if I could hear anything. Off in the distance, there were men's voices that rose and fell as though in a heated argument. I wasn't close enough to hear what they said, but figured I had to take a chance. Using the flat of my palm I shoved hard against the screen. It fell away. I eased my head out the window and saw it floating on the top of the water.

I waited a full breath to see if it had been noticed, and so far, nothing. I shoved my head out as far as I could and realized I was on a small yacht. The length of the boat was very long with windows running most of the length of the boat. The water below lapped calmly against the side which meant to me we were likely anchored. I couldn't hear an engine, and we weren't moving.

Using the strength I had in my good arm and the bounce of the bed, I hopped up onto the sill. Thank you, Lord, for making me petite. I couldn't imagine getting through this window if I was an Amazonian like Blessing or Addy.

God, I wanted to see my sisters. By now they would know I hadn't made it to the dress fitting and would be blowing up my phone. At first it would be complaints and griping that would quickly turn to worry. They'd all call. Mama Kerri would be informed. She'd call. And then Sonia would get involved. Which meant Jonah and the FBI would get involved.

"*¡Mierda!* Fuck my life," I whispered as I got my legs up and out to hang out of the window.

I had no time to be scared. I had only escape to focus on.

"*Stay alive!*" Those were the last words Omar had said to me at the bank.

Looking down at the chilly water below, I shivered as the wind blew my hair against my face.

"I plan to." I answered Omar's last words to me and let myself fall out of the window, feet first toward the icy water below.

The freezing cold water of Lake Michigan burst across the surface of my skin, and I cried out under the water as I kicked and clawed my way to the top with one arm.

In a normal setting, I was a good swimmer, but with a bum shoulder, pain, extreme exhaustion, and fear spearheading my ability, I seriously lacked power in my strokes. Still, I pushed on. And on.

Until I got about a hundred feet from the boat, and I heard a man's voice.

"Man overboard!" he called out.

I pushed harder, kicking my feet wildly while screaming as loud as I could in the hopes that someone, *anyone,* would hear and inspect the situation further.

"She's getting away!" someone else cried out, and then I heard the frightening sound of splashing water from not one, but two large somethings hitting the water.

Trying another option, I flipped on my back, floated and kicked as though my life depending on it, because it damn well did!

Using my one good arm the best I could, I didn't so much as look toward the boat I'd been on, just wanting to put as much distance between me and my captors as possible.

Water kept flowing into my mouth as I kicked and screamed and pushed on. It felt like hours had gone by as I swam, but it was probably only five minutes tops when I was yanked by the ankle and tugged down into the water, my head going under fully.

I came to the surface, sputtering and crying out as I thrust back and kicked hard at my attacker, slamming my foot into one of their faces as I scrambled to swim away, gain some distance.

They were too fast.

Too strong.

In seconds I was being pulled by both arms. I shrieked as something popped in my shoulder. My vision went in and out as water poured into my mouth and I coughed and hacked while being dragged back to the boat I'd just escaped.

When they got me to the wooden platform at the back of the boat, the two other guys, still in masks, dragged me by the underarms up and out of the water. I hacked and spat water from my lungs, striving to bring air back into my body.

"Are you okay?" one of them asked.

I turned my head, my curls plastered to my cheeks and neck as water dripped down my face. I looked directly at the man who addressed me. I couldn't understand what I was seeing, my mind swirling with fear and the instinct to survive. Once I was able to catch my breath, I looked more closely at the two men watching me wearing masks. It hit me like a ton of bricks what the mask was. It was that guy on the game, the face of the Monopoly Man. The cartoon character that doesn't let you pass go and sends you straight to jail. That face.

Maybe I was hallucinating? I blinked several times and shoved at the hair and water still soaking my face.

My stomach churned woefully as I stared but before long, I couldn't function at all, and I bent over and vomited on the wooden planks. Lake water and bile poured from my mouth as I gagged and choked, unleashing everything in my gut.

Before long, someone was covering my wet form in a warm beach towel. My hair fell in front of my face as I clasped the towel to my shoulders. My teeth chattered, but while I cowered, I noted that my shoulder no longer threatened to make me pass out in agony. It hurt. A lot. But it wasn't that bone-cutting pain I'd felt when it was out of place.

They popped it back in place when they grabbed me out of there, I thought. Small favor, I guessed. Now what were they going to do with me?

I rubbed my face with the dry towel. "What do you want from me?" I asked the man who brought me a towel.

"What's your name?" he asked, ignoring my question.

"Lily," I stated, not giving them my full real name. If they found out that my sister was a United States Senator and my family were very public, things could go very bad.

"Lily. Pretty name for a pretty lady," he said, holding out a hand. "I won't hurt you. I promise."

I licked the water off my lips and took his hand. He pulled me up to a standing position and led me over to a circular booth of seats that was out in the open overlooking the water.

Once seated, I held the towel to my form and waited.

"You were not supposed to be a part of this, but one of my men made a bad call. So, for now, you're in it until it's done."

"U-until w-what's done?" I asked through chattering teeth.

He moved across from me and got another beach towel and handed it to me. "I'll get you something dry and warm to wear. I'm sorry you were taken, but by the time I realized you were tied up in the back of the other SUV, we already had the cops on our tail."

"What about the other hostages? Did you kill them like the guard, bank manager, and that one young guy?"

The masked man didn't say anything for a full minute. "I deeply regret that those people died today. I underestimated my team's ability to do harm. That won't happen again."

"And why would I believe you? I'm the one who was just kidnapped, hurt, tied up, and brought onto a boat, away from my family and everything I know that's safe," I countered.

He crossed his arms over one the other as another masked man came forward wearing the same weird cartoon Monopoly Man mask. It didn't cover their entire heads, just their faces like one of those old school masks I used to wear as a kid before the Halloween enterprise got fancy. Now I knew that two of the men were white. These had dark blond hair. Unfortunately, I didn't see what the men looked like who pulled me out of the water, and the ski masks they wore to the bank before didn't show anything other than one of them had blue eyes and another had dark ones.

"I don't normally do business this way. Ever. Loose ends and miscalculations aren't my thing. And I always keep my word. If I tell you that you will not be hurt or mistreated during our time together, you can trust it."

I jerked my head back. *"No puedo confiar en ti,"* I huffed, slipping into Spanish, something that was familiar and comforting to me. I basically stated that I couldn't trust him.

"Sí. Puedes. Lo juro." He shocked me by speaking in perfect Spanish stating, "Yes. You can. I swear it."

"And I'm supposed to believe you? A bank robber. Murderer. Kidnapper. Who apparently is rich enough to own a fancy yacht on Lake Michigan?"

He shook his head while the man next to him chuckled. He laughed.

Oh boy, I was in some serious shit.

The leader guy ignored the man next to him.

"Look, just let me go. I'll swim to safety. You can drop me off at a random harbor. Whatever you want. I won't say a thing. I'll just go home and live my life like I would have any other day. *¿Comprendes?* Does that work?"

The guy next to him bent over and full belly-laughed. I was not impressed.

I glared at his doubled-over form.

"Cool it, kid," the man in charge barked.

He stood up and his body continued to jerk with laughter as his intent to hide his response failed miserably.

"Jesus, I can't deal with you. Go check on Four." He lifted his chin to another area of the boat.

"Four?"

"It's what we call one another. I'm Primary. My brother is Second. The rest go up from there."

His brother. I didn't think he meant to share that bit of information, especially with me, but I held it close and didn't bring light to it.

"Why would he need to check on Four? Was he hurt in the robbery?" Not that I cared, I just knew from Jonah and his FBI partner's kidnapping training that you kept your captor talking. If he was talking, he wasn't killing you.

"He was grazed by a bullet in the neck, but that's not my concern. He's unhinged. I need you to understand what happened today was through no fault of mine, the second, or the third. The bullets that killed those three men today came from one gun."

"Oh, and who gave him the gun in the first place?" I fired back.

His head dropped forward a bit and I cursed myself for making the comparison. If this man thought he was a good guy in all of this, that meant he really didn't intend to harm me further and would ultimately let me go.

"Look, I don't know what to say. I just want to go home. I'm sure you can understand that. The need to be with your family." I tried to appeal to his humanity.

"Funny word, *family*. Never quite means what people think, does it?" he stated cryptically.

I swallowed down the little bit of fear that started to creep back in as I noted Primary's body language was becoming frustrated. His muscles were flexing beyond the thin black T-shirt and pants he wore. And he stopped speaking.

Too many beats of silence flowed between us, but I pushed on, needing to know my fate.

"Are you going to kill me?" My words felt nasty on my tongue.

"No. I already told you that I wouldn't hurt you. Regardless of what you think, you don't know anything. I am a man of my word."

"Okay," I hedged. "Are you going to let me go home?"

"Yes."

"Now?" I asked hope coating the single query.

He shook his head. "No."

"Please," I begged as my body started to tremble.

"I'm sorry. We have to stay the course. There's work to be done. When it's over, I will personally set you free."

I slumped against the back of the seat wondering if I could jump back out and swim faster now that my arm wasn't holding me back.

"Don't even think about it, Lily. My brother is practically an Olympic swimmer."

We'll see about that. I'd have to wait for another moment. Plan it out even better. If I'd left at night, they wouldn't have noticed me go.

"Come." He clapped, and I jumped up and stood, my body responding on autopilot. "Let me show you back to your room."

On wooden feet, I put one foot in front of the other.

If I could escape once, I would escape again.

Chapter
TEN

KEPT THE TWO TOWELS WRAPPED AROUND MY SOAKED BODY AS the laughing masked man led me through the spacious, swanky, living room area of the boat and then down into the belly of the beast. The stairs opened up into a hallway filled with a few doors. One was open, and I noted a man going through stacks of money wearing a Monopoly Man mask. So weird.

Next, we passed a door where I could hear someone raging. "Let me the fuck outta here!" Then I could hear a banging sound as if a booted foot was knocking against the wooden floor.

"Looks like there is another unhappy guest on the boat," I murmured.

"That would be Four. He will be there until I've decided what to do with him," Primary said from where he followed behind.

I stopped in my tracks and pressed my back against one of the walls so I could see both the Primary and Second who both stopped and stared at me with those masks.

"Are you going to kill him?" I gulped.

"Why do you care? He killed three innocent people. Ruined everything we've been planning for years," Primary retorted with bite.

"You robbed a bank. Bad things were bound to happen."
I stated the obvious.

Primary shook his head and the mask wobbled from side to side freakily. I looked away and down at my wet bare feet where water was puddling around me.

"Not like that. We do not harm others. Our goal is specific and important but not at the cost of lives." He said the words with a cutting edge, as though there was a possessive need pushing them to act in such a manner.

"And he messed up." I nodded. "What will you do with him? With me?" I choked back the fear, lifted my chin, and straightened my spine, trying to show that I wasn't scared even though I was terrified. I wanted to present confidence to my captors, even though I had no idea what my fate would be.

"You'll be fine. Unfortunately, you'll be staying with us for a while, but I promise you will come out of this unscathed. You just need to wait it out," Primary answered.

"Wait what out?"

He shook his head. "The less you know, the better."

I closed my eyes and nodded.

The Second captor pressed open a door that I realized was the same room I had escaped from. The window had been boarded up with planks of wood and nails. The nails ran every couple inches, making it almost impossible to remove.

"I'm sorry to have to do this to you," Primary said, as the other man went over to the wardrobe and pulled out a pair of sweats and a T-shirt. He took them into the bathroom and set them on the counter. "Go take a shower, warm up, and get refreshed. The Second will be waiting when you're done to make sure you're not capable of getting away again."

"What do you mean, make sure?" my voice trembled.

Primary nodded to Second who had tied ropes to the right and left rungs of the headboard.

I shook my head and backed away from the bed. "No, no, no, please. I'll stay in here and wait, just please don't tie me to a bed." I couldn't help the natural dread running through my veins at the visual of me tied with my arms spread wide. "Four dislocated my arm." I cradled it in front of me. "Then when they got to me in the water, they somehow popped it back into place but it's useless. I mean it."

Primary stared at me for a long time with that freaky Monopoly Man cartoon face and then gestured for Second to approach me. "Check her out."

He came over and I let the towels fall to the floor as he assessed my arm, touching here and there over my wet clothing, the same way a doctor would.

"She'll need a sling for now, and an X-ray to determine damage. It seems to be back in place, but there's no telling if anything within is broken or fractured." He then took both of my forearms and lifted them up. I hissed at the movement of my bum arm but let him do his inspection. He traced the skin around the zip ties. "These are going to get infected if we don't treat them. I have some antibiotic ointment in my medical bag in my room. Take a shower, get warm, put on the pants and T-shirt, and I'll get you fixed up," he stated and then let me go and left the room, I assumed, to get his bag.

"I'm sorry you were mistreated. Again, my brother and I detest violence of any kind." Primary seemed really disturbed by my injuries.

"Then why did you rob a bank with a bunch of guns? That's pretty violent."

"We have our reasons, but ultimately, no one should have

died, and you shouldn't have been caught in the crosshairs. I'm so very sorry. I know that doesn't mean anything to you now, but in time, I hope you come to understand that none of this was our intention."

"Then let me go. Drop me off at the harbor. I'll find my way home."

"I'm sorry, Lily. That isn't possible at this time. Please, go take a shower and clean up. There are amenities in the shower already. Feel free to use whatever you wish."

"But…"

"Go now." His voice rose to that of a demand. "I will not ask again."

For the first time since being in this masked man's presence I felt true fear. He was at his limit and the last thing I needed was the nice one who called the shots to be angry with me.

"Okay, I will. Please, think about not tying me up. It scares me. Makes me think I'm going to be raped." I put the most heinous thing I could think of out into the open. It was the truth. As a woman, the first thing we believe will happen if a strange man got to us, and especially if he tied us to a bed, was that we were going to be defiled.

As I expected, Primary reacted instantly to that concern with a gasp. He physically put distance between us by taking a step back while lifting his hand to his chest, in affront. "On my honor, no man will touch you in that manner."

"I didn't know thieves could be honorable," I muttered before I entered the bathroom and closed the door softly behind me. I looked for a lock but there wasn't one. Dammit.

Weighing my options, I turned on the water in the shower and let it warm while awkwardly removing my clothing with one arm. Then I stood under the heated spray until I could finally feel my fingertips and toes.

God, please help me find a way to escape again. This guy thought he was a good human, but his actions said otherwise. Robbing a bank was not something a good person did, no matter what the reason.

Once showered and dressed in dry clothing, I took a deep breath and opened the door to my cell. Second was waiting for me, his bag open. A few medical supplies sat on the corner of the bed on top of a clean towel.

"Sit here and I'll wrap your shoulder and arm to your chest for now, until I can get you a proper sling."

"Why not just drop me off at a hospital? I haven't seen any of your faces, I don't know who you are, nor do I want to. I just want to go home." In the shower I came up with the plan of making the two nice ones feel badly for me. They truly didn't seem to want me hurt and stated more than once that I would be set free after their work was completed. Whatever that work entailed, I didn't know. Heck, I didn't want to know either.

"I'm sorry, Lily, that's not going to happen just yet. Please, sit down." He gestured to the space near the medical supplies.

Once I sat, he treated the raw, jagged edges of the cuts around my wrists by bandaging them up with some ointment and gauze. Then he expertly maneuvered an Ace bandage around my ribs and up and over my shoulder and forearm to keep the wounded arm protected, in place, and out of harm's way.

I actually felt like I could breathe easier once it was bandaged to my body securely. *"Gracias.* I mean, thank you," I murmured, exhaustion hitting me as I sat there.

"You're welcome, Lily," he said staring at my face with that cartoon mask. "You look so familiar. Like I've seen you many times before." He shook his head.

I'm sure he had. If he'd picked up a newspaper or watched the news and/or gossip channels like TMZ within the past six months, the odds were good he'd seen pictures of me with my sisters. Most specifically with Sonia, a United States Senator, or Addison, the top plus-sized model in the world right now. Both were my foster sisters. And with all of us staying on and off at Mama Kerri's, the press had a lot of images of us coming and going.

"I think I just have one of those faces. Everyone always tells me I look like a friend or a family member." I swallowed down the lie and stared at the bandages on my good arm.

Before he could say more, Primary entered with a wooden tray holding a plate of food. Looked like a mouth-watering plate filled with alfredo pasta with chicken and veggies on the side. A big glass of water came with it for which I was grateful. I'd drank as much as I could in and after the shower, but my body needed fluids.

Primary set the tray where the other man had just cleared his medical supplies.

"Go, check on Four," the Primary instructed.

Second nodded and left the room, bag in hand. I had been hoping he'd forget the bag and I could score a scalpel or something equally worthy as a weapon. Apparently, these guys were smart, but I'd been trained by FBI agents on what to do when kidnapped. Jonah and his partner Ryan had hammered the information into our heads regularly because of the risk we'd been in for the past several months.

We lost Tabitha during Simone and Addison's kidnapping. They were hell-bent on keeping the rest of us safe. And here I was, kidnapped. I could swear our family was cursed.

"You must be hungry." Primary broke me out of my thoughts and continued. "The sun has set. It's been a long day for us all. I've agreed to allow you to stay in here untied on good faith. The door will be locked, and the window you alighted from earlier," he pointed to said window, "will be monitored form the outside at all times throughout the evening. So don't try and rip the wood off and escape through it. You'd only risk hurting yourself more."

I nodded. "Okay, I won't mess with the window. I promise." I lifted my head. "Thank you. For being kind even through all of this."

"How do your arm and wrists feel?" he asked.

"Better. He's a good doctor," I added to see what he'd say.

"Yes, he is. The best in my opinion. Now please, eat." He gestured with a hand to the food next to me.

"I will." I was starving. I hadn't eaten lunch, and after the bank and the attempted escape, I was ravenous.

Primary walked to the nightstand where he grabbed a remote. Across the room a flat screen TV came on to a channel menu. "Watch whatever you like. We'll talk more in the morning." He tossed the remote to the center of the bed.

"Are you going to let me go tomorrow?" I asked, not hiding the hope in my question.

He shook his head. "I'm sorry, Lily, you will not be going home tomorrow. By the week's end we should be done with our business. Only then will I make arrangements for you to be found."

"Found? What does that mean?" Being found could have meant anything depending on the context.

"You're a smart woman. Figure it out," he said on a frustrated sigh. "Goodnight. Get some sleep."

I nodded as he turned around and left.

The click of the lock sounded like a gavel coming down in a quiet courtroom. My fate had been sealed. This guy wanted me to ride it out until he could put me somewhere safe where I'd be "found."

Found in what way? Was he planning to leave me on the boat and then call the Coast Guard or police and tell them where I was hidden away? Would he put me in the trunk of a car and wait until some innocent bystander could hear my screams and get me out? My imagination ran wild, coming up with a hundred frightening scenarios where my lifeless body was found dead, not alive.

I picked up the plastic fork and dug into the pasta, shoveling a huge bite into my mouth. Buttery, creamy alfredo sauce burst across my tastebuds, and I chewed and swallowed, greedily digging for more. It was delicious. Better than I could have expected, but I was on a yacht. Didn't rich people hire special chefs? Were there other people on the boat who might not know what was going on and be willing to help me? Maybe I could break out of the room somehow and get help from someone already on the boat?

Primary told me to wait it out and I'd be set free.

But could I trust a stranger?

Hell no, I couldn't. Three men were dead because of a man who'd helped this Primary and his brother rob a bank.

Omar had been shot in the shoulder. I'd been kidnapped. No matter what they said, or how well they treated me, I was in danger. Period.

While I ate, I thought about what I knew so far.

I knew Primary was in charge. I knew that Second was his brother. Second was also younger because he'd been referred to by the Primary as "kid" at one point, and he seemed to defer to everything Primary said and did. Second had medical knowledge, and when I made the doctor comment, Primary not only agreed, but he also boasted that Second was the best doctor. He'd also mentioned that he was an Olympic-level swimmer.

What if he wasn't kidding? Maybe the Second practiced medicine? Maybe he *was* an Olympic swimmer. They certainly had money since I was being held on a pricey yacht. Then again, they could have money because they were bank robbers by trade. Maybe they did this all the time all over the nation or heck, the world.

What else?

I knew the bad guy they called Four was also being held captive. So, they were mad enough at him that he was now a prisoner and not part of the crew. I wondered for a second what they would do to him, since he'd supposedly acted off plan. I knew that one of the rooms had the third masked man or maybe another member of the crew, because I'd seen someone counting the money. The last thing I knew was the food was amazing, which meant there could be other people here.

I finished everything on the plate and drank all of the water. Then I went into the bathroom and refilled the water glass and brought it back to the bed with me. One-handed, I bent low and hefted the tray onto my hip and set it on the end table out of the way. Next, I grabbed the remote and put the news on, desperate to find out anything about the robbery.

It took a few minutes, but eventually I was able to find a report.

I scrambled close to the flat screen on the wall and turned up the volume enough that I could hear it clearly. I didn't want it to be so loud that the noise carried through to the other rooms.

A woman with a short blonde bob and a boring royal blue suit spoke directly to the camera. "Earlier today, four masked men entered Liberty National Bank in downtown Chicago carrying automatic deadly weapons. Their intent was to rob the bank. In doing so, three men were killed. The security guard, the bank manager, and one of the hostages. Another hostage sustained a bullet wound and was taken to Sacred Heart hospital. He is expected to make a full recovery. We do not have any information on how the robbers left undetected nor how much money had been stolen."

"What we do know is that at the same time the robbery was occurring, two additional banks in Chicago had their alarms triggered. While the police were called out to the two false alarms, Liberty National Bank was being robbed. By luck, a citizen attempting to deposit a check peered into the windows of the bank after they found the front doors locked during regular business hours. We go now to Tom Conners who's with our local hero now. Here's what young Ricky Lowe had to say about his experience today."

The camera switched to a young man of about twenty or so wearing a black T-shirt that had "Ultimate Gamer" written in neon green across the chest.

"Yo, bro. I went to the door of the bank and tried the

handle, and it was locked. A few people were standing around leaning against the bank as if waiting for it to open. I had to get my check in quick because I was in a hurry to get back to my campaign on Fortnight, ya know."

"And did you see anything suspicious?" Tom Conners, a reporter for the station, held a microphone up to the young man.

"Nah, man. I was going to use the ATM but for some reason they were all down. But I needed to get my check from the pizza place where I work deposited in the bank, or my rent would be late to my mom, and she'd ride my tail for a week. You feel me?"

"Um, I, what happened with the bank?" Tom Conners steered the kid's commentary back to the matter at hand.

"Yeah, bro, I banged on the glass and peered inside. I saw a person all in black in the distance. I banged harder but he kept walking until he disappeared from view. So, I cupped my hands and looked into the lobby which is when I saw the red streaks of blood next to a big puddle of it, man. I knew that wasn't supposed to be there, bro, so I showed a couple of the other people waiting. Then we heard a gunshot, and we all ran. When I got down the street and behind a car, I called the cops. Told them I thought the bank was being robbed."

"That must have been very frightening," the reported said.

"Well, duh, but I was more concerned about whoever lost that blood, yo. That didn't look good at all. Besides, I still needed to deposit my check, or my mom would be pissed."

Tom Conners blinked and frowned at the guy as if he couldn't believe how incredibly unbothered the kid was before getting his expression back to something more neutral. "Well, there you have it, folks. A young man, doing what was right, calling the authorities at the first sign of trouble. Well done." He clapped the boy on the shoulder in thanks.

"Yeah, cool. Shout out to my mom! I love you, Mom. Don't kick me out!"

"Okay, well, that's it, direct from Liberty National Bank with the first eyewitness to today's bank robbery where three innocent lives were lost."

"Yes, thank you, Tom. Our thoughts and prayers go out to the families of those men who lost their lives and the single man who was injured. We'll continue to share updates on the bank robbery as the story progresses into the night and morning. The police chief promises an update tomorrow afternoon with information on who was killed, injured, and what happens next. Thank you all for joining us for this special broadcast. We will now return you to your regularly scheduled programming."

The story disappeared and went to commercial.

I went to the bed and sat down, resting my back against the headboard. There was no mention of my kidnapping, which meant the cops were keeping it hush-hush. I took a full breath and let it out slowly. My sister Sonia would be all over this. Jonah, my soon to be brother-in-law, would stop at nothing to find me.

For now, I was somewhat safe. Tired, stressed, in pain, but alive.

There were people looking for me. That I knew with my whole heart.

I eased my sore body down onto the bed and closed my eyes. I'd just rest a bit and then hope a new plan of escape would come to me by morning.

There had to be another way to get out of here.

Chapter
ELEVEN

I WOKE DISCOMBOBULATED WITH MY SHOULDER THROBBING IN TIME with my heartbeat. The TV was still on, and the room dark. Without being able to see out the boarded-up windows above the bed, I had no way of knowing what time of day it was. I knew I was out like a light the moment I closed my eyes. Exhaustion had finally taken its toll.

Rolling to my good arm, I wiggled to the edge of the bed and flung my legs over the side. I stood up and waited for my balance and equilibrium to settle before I padded into the bathroom. I did my business, then looked out the porthole and noted the sky was still black and the lake shimmering in the moonlight.

I clenched my teeth and firmed my jaw. *Time to think, Liliana.* There had to be a way to escape this room.

My wet pants were still hanging over the shower rail drying. Seeing them, it came to me.

The nail clippers!

I yanked the still-damp denim off the rod and set them on the vanity. I was working with one arm, but I'd make do. In the back pocket I found the slim metal tool that had gifted me my freedom the first time.

"Let's see if we can go for a second time." I snickered wickedly feeling the thrill of escape seep into my veins.

I fingered the tool until the metal hook that people used to dig out their toe jam was at the ready. Worst case, they heard me trying to break out and decided to tie me up, rape, and kill me. Since I really didn't believe Primary or Second were that evil, I figured I'd take my chances.

The smart thing to do was try the doorknob to see if it was unlocked first. It wasn't. Okay, so they weren't dumb. Still, they were dumb enough to leave me untied and I needed to use that gift wisely. For a solid thirty or forty minutes I prodded the key slot with the hook, trying to manipulate the lock. Nothing worked. My arm was tired, and I wasn't getting anywhere.

Moving to the door hinges, I ran my fingers across the stainless steel bars and was able to feel the lip of the middle pin wobble. Holy shit! Immediately I went to work, yanking with my nails at the pin until it loosened and came out. There was another top hinge and a bottom hinge. As quiet as a teenager who'd come home from a party trying to sneak up a squeaky staircase, I tugged at the bottom hinge closest to the floor. It wasn't loose at all.

I got onto my knees, wincing at my bruised kneecaps, the same that were damaged when Omar and I were shoved onto hard marble yesterday at the bank by number four bad guy. I hissed at the throb of pain and dipped my head toward the floor so I could see under the hinge. It was hollow.

"*¡Fantástico!*" I whispered against the floor and then held my breath on a shocked gasp as I saw the shadows of booted feet come to a halt before my door.

Please don't come in here. I prayed silently.

Then I heard voices.

"I'm going to get you out of here, cousin, I swear." I heard whispered in a harsh male voice I didn't recognize. It definitely wasn't Primary or Second, nor the guy they called Four. That man's evil voice would fuel my nightmares as I relived every moment of the bank robbery and watching that young man die in front of us. That was provided I actually got out of my predicament alive.

I trembled and pressed my lips together so I wouldn't make a sound.

"Before we leave for the bank in Gary tomorrow afternoon, I'll cut your zip ties, man. Then all you gotta do is wait until we leave. Take your cut and run. These guys have more money than God. It's not the money they're after. I don't know what it is they want, but I know they don't care about the cash. Something's off with those two."

"You're the one that got me in to this, Tucker. You need to get me out of it," the other man growled. And there was the voice that scared me stupid. Bad guy number Four.

"I know, Mac. I'm sorry, man. I didn't think they'd hold you captive, but cousin, you killed people," Tucker, who I assumed was bad guy number three, reminded him. Which was a good comeback for sure.

"We have all taken lives, don't act all pious. You're not one of them." His disdain threaded through every word he spoke. "All those soldiers that didn't make it home on the enemy's side. They had families, loved ones. They were just doing a job. Well, you know what, cousin, so was I," he grated nastily. "I did the job that needed to be done yesterday. The job that none of you could do. We made it out alive because of me and my actions. That guard had a gun. That guy in the room with the bank customers had a gun!" His words got more heated as they conversed. "Those two should be *thanking* me for saving their asses, not locking me up!" His voice rose and I knew he was about to attract some attention.

"Shh, man. Shit!" I heard a rustling sound and then the door across from mine clicked shut at the same time I heard feet barreling down the stairs at a fast clip.

I knew that was my cue. I shoved up off my knees from my hiding place where I was eavesdropping and dashed to the bed. I lay on my back and tugged the coverlet over my body and tried to slow my erratic heartbeat and heavy breaths. Adrenaline was pumping through my system, and I needed to calm down if I were going to stay off their radar.

As I suspected, voices could be heard arguing outside my room, but being this far away, I couldn't decipher what they were saying.

Much to my extreme shock, there was a knock on my door before it popped open. Playing the game, I blinked rapidly and rubbed at my eyes as though I'd just been woken.

"What's going on?" I asked the masked man I knew was Primary based on his silhouette in the shallow light of the room and hallway behind him. Primary was a large guy. Not as muscular as Omar, more lean and fit. More like Jonah than my man.

My man. Ugh. Not. Where the hell did that come from?

"Nothing that concerns you, Lily. I'm sorry you were awakened," the Primary apologized.

"Was that arguing?" I pressed and yawned for effect.

"Like I said, it doesn't concern you. The less you know, the safer you are," he answered.

Yeah, right. I'd believe that like I believed I needed a man to make my life complete. Not at all.

"Go back to sleep. I'll come and get you in the morning to have breakfast and discuss…things," he said cryptically.

I nodded and tugged the covers up to my chin as a sign that I was being good and following his instructions. I glanced over to where the door was opened, the loose pin lying across the floor. If he stepped forward a foot more, he'd step on it and my hopes would be dashed.

My heart beat a mile a minute as my gaze flicked from that single pin to the Primary.

"Goodnight," I croaked, thankfully sounding tired not scared out of my *cabeza*.

He stared at me with that freaky mask face for longer than I could hold without shaking. So, I shifted to my good side and closed my eyes.

The door shut a second or two later and I was back alone in the room with only the light from the TV casting everything in an ominous glow.

Back to work.

Figuring he wouldn't come back right away, I tiptoed back to the door, got down on my knees, and peered under. I could only see through an inch of space between the door and the floor, but it was enough to see there wasn't a person standing in the hallway. At least not directly in front of the door to this room.

While I got my clippers back into place, shoving the hooked end up the inside of the hinge to help push the pin out the top, I recalled what more information I'd learned.

Tucker was the name of bad guy number three.

Mac was the name of bad guy number four.

They were cousins. Tucker was clearly the submissive to Mac's alpha.

They were veterans who'd killed enemy soldiers.

Mac insinuated that they were different than them, meaning the Primary and Second. Did that mean they were the enemy? Were they soldiers at the same time, possibly in the same unit? Had they an ongoing beef that was still toxic between them now? Or were they different in the ways of rags and riches? The way the Primary spoke seemed more educated, compassionate, and cultured. He knew Spanish. The Second was a doctor and a great swimmer. Maybe they grew up rich together and hired out the two soldiers.

I wanted to remember every detail I could about this experience so I could reiterate it back to Omar and the cops when I was either found or when I escaped. Death wasn't even on the table. I was smart and crafty. I'd come out of this on top. There was no other option.

Finally, the bottom pin sprang free from the hinge and clunked to the floor. I immediately pressed my cheek to the wood and scanned under the door in front of me. Waiting to see if they'd heard that small noise.

Nope. I was *almost* home free. All I needed now was to get the top one out and then remove the door from its hinges. Somehow. I wasn't quite sure exactly how I was going to make that happen, but I'd deal with it when I got there.

One step at a time.

Getting off the floor I looked around the room. There wasn't a chair in sight.

There was no way in hell a five-foot-three woman was going to be able to remove the pin from the top door hinge without something to stand on.

I tapped on my chin and scoured the room. Then I grinned as I went over to the nightstand, removed the lamp and tissue box, and set them both on the floor. The nightstand wasn't super heavy as I pulled it toward me, but it was louder than I'd hoped as the four feet scraped across the wood in a high-pitched sound that pierced my eardrum like nails on a chalkboard.

Maybe I could lift it?

Using all my strength I pressed the front of my body to the flat top, my damaged arm preventing a good hold, but that wouldn't deter me from trying anything and everything. Even with my arm bandaged to me, I pressed my weight against the flat top, looped my good arm around to the underside, and lifted up.

It was a lot heavier than I thought and I couldn't lift to a full stand with my arm in the way. I stayed hunched over the piece of furniture and shuffled a couple feet at a time, stopping to catch my breath and bite back the pressure and pain I was putting my wounded shoulder through, then I'd go another couple feet carrying the nightstand. I repeated this process across the entire room until I got the nightstand in front of the door. Once there, I did my floor check and was relieved to see and hear nothing.

Hoping all of the crew were sleeping, I braced myself on the wall next to the door, put my bare foot in the center of the end table and pushed off the floor, bringing my other foot to balance on top. I stood unbreathing for a few beats praying the wood would hold my weight.

It did.

Digging back in the sweats pocket I wore, I pulled out my trusty nail clippers. When I got out of this, I'd have them encased in gold and hung on my wall in gratitude for helping me escape the most frightening situation of my life.

The pin was much harder to get loose than the previous two. Still, I worked on it for a good hour, until all of the nails on my good hand were completely shredded. The tips of my fingers sore from yanking at the pin for so long, and my good arm ached from being held above my head for an hour.

Finally, I managed to the remove the final pin, holding the damn thing in my fist and over my heart as I silently celebrated.

Thank you, thank you, thank you, I chanted to God over and over in my mind as I made my way down from the night-stand and shoved the pin and the remaining two along with my trusty clippers in my pocket.

Which is also when the door came unstuck from its position connected to the hinges and jolted that single inch, falling to the floor making one loud *crack.*

¡Mierda!

The door wavered and I shoved the nightstand away with my leg much more noisily than I wanted to but kept my palm against the door. For some reason the damn thing was practically falling into the room.

I used my body and wrapped my bum hand around the doorknob and wrapped my good arm around the door and shimmied until the door was completely open.

As fast as I could, I maneuvered the door against the jamb and the wall and slipped around it and down the hall. Knowing that the rooms were downstairs, I climbed up the staircase as fast as my feet would take me while being as quiet as I could manage while rushing. Someone had to have heard the door come off the hinges and would be out soon to check out the noise. I just knew it.

Every step sounded like a sonic boom in my head as I

padded up. I finally made it to the top and peeked overhead and back down below.

Nothing yet.

The Primary had said someone would be watching my window all night meaning they had more crew members. Getaway drivers had to have been in the two SUVs while the four robbed the bank. That meant there could be two people watching over the side of the yacht where my room was situated, so my best bet was the opposite side. Ducking down, I snuck through the living room area scanning both sides of the windows as I did. The sky was still dark but I could see a lighter color coating the sky off toward the horizon where I peered through the glass doors.

I was almost free.

Get through the glass doors, avoid whoever was outside, and jump overboard. Swim to shore or another boat. That was my plan.

I made it to the glass doors of the living space that opened out onto the deck. I glanced around one last time before I pulled it open.

A screeching banshee-style alarm like an ambulance racing down the road at seventy miles an hour tore through the entire boat. It announced my escape before I even made one step outside.

I ran as fast as I could across the open deck glancing back as someone from a higher position than me shouted, "Hey! You! Stop!"

I didn't stop. Nothing would prevent me from making it out. Running as fast as my bare feet would take me, I flew up the seated area and onto the hull. I wasn't watching where I was stepping and landed the arch of my foot on a cleat, the metal T-shaped thing they tied boats to at the harbors. It banged into the bottom of my foot, and I screamed as my momentum barreled me toward the choppy waves of the lake.

I didn't even feel the cold of the water this time as I rose to the surface fighting the waves as the boat raced past me. I flipped on my back and kicked as hard as I could, regardless of the pain in my foot.

I kicked and kicked, using my one good arm to keep me going toward shore. I could see the boat slowing down and one man dove into the water after me.

Why couldn't they just leave me alone! I doubled my efforts kicking and swimming backward. I couldn't see the person behind but that didn't mean he wasn't there.

Unfortunately, my foot was becoming useless, going numb from the pain and cold. My chest was hardly able to stay above water and I gasped as I started to sink under.

The water was pitch black as I fought to climb up. I'd get my head up and sucking in air and then a large wave would take me under again. The water was so active I could no longer see where the shore was in the dark of night. Everything seemed black, except for the moon.

I was taken under the water again, my breath bursting out of my lungs as I tried to get back to the top, the moon flickering in my vision as I failed to reach the surface and sucked in a mouthful of water.

My body convulsed as more water came rushing in and the air within me went out. I felt like I was being pressed between two plates of glass as my body started to twitch and fight against the invasion.

I was drowning.

A dark shape approached, maybe a black fish or a shark

came at me as another oxygen-deprived gasp stole from my lungs bringing more water with it.

I was losing consciousness, my body going light as a feather as the last thing I saw was a pair of very pretty blue eyes against a handsome Disney Prince hero face floating in the water before me.

Then the water took me deeper into the darkness.

I thought I'd died.

Everything hurt.

Why would I hurt if I was in Heaven? That seemed counterintuitive to everything I believed the Holy Father would do for one of his children upon their death.

The pain, however, exploding through my body was intense, my entire form one throbbing, endless ache.

I tried to open my eyes, but they were so heavy and I was tired. Bone tired.

Something caressed the side of my face.

"Omar," I mumbled through the fog wanting to get closer to that sweet touch.

"You're okay. You're safe."

I knew that voice.

The Primary.

I definitely was not dead but at that moment I wanted to be.

"Hurts," I croaked and eventually was able to get my eyes half-open on a pained groan.

The light was on low, and I was in a different room, on a bigger bed. I tried to shift but realized I couldn't. Not because

I was hurt, which I was, but because my legs and good arm were tied to something.

"What have you done?" I pleaded.

"Saved your life." The voice of the Second came from down near the foot of the bed where I could feel a bandage being spun around the arch of my foot and around my heel, and then over my foot and ankle. "You sprained and bruised your ankle. You almost drowned and I had to reset your arm, bandage it, strip you, and put you into warm, dry clothes."

"Lily, why do you keep trying to escape? I promised you we'd free you when our business was done at the end of the week."

I licked my dry, cracked lips, and moved to speak, but was stopped by a coughing bout the likes of a forty-year smoker.

The Primary lifted my upper body as far as the tie to my good wrist would allow while the Second brought me a cup and helped me drink. Once I'd gotten through the congestion in my throat I flopped back down.

"Tell me why?" Primary asked again, his question more of a demand.

"I'm not the kind of girl who sits back and just takes being *kidnapped*. ¡ *Jesús, María y José!* For kidnappers, you're pretty thick." I winced as the pain in my body radiated up to my head and I had to close my eyes against the sheer need to pass out again.

"We're not kidnappers." The Primary's voice was scathing as if he couldn't fathom being labeled such a term.

"Says the man who tied me up after promising me you wouldn't," I bit out snarling.

"You broke your promise first," he quipped.

"No. I didn't. I promised not to try escape through the

window. I never said I wouldn't use the door, or leave the room, or the boat."

"Do you realize that if my brother hadn't been such an amazing swimmer that you would have drowned out there? Did you even look to see we weren't in Chicago anymore but in the middle of Lake Fucking Michigan on our way to Indiana?"

I looked at his form and tried to ignore the mask.

He wasn't wrong. I assumed the shore was in the same place it was yesterday. Didn't even make the connection that the engines were running, and the boat was moving, until I'd jumped off of it.

"We had to give you CPR. You could have died, and I don't need another innocent life on my conscience." He pushed a curl of my hair away from my face and off to the side.

"Then let me go," I begged.

He shook his head and looked down, seeming sad. "I'm sorry. We can't yet. Our goal is too important. There are more lives at stake than yours or mine, or any of ours. Please, just do what we say, and you'll be safe. I swear."

"And if that guy number Four gets out like his cousin Tucker plans to do before you leave today, what then? You think I'll be safe then?"

"What are you talking about?" he growled.

"I heard them before you came into my room earlier. Tucker was talking to Mac. Saying he was going to clip his ties before you leave today. You leave me here and that guy *will* kill me. He plans to kill you." I gestured to him and then the Second who was pacing back and forth at the end of the bed rubbing at his neck. "And you."

"We'll handle it." The Primary stood and gripped his brother's bicep, leading him toward the door.

"No! What about me? Let me go! Please!" I tugged at the ropes anchoring me to the king-size bed.

"You'll be safe here. We're locking you in and leaving guards on watch. Mac will not get to you. No one will." That was the last thing he said before he shut off the light and closed the door.

The second escape attempt was a fat failure. I was beginning to think it would be wise to listen to them and wait out their plan, hoping I'd make it to the end of the week.

Unless Omar and his team, the FBI, and Sonia's people or the cops found me first.

God, I hoped they'd find me first.

Chapter
TWELVE

THE NEXT DAY, THE DOOR TO MY ROOM FLEW OPEN AND I jerked awake. It was much later in the day based on the lighting streaming in through the windows. I must have slept a long time, which made me wonder if they drugged me last night.

The Primary pointed at me. "You haven't been honest with us," he grated angrily as he stormed over to the nightstand, picked up the remote, and hit the button.

The TV came to life, and I waited as my heart pounded rapidly against my chest. The Primary pressed buttons as the Second entered, leaned against the wall, and crossed his arms over his chest, not saying a word. The channel stopped on a local news broadcast. I noted the time stated it was four in the afternoon.

My smiling face appeared in a picture on the screen. It was a headshot from our school yearbook.

"Breaking news! We have been informed that twenty-eight year old Liliana Ramírez-Kerrighan, Spanish school teacher at Franklin D. Roosevelt High School in Chicago, Illinois, was the single hostage kidnapped in the Liberty National Bank heist where the robbers killed three men, injured another, and absconded with just over two million in cash. We know very little about Ms. Ramírez-Kernighan's abduction, but we have United States Senator from Illinois live at a press conference in front of the bank now."

"The fucking Senator," the Primary barked.

I trembled where I lay tied, but couldn't help soaking in my sister's beautiful face. Her hair was sleek and neatly pulled back away from her face. She wore jeans, a white silk blouse, and a navy blazer. Her face was blotchy and devoid of makeup. The normally pristine, elegant, and sophisticated Sonia the Senator was gone. In her place was my big sister. The woman who held me when I cried at night because I missed my mother and father when I first arrived at Kerrighan House. The woman who made sure I had extra money for fancy drinks from the coffee cart back when I was in college getting my teaching degree.

"My name is Sonia Wright-Kerrighan. The woman abducted in the Liberty National Bank heist two days ago is my foster sister Liliana." Sonia's eyes shimmered with tears as she swallowed and cleared her throat. The camera panned back. Standing next to her were Mama Kerri, Simone, Addison, Genesis, Blessing, and Charlie. Directly behind Sonia stood Omar, in a black suit with his arm in a blue sling, looking angry and so handsome my teeth ached. I ground down on my pearly whites as I watched. Thank God he was okay. He was with Holt, Jonah, Ryan, the police chief, and a bunch of others I recognized from my sisters' tragedies.

Tears filled my eyes and fell down my cheeks at the broken, dejected faces of my family. Mama Kerri looked haggard, her eyes red-rimmed and bruised a dark purple underneath as though she'd had no sleep in the past two days. The rest of my sisters looked no better except Blessing's cool demeanor and pinched brows proved she was ready to murder someone with her bare hands.

"Please, whoever has my sister Liliana, we are begging you, *begging* you to bring her back…" Her voice broke and tears fell down my stoic sister's cheeks. She didn't even take the time to wipe them away. She looked straight into the camera and continued on bravely. "We have been through so much the past several months. I have already lost one foster sister to a madman. Please, if there is anything human and decent within your heart and soul, bring back Liliana. Call the police. Call my office. We have people manning the phones 24/7. One phone call telling us where to get her is all you need to do. That's it. That's all we need. Please, *please* bring my sister home to us alive." Sonia choked on a sob and covered her mouth, dipping her head down and away while Mama Kerri tugged her into her arms.

Jonah approached the microphone next.

"My name is Jonah Fontaine of the Illinois Federal Bureau of Investigation. My team hunted down the Backseat Strangler and the copycat killer this past year, both of whom targeted this family. Both of whom are now dead. You kidnapped the wrong woman," he growled, his face twisting into a nasty scowl the likes I've never seen before. "The FBI, the Chicago Police Department, and a specialized team of highly trained bounty hunters have been tasked in finding *you*." He pointed directly at the screen. "And we will find you. I will not stop until Liliana is safely within the arms of her family. You better drop her somewhere safe and leave town. There is nowhere you can hide that we won't go. No dark hole we won't scour. Bring her back. Her family needs her home." His nostrils flared and his dark brown gaze seared straight into the camera.

I shivered at the anger in his expression. The man was going to come unhinged. Then he turned around and pulled a crying Simone into his embrace. My heart ached for them. My family, my sisters, and Mama Kerri were in such turmoil. It wasn't fucking fair! We'd been through enough already.

When the police chief approached the microphone, the Primary cut off the TV and turned to me.

"You might have mentioned that your fucking sister was the United States Senator of Illinois," he accused.

I shrugged my good shoulder and bit down on my bottom lip, trying not to let the fear of this damming information leak into my face.

"You didn't ask," I whispered.

The Primary threw the remote control across the room, and it shattered against the wall, the plastic pieces falling to the ground like confetti.

"Fucking hell! This just got a hundred times more complicated!" he roared.

My temperature rose and more tears fell down my cheeks as fear slithered over the surface of my pores. The shit had finally hit the fan. Would they kill me now that they knew I was connected to high profile people, or would they finally let me go?

"Brother, they are going to be looking *everywhere* for her. Traffic cams have to be showing our license plates by now, and even though the plates are fake, it won't be long before they figure out we headed to the harbor and loaded the money on a boat. Especially after the heist today. Sure, things went smoother there, but anyone could have caught something on camera at this point," the Second explained.

"*¡Dios mío!* You robbed another bank today? While I

freaking slept?" I gasped, realizing I probably wasn't supposed to call attention to that information.

"Christ!" The Primary paced in front of the bed I was tied to with his hands locked behind his head.

"And what do you want to do about it now?" Primary seethed, and I could almost see spittle flying out the bottom of his flimsy mask when he spoke.

"We're going to have to drop her and the money somewhere at the next stop in Holland, Michigan before moving to Plan C."

"Plan C? What was Plan B?" I asked.

Primary ignored me. "Fine," he growled. "Get Six and Seven to deal with Three and Four. Those two can't be trusted after what Lily shared yesterday. They're going to be a problem."

"What's Plan C?" I asked. I felt more hopeful after hearing him say "Fine," to me being dropped somewhere in Michigan. Hell, they could drop me at a dirty gas station bathroom, and I'd give them a round of applause.

"You'll see soon enough," the Primary answered once again ignoring me. "Untie her. Let's bring her to the front to eat. Can we trust you not to jump overboard or scream your lungs out if we bring you above to the deck?"

"Are you really going to set me free today?" I asked.

He nodded. "Yeah, *Liliana*." He enunciated my name as though it were dipped in pure acid. "We really are going to let you go today."

"Then yeah, I'll be good." And I would. I wanted to go home to my family. Wrap my arms around Mama Kerri and cry until I couldn't cry anymore. I wanted to see Omar, make sure he was okay and then slap him silly for making me fall for his charms when he had a woman and baby on the way. I wanted to feel safe again.

The Second untied each of my ankles as Primary released my good wrist. Second put pressure on my foot and I waited while he assessed the sprain. He flexed my foot forward and back. I sucked in a sharp breath when he manipulated the ball and arch of my foot where I'd sustained the most damage from the cleat on the boat.

"When you're picked up, tell them to give you an X-ray of both the shoulder and foot to ensure neither are fractured or broken. I did what I could, but you may need a surgical consult."

I nodded. "Okay. I will."

"First, let's break bread together and talk," the Primary ordered.

With the Second's help, I got out of bed and limped along beside them. We'd just made it out of the bedroom at the end of the hall when the door to where they were holding Four flew open and another masked man stood in front of us.

"I'm going to kill every last motherfucking one of you!" Four bellowed from behind the new masked guy.

I couldn't help but peek around him and look through the door. My gaze went straight to his familiar, scary, dark blue eyes. The same I remembered seeing when he tossed to me to the ground at the bank. Put a gun to Omar's head and mine too. The same I looked into when he killed that young man in the office. The same that knocked me out at the bank.

Four had long, dark, stringy salt-and-pepper hair that came down to his shoulders. A scruffy matching beard and mustache were unkept and matted with what I assumed was sweat or something gross. His nose was big and bulbous, dripping snot from one nostril. He hissed and grinned manically right at me.

"Hey there, little princess, how about you come over here and sit on ol' Mac's lap, eh?" he taunted.

"Mac, shut up!" Tucker, who I knew was the third bad guy, was also unmasked and tied to a chair next to his cousin. He had reddish brown hair that was buzzed so short on top I could see his white scalp through it. His jawline was prickled with reddish hair and unshaven. His eyes were a dark brown that I remembered seeing at the bank through the ski mask too.

"Take a good look, pretty, pretty princess. It's the face you'll be seeing not only in your nightmares, but wherever you hang your head at night. As soon as I get out of here, I'm going to slit that pretty head clean off your neck. Maybe I'll keep your head as my prize." He lifted his chin.

"Shut up!" Tucker begged next to him.

"You're all dead. Mark my words. I will kill every last one of you!" Four sneered and another masked man entered from a door in the back of the room. I couldn't recall seeing a tall, skinny guy before and didn't get a good look before he slammed the door cutting off our view.

"Sorry, boss," the man before us said in a booming, deep, gravely tone I'd not heard before.

"It's okay, Five. Gag them both and sedate them. We'll be getting ready to transport when we reach the Holland harbor."

"You got it, boss," he said, then went back into the room.

"Fuck you! Get away from me with that needle, you pansy! Fight like a real man!" I heard Four shout before everything went silent.

"Come. Let's get you settled before we transport you."
The Primary took over leading me up to the deck.

I moaned around a bite of the most delicious sea bass I'd ever tasted. It was buttery, fluffy, and melted in my mouth. "Wow, for bad guys, you sure know how to eat," I said adding another forkful of cheesy risotto. The meal was paired with grilled baby asparagus, and I ate like I hadn't had a meal in a week. Then again, I'd slept the day away.

"We're not bad guys," Primary groused.

They must have already eaten because they were both just sitting with me at the table overlooking the water, watching me eat. I pointed my fork at both their masked faces.

"Kidnapping. Robbery. Those are not things good guys do," I reminded them, not that they could forget.

The Primary sighed and got up, taking his untouched glass of white wine with him to the boat's edge, showing me only his back. He lifted his mask and, I believe, took a sip of his wine. Then he turned around, mask back in place, crossed his ankles over one another, and focused on me.

"Liliana, we had to do what was done. A very bad man was ruining a lot of lives."

"So, you stole two million dollars to make it right?" I snort-laughed.

"We stole more like a total of six million after today's haul, not to mention the others we'd already hit that didn't receive the same amount of press," he corrected.

"O-kay, six million. How does that help all the ruined lives related to this bad man?" I countered.

169

His shoulders dropped and he sighed again. "All the money will be returned. It's part of why we wanted you to come have dinner with us. So we could share where we'll be leaving the cash. The money was never the goal. We just needed it to be stolen in order for a massive audit and investigation of each of the banks we hit, as well as those we set off with the fake alarms."

"But why? Three people died!" I shoved my plate away, the food now tasting like sawdust on my tongue when the memory of that bank manager's lifeless eyes staring out at nothing entered my mind.

"I'll admit the MacCreedy cousins were a bad idea. Tucker and John 'Mac' MacCreedy were suggested to us by a solid source. A source that has since disappeared into the ether. We trusted this person at his word as he'd served with the two. They were brothers in arms. We trusted that resource, that connection, and planned to pay them all handsomely for it, from our *own* money. Not the banks'. The plan was always to return what was stolen. And now my brother and I have to live with the unfortunate choice, but we didn't pull the trigger. Our guns weren't even supposed to have ammunition in them. Frankly, I don't even know how to shoot the gun I held. The MacCreedys must have loaded them on their own."

"So, the guns were for show?" I clarified.

He nodded. "That was the plan, until it went straight up shit's creek."

"And the robbery today?" I asked.

"No one got hurt. Not so much as a scratch."

"The others?"

"Same. No issues," he sighed.

I nodded. "What now?"

170

"When we get to Holland, Michigan, we'll hide you away at one of the houses we rented via a dummy corporation. Then we'll place an anonymous call to the authorities with your location."

"And the MacCreedys?"

"They'll be left in the trunk of a car, parked in a storage unit next to where we'll leave the cash for the police to find. We'll give you a note with that address and we ask that you share it with the police." Primary came over to the table and sat across from me. He took my hand and held it between both of his gently. "I'm sorry all of this happened to you, Liliana." He squeezed my hand, perhaps signifying the truth behind his words. "None of this was supposed to happen. I hope one day you'll understand and be able to forgive me and my brother for what had to be done." Finally, he patted my hand kindly and then let me go.

The Second, who I hadn't realized had left the table, pointed out toward the horizon from where he stood near the small bar setup. "There's the Big Red Lighthouse of Holland, Michigan."

I looked where he pointed and noted a two-story lighthouse that was indeed a bright, stunning cheery red color. It was beautiful, like a beacon to my upcoming freedom.

Within thirty minutes the men were running around the boat, getting ready to dock. Which is also when Second came over to me and offered me his hand. He helped me stand and I looked into his masked face.

"I really am sorry for everything, Liliana. I'm also sorry for this," he stated, and then I felt a needle jab the side of my neck.

"You drugged me?" I mumbled as my tongue got thick and I started to sway, my knees suddenly feeling like Jell-O.

Within moments, I was unable to hold myself up. I smacked Second in the chest and held on. I looked into his masked face. "You suck," was the last thing I got out before once again, I was lights out.

It was dark when I awoke to the sound of a loud pounding. I was lying on an unfamiliar bed, my ankles and arm once again tied to the headboard and footboard. A comfortable quilt had been thrown over my body.

The banging got louder as I noted red and blue flashing lights streaming through the windows, casting an eerie glow on the ceiling.

I opened my mouth and tried to speak, but the sedative was trying to pull me back under.

"Help," the word lulled out of my mouth sounding more like "Hep."

There was another huge bang and then the sound of wood splitting as something smashed open. My eyes rolled around the room as I tried to keep them open, but I was sooooooo tired.

"Liliana!" I heard yelled throughout the strange space.

"Liliana!" A bit louder and closer.

"Help!" I croaked and tried to pull at my ties with no success. My limbs were wet noodles as I fingered the rope tying me to the gold antique metal headboard.

"Liliana!" I heard even closer, coming maybe from just outside the room I was in. I knew that voice. It sounded... like Omar.

"Omar!" I called out just as the door burst open.

There he was.

My knight dressed all in black, looking deadly and wild.

"*¡Mi lirio!*" he gasped as he came to the bed and cupped my cheeks. He kissed my lips hard, and I tried to kiss him back, but I was sloppy due to the drugs. He pulled back and kissed my cheeks, my forehead, my chin, and then my mouth. "You're alive. Thank you, God. You're alive, baby." He kissed me again. "I'm never letting you go again, woman. Never." He growled and pressed his forehead to mine.

"Omar," I choked back a joy-filled sob.

"Liliana!" I heard another voice I recognized as Jonah's coming from outside the room.

"In here! She's here. Alive!" Omar hollered.

"Untie me, please," I mumbled, my mind slowly coming out of the drugged haze.

Jonah entered the room, and his hand went right over his heart. "Oh, sweetheart, am I glad to see you!" He smiled wide and came over to me.

"She's tied up. Get her other foot," Omar ordered, his sling nowhere in sight, even though I knew he'd been shot a couple days ago and saw him wearing one on the footage earlier today. How was he even here? Not that I wasn't immensely happy to have him where I could see, feel, and touch his powerful frame, but how did they find me so fast?

Jonah and Omar untied me and then both men bumbled around the bed to help me sit upright.

"Why are your foot and shoulder bandaged?" Omar asked the second the blanket was removed, and I was in a seated position.

"Just get me out of here." I cupped his cheek. "I need to be home." My voice cracked as tears fell one after another down my cheeks. Emotions so intense built up like a simmering volcano, needing to escape. I could feel myself losing it, the tidal wave of suppressed emotions building at a rapid pace at the knowledge that I was finally within the safety of people who cared about me.

Omar moved to lift me up into his arms and Jonah slammed an arm against his chest. "Omar," he reprimanded. "You sustained a gunshot two days ago. I'll carry her."

Omar's nostrils flared and his jaw went tight before he nodded once sharply.

I was bundled in a blanket and lifted princess-style into Jonah's arms. He carried me out of the room my captors had left me in, down the stairs of the strange house, and straight out into a forest. There was nothing but trees as far as the eye could see.

"Where are we?"

"A vacation rental on Waukazoo Street in Holland, Michigan. Do you know how you got here?" he asked as he carried me straight toward an ambulance.

"Kinda, oh! We need to check my pockets or the room. My captors said they'd leave a note."

"A note?"

"To where the bad guys and the money are." I breathed. "We need to check my pockets," I screeched. Fear overtaking what I now knew to be the illusion of safety. "Those men want me dead. At least one of them does. He said he'd cut off my head," I cried, my body started to convulse as the sheer fear of what he threatened and how serious he was in that threat hit me full tilt. What if he got my family? Mama Kerri...

I gagged in Jonah's hold at the frightening visual of Four or "Mac" getting to my loved ones.

"Your captors?" Jonah asked.

I shook my head as everything came at me from every angle. The blinding brightness of the flashing police and emergency lights, the pain in my shoulder and ankle. Omar's kisses and his handsome face. Jonah holding me as though I were precious cargo. And the men who wanted me dead, along with the men who ultimately saved me.

It was all too much. Everything coalesced and blurred into a great giant ball of fear.

I was suddenly consumed with bone-breaking, agony inducing panic.

"Omar! I need Omar," I screamed, thrashing in Jonah's arms, forgetting who he was, where I was, and what was happening. All I knew is that it was all too much. I was going to die.

"Baby, I'm right here." He pulled me out of Jonah's hold, and I tucked my face into his neck and held on to him with my good arm, digging my nails into his shirt. "Don't let them get me. Please, don't let them take me again. He wants my head." I shook so hard I couldn't catch my breath.

"She's in major shock, sir. Please set her on the stretcher," someone said.

I held on tighter. "No! Don't touch me!" I screeched like a demon being exorcised.

Omar wrapped his bulk around my form so completely I curled even smaller against him, cowering against the only source of safety I believed in.

"You're okay, you're in my arms. Right where you're meant to be, *mi amor*. Shhhh, let them see to you."

I shook my head over and over and clung to his strength,

his voice, his smell, his feel, his *everything* surrounding me. I wasn't safe anywhere. Not anywhere but in his arms.

"They're gonna find me. Jonah has to find them. They want my head," I croaked and shook so hard my teeth chattered. I peered desperately into the most beautiful brown eyes I've ever known. "Please. Don't let them get me, Omar."

"No one is going to touch you ever again, Liliana. I'm here now. I've got you. Hold on and breathe. Just breathe for me, baby."

Eventually he sat on the stretcher with me curled in a ball in his lap. The ambulance closed the doors and jetted off, alarms blaring.

I twitched, remembering the alarms that rang out into the night at my second escape attempt from the boat. The night I almost drowned.

"I've got you. No one is going to hurt you, ever again. Not ever. I promise, *mi amor.*" He curled his big hand in my hair and kissed my entire face in small presses of his warm lips. I focused on each press of his soft skin to my eyes. My cheeks. My forehead. My nose. Finally, he kissed my lips softly until I started to warm up and respond, breathing more normally even while I trembled in his arms.

"C-cold," I murmured against his lips.

He nodded. "Okay, Liliana. We'll get you warm, but you have to let the paramedics take care of you. I'm right here."

I clung to his T-shirt, keeping him curled over my form and shook my head, tucking my face against his chest and listening to the beat of his heart.

"She needs a little more time. We'll try again at the hospital," he told the people who wrapped a warm blanket around the both of us. I snuggled more deeply to his chest.

"You have to find the note," I whispered.

"Where is it?" he asked as I held on.

"Pocket?" I responded with a question because I wasn't sure where my captors would have put the information since I'd been drugged.

Omar ran his hand up my thigh to the side of the loose men's sweats I wore. He tugged something out. It was a folded piece of yellow lined paper.

"I got the note, honey. Just rest. I'll take care of everything."

I pressed my ear to his chest and breathed in his scent, letting it comfort and sooth the shivers that hadn't slowed down since I'd been found. I focused on that smell and his heartbeat and closed my scratchy, tired eyes.

Through my woozy half-sleep drugged state, I could hear Omar speaking.

"Yeah, Jonah, this is Omar. You need get your team to Holland Boat Storage Units 105 and 106. The kidnappers left a note in Liliana's pocket. Go in hot. There may be two men that took part in the bank heists and her kidnapping. They could have weapons. One of the units may have money in it. Yeah, okay. She's not good, no, but she will be. I'll make sure of it." He curled his arm around my back and wedged me closer to his warmth.

As long as I was in this man's arms, I knew with my entire being that I would be just fine.

Chapter
THIRTEEN

I WOKE TO THE FEELING OF SOMEONE RUNNING THEIR FINGERS through my curls. I hummed and sighed, snuggling closer to the warmth running down the front of my body.

The warmth started to quake as hushed laughter weaved into my sleepy, happy place.

"You gonna open those beautiful eyes for us, *mi amor*?" I not only heard the deep rumble but *felt* that voice against my chest and legs.

I blinked open my eyes and found I was pressed from head to toe against a male body. Omar's lush, freshly washed soap mixed with a rich, earthy cologne scent, filtered through my lungs. My good arm was wrapped around his waist keeping him close.

"There she is. Hey, baby, how are you feeling?" he asked and nuzzled my forehead with his own.

I swallowed and took stock of how my body felt. My ankle and shoulder throbbed but for the most part, I was good. Last night when we got to the hospital, I wanted no part of being evaluated until I was able to calm down and see things more clearly. My overall health and vitals were good, but the doctors were worried about my mental state and chose to keep me overnight. If they hadn't let Omar stay, I would have lost the plot.

"Chicklet." Mama Kerri's sweet voice entered my hazy mind, and I turned toward the sound.

"Mama?" I gulped seeing her beautiful face.

Tears fell down her cheeks as she smiled wide.

"Mama!" I croaked as the overwhelming sensation of love filled the room and eased any remnants of tension I may have had at waking.

Omar eased us both up to a sitting position in the small hospital bed where I'd slept soundly against his form. He slipped out of the side of the bed as Mama came around and took his spot. The moment her essence surrounded me I burst into joyful tears.

"Oh, my girl, I was so, so worried," she admitted and kissed the crown of my head.

I nodded against her, breathing in the only parental unit I'd had since my biological parents died almost twenty years ago.

"I was so scared, Mama," I confessed. "But I tried to get away. I escaped the yacht twice but was brought back each time."

"Yacht?" Omar questioned. "You were held on a yacht?"

I rubbed my runny nose along the hospital gown sleeve and wiped at my eyes. "Yeah. It was fancy, too."

"Liliana, you're going to need to give a full report to the authorities. I was able to ward them off last night because you weren't in any state to talk. I'm afraid I won't be able to do the same today, *mi amor.*"

I sighed and held Mama's hand. "I'll tell them what I know. Did they find the bad guys?"

His face went from gentle to granite in a second flat. "Let's have the doctor check on you, yeah? Then we can discuss the rest…"

"Omar, no!" I frowned. "I deserve to know the truth. What did the FBI find in those storage units?"

His jaw firmed and he let out a frustrated breath. "They found all the money. Every dollar that was stolen. And it wasn't from just the two banks that we know were hit. It was from several others spanning the entire Great Lakes area. Looks like all the banks were under the same corporate umbrella. Owned and operated for the last thirty-five years by Gregory Winston."

"Name doesn't ring a bell," I said. "And what about the MacCreedys?"

That time he frowned, his perfectly arched brows furrowing. "Who are the MacCreedys?"

I closed my eyes as pure dread snaked through my system.

"Who are the MacCreedys, Liliana? You mentioned that two men would be in the storage units but all we found was a mutilated storage bay that looked like a vehicle had crashed through it."

"You mean they got away?" I trembled in my mother's arms. "No, please don't tell me they got away?" I gasped, fear settling once again in my bones.

"Honey, none of us are sure about anything at this time. Our focus has been entirely on you. The girls and I have been in the waiting room since shortly after you arrived last night, but they wouldn't let any of us see you. You were in such a state, Omar was the only person you'd respond to in a positive way."

I reached for her hand and squeezed it with mine. "*Lo siento*, Mama," I murmured. "I'm sorry I scared you. All of you." I looked from her sorrow-filled face to Omar's angry one.

"Chicklet, you are alive and talking to me. I'll thank my lucky stars and the good Lord above that He brought you back to me safe and sound and in one piece." She cupped my cheeks and wiped the tears from my eyes with her thumbs. "Everything else we'll figure out. Okay, sweetheart?"

I nodded, trying to focus on the good instead of the fact that the authorities did not have the MacCreedys in custody.

"I'm going to get Jonah and Ryan in here to take your statement. First, I'll bring in your sisters. I'm sure you want to see them. But only for a bit. We need to get a move on with the hunt for those men before they hurt anyone else," Omar shared.

Or come after me, I thought with futility.

Four, or should I say John "Mac" MacCreedy, wanted me dead. He'd made that very clear in his last threat before I was released by my captors and found by Omar and Jonah's FBI team.

What if they too knew who I was? If they didn't, they sure as heck would soon enough. I knew the press would be doing a bang-up job spreading every detail about my family's newest tragedy.

That meant none of us were safe.

I'd looked straight into the cold blue eyes of that monster John MacCreedy and saw nothing but disdain and unadulterated hate.

It wasn't a question of if John MacCreedy would come after me. The real question was *when* he'd come after me. And whether or not I'd be ready to fight back.

Just like on the yacht, I'd do whatever it took to protect my family and stay alive.

After teary hugs and a beautiful reconciliation with my family, I spent a couple hours going over everything I could remember about my time with my captors and every detail I could remember about the MacCreedys. Though for some reason, I kept out that the two main people who kept me under lock and key were brothers, and that one of them was definitely a doctor. Instead, I gave vague recollections of my time with the two men, confirming they wore masks the entire time but treated me well. I did make it clear that I knew there were at least seven men involved but the MacCreedys were the ones who went off script and killed those people in the bank. I also shared how they'd been hired outside of whatever relation the rest of them had with one another.

What I didn't share either was the fact that my two captors were somehow on a vigilante spree to right some wrongs I thought had to do with the bank. I still didn't know their angle, but kept that part of my speculation to myself. Maybe when they found out that the MacCreedys had escaped the storage units, my two compassionate captors would help find them. I knew the Primary and the Second were not only disgusted at what had occurred, but they most likely felt an intense amount of responsibility and guilt regarding the lives that were lost—and could still be lost, now that the MacCreedys were on the run.

I sure as hell hoped those two were running. Definitely made me feel a tad more secure, but nothing right now would make me feel *safe*.

Nothing but Omar.

My sisters agreed to go home and await my release from

the hospital later today. Mama Kerri however flat-out refused to leave without her daughter by her side. She did agree to getting a cup of coffee and a bite to eat while Omar and I waited for the doctor to discharge me officially. I'd given what information I was prepared to give to the authorities, and the rest would be kept to myself.

Omar removed a pair of men's sweats from a clear bag that held the things I'd been wearing when I came into the hospital last night.

I shook my head at the sight of those clothes, knowing they were the Primary's. "I won't wear those. They belonged to one of my captors," I declared with a curl of my lips.

"No problem, *mi amor*, you can wear my clothing." He pulled out a black duffle that had the Holt Security logo emblazoned along the side in big, slanted letters. Omar unearthed a pair of men's pajama pants that were a dark forest green and made of the softest T-shirt material ever. He handed me a folded black men's V-neck T-shirt that was also super soft.

"*Gracias*. Um, do you think you could help me?" I bit down on my bottom lip hating that I needed his help, but even more upset with myself that I *wanted* it. Wanted him.

Omar nodded and removed the blanket from my legs. He then helped me shift to the side of the bed. He stood in front of me and reached around my form to untie the hospital gown. He slid the fabric away which left me sitting completely naked before his eyes. He didn't so much as look down, his gaze set above my neck.

However, I did look because I hadn't evaluated myself since the day of the bank robbery when I got out of the shower. I had aches and pains everywhere.

I gasped at the blackened, bruised color of my kneecaps where I'd hit the floor at the bank.

Suddenly Omar was there, his thumbs tracing the large marks. His big body dipped low, and he placed a soft kiss on one knee and then the next, before his gaze lifted to meet mine.

Then I watched silently as his eyes traveled from one injury to another. The next was at my thigh where it was clear I'd been manhandled by a brute. Black thumbprints trailed up the sides of my legs. Each print got a feather-soft kiss from Omar that sent my pulse soaring.

I threaded my fingers through his thick, black hair. It was as soft as I knew it would be, like silky onyx ribbons.

Omar's hand slid up to my ribcage and he dipped his head, placing a kiss just under my bare breast where another ugly purple bruise had formed.

I gasped and his gaze shot to my breast and then to my face. With those stunning brown eyes on mine, I watched as they lit with a fiery possessiveness I didn't fear. In this moment he was staking his claim on my body, covering marks that were made in violence not love. Each caress felt as though he was making promises to me through his touch. Each kiss told me how much he cared. How much damage he would do to those who had hurt me.

"Omar." I licked my lips as he inhaled deeply near my breast, the heat of his breath stimulating the tip of one erect nipple. For a full heartbeat he stared straight into my eyes. I'm sure he saw all my need, hope, and desire. I tightened my grip on his hair, bringing his face closer to my naked breast, an offer he took greedily, first with a closed mouth kiss directly over my nipple, then by taking the entire peak into the heat of his mouth. He swirled his tongue against the burning tip and sucked until I moaned at the decadent sensation of having his mouth *there*. Finally.

I groaned, arching into the pleasure and wanting more as he teased my nipple, licking, flicking, and sucking in a dizzying rhythm that made arousal coat the space between my thighs.

He pulled back and I almost cried out in frustration until he shifted that gifted mouth to the other breast and repeated his attentions. By the time he kissed his way over each fleshy globe, over my shoulder, and up along my neck, I was a ball of sexual need. I sighed into the warm, pleasurable feeling. It was so far beyond the opposite of the ugliness I'd experienced the past few days, I craved *more*.

Instead of kissing me like I wanted him to, he stood and tugged the black T-shirt over my head and helped me get my bad arm inside before I was able to shove my good arm through the sleeve on my own.

"Omar?" I questioned, all of a sudden feeling shy and unwanted after he'd stopped the festivities.

He stood before me, fisting his hands at his sides. "Liliana, I want nothing more than to spread you out over this bed and sink so deep inside you we become one. But I don't want our first time to be when your emotions are all over the place. When you decide to make love with me, it's going to be because you want it more than anything. Not because you need to replace the scary emotions you are dealing with right now."

"But I want you," I admitted for the first time since we met all those months ago.

He cupped my cheeks. "I know you do. And I'm happy about that, *mi amor*, but our first time will not be in a hospital bed after you've been kidnapped, are scared, and are healing from your injuries."

I blew out an angry breath because he was right. The moment his lips touched my knees, the hospital disappeared, and it was just us. Being with him made entire rooms disappear. And stopping was the right thing to do. Not only because of the things he noted, though all those reasons were good ones.

"And what about the pregnant woman I saw you with three months ago? She still in your life?" I snapped, my original reason for pushing him away suddenly coming back to the surface.

He tilted his head and scoured my face with his gaze. "What woman?"

I glared, my ire coming back full force now that his mouth wasn't on me, and I was thinking more clearly.

He reached for the pajama pants and brought them to my feet where he pulled them up my thighs. He helped me stand and covered my bare lady bits and ass then rolled up the waistband until the legs weren't so long and the crotch didn't hang down to my knees.

"Charlie and I saw you at Old St. Patrick's Church a week after Addison's situation ended. The same week you claimed to want to take me out, to want a relationship with me. You were at church with a gorgeous woman with long dark hair who was about ready to pop. You were loving on her, holding her, touching her belly." I coughed trying to hide the sadness in my tone.

Omar put one of his hands to my hip and the other to my cheek, forcing me to lift my head and look into his eyes.

"The only pregnant woman in my life is my twin sister Ophelia. Yes, she is gorgeous, but I'm biased. She is also raising my nephew alone. I was her birth coach. She and the baby currently live in the apartment across from mine so I can keep an eye on them."

"Your sister?" My bottom lip trembled at the truth behind his response.

"Yes, *mi amor*. I would not pursue you so completely like I have if I had another woman in my life. Since the day I laid eyes on you I've been under your spell. Other women ceased to exist. No woman could compare to your fire, your beauty, your spirit."

"Twin sister?" I gulped back the sadness threatening to claim me once again into a weepy mess.

"Ophelia knows all about you. She calls you '*la fiera*,' my spitfire." He grinned. "She'd be thrilled to meet you. Prove I'm not lying." He chuckled.

Tears filled my eyes, and I wrapped my arm around his shoulder. "I'm sorry, Omar. I thought..." I closed my eyes. My past was messing up the potential for my future.

"You thought you were the other woman?" He grumbled under his breath. "I called, texted, left voicemails, dropped by your house. You avoided me. I thought..." He shook his head. "I stopped coming because after trying for a month..." He shrugged. "I believed that maybe I'd imagined our chemistry. After trying so many times, I figured you really didn't want more."

I grabbed his wrist and rubbed my cheek into his hand. "I did want more. But in the past I've been hurt by men I loved. Hurt badly. Lied to. Cheated on. I saw you with that woman..."

"My twin sister." He unhelpfully interrupted, making the knife of regret sink even deeper into my heart.

I swallowed down the pain of that mistake and nodded. "I saw you with your sister and I just snapped. I did everything, *everything* I could to avoid you. Until the universe put us at the bank at the same time."

He stepped back and rubbed his chin. "I shouldn't have stopped trying. I should have made you talk to me. *Mi madre* thought maybe I reminded you of the danger you were in. That was when I decided I'd give you some time. Wait a few months and try again when you were in a better position emotionally."

God, I was so stupid. He was such a good man.

"I'm so sorry. I don't..." My bottom lip trembled. "I don't deserve you," I finally croaked.

He pressed his fingers to my lips. "We'll talk about it more when you're safely in my arms and we're settled in for the evening."

"We?"

His eyebrows rose up into his hairline. "You think I'm going to let you out of my sight any time soon, *mi amor*, you are very, very wrong. Especially now that I know why you have been avoiding me so completely the past three months. Ophelia is going to laugh herself sick when she finds out."

"Sounds like you have a really close bond with your sister."

He nodded. "Like you with yours. Only it's just me, Ophelia, *mi madre,* and my brother Arturo. They run our family restaurant downtown."

"Family restaurant?"

He smiled wide. "As soon as you are well enough, I will take you there. You will have the best tortilla soup you have ever tasted," he boasted with great pride.

I grinned then narrowed my gaze. "I'm known in my

family for my traditional Mexican cuisine, so your family has a lot to live up to," I touted, feeling the shimmering whisps of excitement at the idea that I'd have such an experience with him and his family.

He cupped both of my cheeks, rubbed his nose against mine, and whispered against my lips. "The cookoffs will be exciting, *mi amor*. I look forward to the challenge."

A man that not only protected but loved his family, and cooked too? I must have been dreaming.

Omar pressed his lips to mine and kissed me stupid. Letting the past go with every sigh and press of his tongue to mine, I gave him my all. Filling up on his desire and clear devotion to me and our future. For him it's always been a foregone conclusion that we'd end up together, and for the first time, I believed him.

We kissed for so long and so completely that we were bombarded by the discharge nurse and Mama Kerri entering at the same time.

"Oh... Um, sorry, my dears. But it's time for our girl to go home." Mama Kerri's cheeks were tinged as pink as I'm sure my own were after I watched Omar lick his lips as if tasting me a second time. The heat in my cheeks ramped up a thousand degrees when he gifted me that sexy smile and jaunty wink before letting the nurse discuss my home care.

In the end, my ankle was not broken, just badly sprained and bruised from the cleat. My shoulder wasn't broken either, but I'd need to stay in a sling for at least two weeks, and then follow-up with my regular medical practitioner to be sure everything healed well.

Once Omar got me into the zip-up hoodie that smelled

amazingly of him and into a hospital wheelchair, we made our way out of the hospital and into a sea of paparazzi.

The cameras flashed, setting off a thousand tiny stars behind my eyelids.

"Shit!" Omar cursed and started to back up my wheelchair in an attempt to return to the hospital and away from the mob.

Mama Kerri lifted her hands in front of her eyes while keeping her head down and made a shooing sound. She tried to wave away the photographers, but they didn't budge.

"Have some respect!" she demanded, but they ignored her, continuing to hurl question after question our way.

"Liliana, what happened during your kidnapping?" one hollered.

"Ms. Ramírez, is that your boyfriend?" another asked.

"Can you ID the bank robbers?" I heard next.

"Are you scared the robbers are going to come for you?" Another reporter questioned and I flinched, because I was terrified of that happening.

The more questions that were thrown at me, paired with those nauseating camera flashes, the more frightened I became, cowering within myself. I put the hood up, obscuring my face, and ducked my head and upper body and brought my legs up, making myself as small as possible.

"You all should be ashamed of yourselves. My daughter has been through enough. She needs to go home to heal, you vultures!" She sobbed, her tears threatening my own.

Eventually Omar got us back into the hospital and we waited in a corner as Jonah and Ryan stormed through the entrance. They must not have been far away since they were able to get here within fifteen minutes, and I knew we were over a two-hour drive from Chicago.

"I'm so sorry," Jonah stated as he made it our way. "We had no idea they were discharging you so quickly. Usually it takes hours." He pushed the hair out of his tired eyes.

It did in a busy Chicago hospital, that's for sure. But here in the smaller hospital, they'd been fast and efficient. Though it would have been nice to be forewarned about the media.

"We were at the hotel packing up when your call came," Ryan explained. "I'm really sorry too. We'll take over here. Why don't you bring your truck around to the back private exit, and we'll get you guys out of here and on the road."

Mama Kerri reached out and squeezed Jonah on the shoulder. "That would work perfectly, son." She smiled sweetly.

Ever since Simone announced her engagement to Agent Jonah Fontaine, Mama had been calling him "son." She did the same to Killian when he proposed to Addy, too.

It made me wonder if she'd one day call Omar that.

A shiver of excitement raced down my spine, making the unsettling experience of the paparazzi fizzle away into something much less important.

I was safe.

I was going home.

I was with Omar.

I would take the wins that came my way, because now I knew how important each day was. How quickly life could be snatched away. I'd never take a single day for granted again. Not after what I'd lived through.

A warm hand covered the back of my neck. "You ready to go home?" Omar asked.

"Depends on what home?"

"I figured you'd want to go to Kerrighan House, chicklet.

Your sisters are all there and they'll need some time with you," Mama Kerri stated.

I shook my head. "I can't go there. I can't go to my childhood home."

Omar crouched down and took my hand. "Why not, baby?"

"By now they know who I am. All the press. Everything leads back to Kerrighan House. None of us are safe. I just know it." My voice shook as I held on to his hand. Renewed fear, anger, and hopelessness washed over me. "None of us are safe," I repeated.

"We'll meet there, talk to everyone, and then decide what to do, okay?" Omar suggested. Then he stared deep into my eyes. "Remember I promised you I wouldn't let you be hurt again. They will not get to you."

My bottom lip quivered. "What about my family? They'll hurt them to get to me."

"Not on my watch." He said the words as though they were fact.

At that moment, I had no choice but to believe him. I surely believed he'd try, but I also knew John MacCreedy was psychotic. And nothing fueled a psycho like revenge.

Chapter
FOURTEEN

Entering Kerrighan House, even while being carried princess-style from Omar's SUV, brought tears to my eyes. It was as if I was wrapped in a warm blanket of nothing but love and affection after having been so damn cold on that boat and in the icy depths of Lake Michigan. Reminded me of inhaling the ocean breeze after a year of teaching other people's children and finally getting your summer break.

It was home.

Omar set me down with such care, it was as if I were a treasured Fabergé egg that might break on contact. All my sisters watched in what I could only call hushed anticipation as he tucked the throw blanket that had been hanging over the back of the couch around my form. Then he dipped his head, lifted my chin, and took my mouth in a sweet kiss.

"Talk with your family, *mi amor*. I'm going to touch base with the guys on your case."

I gripped his hand and squeezed it. "You're not leaving, are you?" I asked, trying not to let my desperation leak into the question but knowing I failed miserably.

"Not without you, I'm not." He stared straight into my eyes until I could see the severity and truth behind his words.

I nodded, and he ran his hand from my temple down the

side of my cheek and chin in a feather-light caress before he left to enter the kitchen.

I let my shoulders fall, took in a breath, and then realized I had a room of shocked sisters all staring at me.

"Hey guys, it's so good to be home…" I started before Blessing cut me off.

She held out her hand and then waved it wildly. "Mmm hmm. Nope. Not happening. We're starting with the kiss," she blurted, having none of it.

"Or maybe the caress?" Simone giggled and came to sit right next to me on the couch, taking my hand with both of hers.

"I wanna talk about the *mi amor* business," Charlie announced. "Let's start there. *My love.*" She gushed, enunciating the endearment Omar chose for me. Every time he called me that my heart swelled to twice its size.

"You guys, leave her be. She's been through hell and back," Genesis offered. "She'll tell us all about her brand spanking new boyfriend that she somehow secured—while being kidnapped and surviving a burglary—in her own time…"

"The fuck she will," Blessing sassed. "Sister, spill!" she demanded.

"Blessing!" Mama Kerri hollered. "Watch that mouth. My goodness me, you've lost your mind."

"I have lost my mind, Mama! My sister was just carried in like a bride on her wedding day by a hunky guy who called her my love AND kissed her in front of all of us. Like he had the God-given right to do so. I'm shook! You shook?" She pointed to Simone, who nodded. Then to Sonia who did the same and so on with all of them until she got to Mama Kerri.

Mama sighed. "I'm not surprised at all. The writing was on the wall the day they met. Anyone could see it."

"I mean, she's not wrong. They have been fire since he was assigned to protect her body. Now he wants to do all kinds of things to that body…" Charlie teased.

"Charlie…" Mama warned.

I pressed my lips together and tried not to burst into laughter. These women were the world to me.

I held up my good hand. "Okay, so obviously a lot has happened in the past several days. Most of it was horrible, scary, and a nightmare I don't want to relive. The only good part was that Omar and I cleared the air."

"Cleared the air? More like filled it with soft romantic music, rose petals, and champagne," Charlie went on. "How in the world did this happen? I thought he had a woman, a pregnant woman to be exact."

Of course, they all remembered what Charlie and I had seen at the church. They had helped me nurse my wounds over being misled and then assisted me in ignoring and hiding out from my once-sexy bodyguard when he continued to chase after me.

"About that… It turns out the pregnant woman we saw was his twin sister Ophelia," I confessed, feeling shame swirl in my gut.

"Twin sister! Shut up!" Charlie blasted. "No way!" Then she nodded and looked off into the distance as if going back to when we saw him at the church. "I can totally see it now. We were sooooooo wrong. Oh my god, that sucks! I was ready to kill him."

"Shoot! Makes you wish you'd cleared the air and told him

what you saw that day, huh?" Genesis frowned and slumped back against the couch.

"Yeah, it really does." I sighed and glanced over toward the kitchen where I could hear the guys debriefing.

Mama stood up from her easy chair. "Well, there's nothing we can do now but move forward. What's in the past is in the past. You can't change it. We can only live with the decisions we've made and focus on the future and not making those same mistakes again. Right?"

Each one of us nodded solemnly. We've all made a lot of crummy decisions in the recent years, and we were determined not to let the tragedies derail our happy futures.

"This little get-together needs tea and cookies." She rubbed her hands together.

"I'll help you, Mama." Genesis got up and followed her into the kitchen.

"So, what's going to happen now?" Charlie asked.

"With the case?" I clarified.

Her red brows came together, and she shook her head and made a stink face. "No, with you and Omar."

I laughed because of course Charlie was only concerned about my love life. Not the fact that we were all back in the thick of a traumatic situation once more.

"Honestly, I don't know. We're, um, together? I think? I'm pretty sure. Just, I don't know what that looks like right now. There's a lot for us to talk about," I admitted, feeling the strain of not knowing where we stood. I mean, the kisses in the hospital were pretty straightforward. Still, it was all so up in the air. There hadn't been time to label anything, and I didn't really want to label it.

"Lil, you have all the time in the world." Addy sat on the

arm of the couch and put her hand to my shoulder. "I know with Killian it just naturally went there. It was fast, but right. Maybe it's like that for you?"

Simone sat up and put her hand to my thigh. "Same with me and Jonah. The chemistry was there but it just clicked into place. Also super-fast, and I have no regrets."

"I regret not talking to him when Charlie and I saw him in the church. We could already be together by now, not having a bank robbery and kidnapping in the way of us starting something serious. Now I worry that his fear of losing me to what we endured in that bank is twisting what his true feelings for me are."

"Is that how you feel? That your feelings are based on relief that he helped save you?" Sonia asked in a gentle tone that was nurturing and supportive, not at all accusatory.

I shook my head. "No, but I can't help how safe I feel when I'm with him. Like as long as I'm in his arms, nothing bad can happen to me."

Addy nodded avidly. "Totally get that."

"Absolutely. Jonah holds me until I fall asleep every single night. He's my security blanket," Simone admitted.

"Exactly," I whispered.

"But, honey, that doesn't mean I don't want and love who he is outside of him being my greatest protector. He's kind, compassionate, loving, ridiculously competitive when playing any kind of game, works too hard, cares too much, and never, and I mean *never* gets his clothing into the laundry bin. That sucker is right there in the corner of our room, but his clothes end up wherever he drops them. He makes a mean grilled cheese that is to die for, can grill anything, laughs too little, despises Amber shedding all over the place, and loves me to distraction."

"God, he's so perfect for you." Sonia sighed and rubbed her sister's arm.

"What I'm trying to show you is that he's so much more than my protector. It may have started out like that, but, sister, it doesn't continue that way. What do you like about Omar outside of his protection?"

"I love how much he talks about his mother and how he can't wait for me to meet her." I smiled shyly.

Simone's cheeks pinked up and she nodded. "And…"

"His body, *Dios mío*, just looking at him makes me crazy. And he has the softest, silkiest hair. And the way he kisses me like I'm important…*special*. It's different than any kiss I've ever had."

Simone grinned huge.

"He's so hard-working. Takes what he does very seriously. The people in his protection mean something to him. They aren't just a job. And he loves children. I could see that when we went to the zoo. He thinks Rory is amazing. He doesn't care that I come from a house full of independent, strong women and genuinely seems to like all of you. There's still so much I don't know about him though. I don't know his favorite movie. What his hobbies are…"

"*Die Hard*. Playing basketball with the boys, cooking, and teasing my sister and *madre*. But feel free to continue sharing how awesome I am," Omar teased while answering my questions. He entered the living room carrying the tea and cookies for Mama Kerri, setting the tray neatly on the coffee table.

Embarrassment rushed over my skin in a wave of heat and pin pricks.

"And now she's all pink. You're just as beautiful with pink cheeks, *mi amor,* as you are naturally." He smiled in that sexy way that made my heart beat faster.

I rolled my eyes. "Charmer!" I fired back, trying to hide just how much he affected me.

"I quite like a charming fellow." Mama Kerri patted Omar's back. "Thank you, my dear."

"After your visit, I think it's best that we pack up your clothes and take you to my place. No one connected to you knows where I live besides Holt. Jonah and Ryan think it's a good idea to keep you hidden away for a bit longer, at least until they can get a beat on the MacCreedys."

"Who are the MacCreedys?" Charlie asked.

"The two we know helped rob those banks and threatened to harm your sister," Omar confided.

"You mean to tell me my sister is still in danger?" Blessing stated with anger in her tone.

Omar nodded as Jonah entered with Ryan at his back.

"It's back to bodyguards for all of you," Jonah announced.

"Seriously?" Charlie grouched and slumped against the cushions with a big sigh.

"When is this ever going to end?" Simone mumbled, closed her eyes, and leaned her head back onto the couch.

"I'm going to go wake Rory from her nap. If you two are leaving soon, she'll want to see her *tía* Lily," Genesis said and took the stairs heading to our rooms.

Blessing stood up and walked around the table to stand directly in front of the men. "What is it going to take to capture these motherfu…"

"*Blessing,*" Mama warned.

She hissed. "What's the plan?"

199

"There isn't one. Our team is hard at work poring over the details of Liliana's statement of events. We know who the MacCreedys are, but we know nothing about the remaining five men that Liliana noted were part of the heist and kidnapping. All we know now is that specifically John MacCreedy was the individual who took the lives of the three innocents at the bank. He was also the one who carried and put Liliana's unconscious body into the back of one of the getaway vehicles. The rest are all accomplices at this time. We've got teams going over the banks' security feeds, management, and ownership. It's odd that all of the banks were owned by the same company. That means whoever stole the money did it on purpose. We also don't know why they returned what they stole."

"Maybe they thought that would get them out of trouble?" Sonia suggested.

"Which may have been the case had three people not been murdered, another wounded, and Liliana kidnapped. All of those things are illegal, and each member of that team will ultimately pay for their part in it."

"I think the banks are the key. As I told you, I overheard the men taking care of me on the boat mentioning that the bank leadership are criminals. I'm not in banking so I have no idea what that means, but it makes me wonder at their motive. Robbing banks to turn around and give back all the money? They didn't have to do that. They even left a note where to find it. That does not say normal bank robbers who are greedy for money."

Jonah nodded. "It's odd, I'll give you that. While we comb over the evidence, each of you need to stick with your bodyguard and preferably paired up. Let's not give these criminals any opportunity to hurt any of you. Got it? We're going to be extremely vigilant."

Jonah looked at each sister until they each nodded.

"I think it's best if you shack up together for now. Except you, Liliana. I agree with your fear that your presence makes the rest of your family a bigger target. If the goal is to get to you, they may try and go after one of you, but they certainly won't when there are FBI agents crawling all over this place. And if they're looking for you, it's best you be hidden somewhere they won't find you."

"With me." Omar pointed to his chest with his thumb.

I nodded. "I'm fine with that. I'll do anything to keep my family safe and avoid ever looking into the eyes of that monster ever again." I shivered.

"Good. Then we've agreed. Ryan and I will stay in touch as things progress," Jonah finished. "Now, I know we're all hungry and tired. I'm thinking pizza and bed. Mama Kerri? I defer to you as this is your home." He smiled.

"Sounds great," she agreed.

"I'm going to get Liliana to my place. *Mi madre* already has a hot meal waiting." He smiled and winked at me.

His mother.

She knows what happened to me.

I can't meet his mother. Not like this. She'll hate me on sight.

"*¡Dios mío!* I'm not meeting *tu madre* like this!" I gestured to my body still clad in his oversized clothing, bruised from head to toe, a busted shoulder, sprained ankle, my hair needing a good washing, dark circles under my eyes, and my mental state sitting between 'more tired than I've ever been in my life' and 'scared out of my mind.'

He smiled softly. "*Mi lirio*, you couldn't be anything but absolutely beautiful. *Mi madre* is going to love you. Do not worry."

"Yeah, Sprite, everyone loves a damsel in distress." Charlie snorted.

I finagled to a standing position while Simone tried to help but I batted her hand away.

"I am not a damsel in distress. I'm perfectly capable of taking care of myself." I huffed, wobbling where I stood on one foot.

Omar crossed those massive arms over one another and grinned, waiting for something, for what I didn't know. I'd been given a walking boot for my sprained ankle, but I didn't see it anywhere.

"Where's my boot?" I grated and narrowed my eyes at the ridiculously handsome man grinning before me.

"What do you plan to do with it?" he asked.

"I'm going to hobble up those stairs." I pointed to said stairs. "Take a shower, wash away all that happened, maybe cry my eyes out, and put on *my* clothing." My bottom lip trembled as I started to get teary-eyed and frustrated at my crappy situation once again.

He nodded as Jonah and Ryan slipped into the kitchen, obviously realizing that I was going to get into it with Omar.

"And how are you going to get into the shower, *mi amor?*" Omar queried.

I lifted my chin and gestured to my sisters. "One of them will help me."

"Mmm hmm. I'm sure they would be happy to, if that's what you want. Is it?" His question was thoughtful, not filled with any expectation which made me feel even more unsettled.

"I don't know what I want anymore." I choked out as the tumble of everything that happened spread over me once again. "I'm so tired. So tired of being scared. So *tired*, Omar. I can't...I can't deal with anything more."

"How about I make sure *mi madre* is gone before we arrive at my home? Would that be better for you?" The clever, clever man. Realizing immediately what the problem was.

One by one, each of my sisters removed themselves silently from the room.

Until it was just me, Mama Kerri, and the rock wall that was Omar left to face off.

"Sweetheart, you know you're forever welcome here. This will always be your home. However, I think you need some time with Omar to get fed, washed, and into bed where you feel safe and protected. Things will feel differently in the morning, chicklet. I promise."

Omar came over and wrapped his arms around me. I pressed my face against his chest and clung to his waist with my good hand. "It's not your mom. I want to meet your mom. Just not when I'm broken," I admitted as my breath hitched.

He tunneled his fingers into my hair and tilted my face up so he could look me in the eye.

"Liliana, you could never be broken. Wounded sure, but never broken. You're too strong for that. And you have too many people who love you to help keep you solid."

"Thank you," I said as a tear fell down my cheek. "I needed to hear that." I sniffed back the emotions threatening to take me down the rabbit hole of stress and worry. "Can we go now?"

He nodded, kissed me softly, and pulled back. "We can go now. Say goodbye to your mom while I get one of your sisters to secure some of your things."

I sat back down on the couch and Mama Kerri came over and sat right next to me so that our thighs touched. She wrapped her arm around my back and let me rest my head against her shoulder.

"You're going to be okay. You know that, right? That man would die before he ever let any harm come to you again. It's written all over his face." She murmured against my hair.

"I just want this all to be over."

"Me too, chicklet. Me too." She played with my dirty hair until Omar came down the stairs with a suitcase in each hand. I watched as he took them through the room and out the front door. The paparazzi roared to life. I could see the camera flashes through the closed sheers of our big window.

"When will they stop?" I groaned.

Mama sighed. "When there's a better, more exciting story to chase after."

Omar came back and Mama helped me stand up. Each of my sisters came from inside the kitchen and hugged me tightly.

Genesis came down the stairs with my niece clutched to her chest, her thumb in her mouth and her wild black curls all over the place.

Her gaze came to mine and she smiled huge, kicking to get down. Her mom put her down and she raced over to me. Omar scooped her up before she could slam into me.

"Hey, little one, *Tía* Lily has been hurt. We have to be very careful when we hug her, okay?"

Her eyes got wide, and she nodded with her mouth in the shape of an O. "*Tía*, you got a boo-boo?" She asked.

"*Sí, mi cielo. Tía* is not feeling too good, but I'm going to feel better real soon." I ran my fingers through her pretty curls.

"And then we can go to the zoo again with *tío* Omar?" she asked excitedly.

I nodded and cupped her cheek. "*Sí.* Now give me a big hug and a kiss because I'm going to stay at Omar's for a little while so he can take care of me."

"I can take care of you. I'm going to be a doctor," she announced with purpose.

"A doctor? I thought you were going to be Queen?" I teased and tickled her ribs.

She giggled and nodded. "Yeah. Queen Doctor."

I smiled so wide my cheeks hurt. It was the first time in days I felt actual happiness.

Omar lifted Rory close so she could hug me and kiss me on the cheek.

"Where does it hurt?" she asked.

I pointed to my bum shoulder.

"Oh, I kiss it." She leaned her little body over Omar's arm, so he brought her closer. She placed a kiss to my shoulder. "Better?"

"*Sí,* it is! Wow. You really are a great doctor."

She shrugged. "I know," she claimed with all the confidence in the world.

"*Te amo*, Rory."

"I love you too, *tía* Lily and *tío* Omar." She smiled and kicked to get out of Omar's hold. He set her down and she ran directly over to Mama Kerri. "Cookies!"

Mama Kerri cupped her grandchild's face as though she were beloved, because she absolutely was. That child was the best of all of us combined. Raised to know her value and worth.

"I'm ready." I took Omar's hand.

He dipped down and lifted me into his arms with a little grunt. "Guys, an escort?" I knew he was told to go easy on that arm since he had a bullet go right through his shoulder but he didn't seem to care or let it prevent him from doing what he wanted.

Jonah and Ryan nodded and followed us out the front door, keeping the paparazzi from getting too close. They shouted question after question, but I just kept my face pressed against Omar's throat and focused on the beat of his heart.

Within minutes we were off to his home.

I needed food. A shower. A bed. And Omar. In that exact order.

Chapter
FIFTEEN

THE GOOD NEWS: OMAR WAS ABLE TO SHAKE OFF ANY paparazzi stragglers that had followed us from Kerrighan House. The bad news: I was about to crash. Between the pain medication I'd taken, the whirlwind of being with my family, and the realization that the drama continued with my situation… Everything finally was taking its toll.

A gritty, raw vulnerability swarmed around my form as Omar helped me exit the SUV. He lifted me into his arms and as much as I wanted to rebuff his Prince Charming ways because I knew he was hurt too, I simply couldn't. I didn't have the energy.

I didn't so much as look around his complex to see where we were. I just tucked my head against his neck and closed my eyes. Keeping them open was taking herculean effort, a battle I was losing by the minute.

My stomach growled as he unlocked his door then brought me into a spacious open floorplan living/kitchen area. I briefly noted a camel-colored leather couch and matching chair with a glass coffee table. Off to the side was a four-person circular dining table and chairs next to a small kitchen. Omar didn't place me on the couch. He took me into his bedroom and placed me on a ginormous bed.

It had a black, button-back headboard that stood almost

as tall against the wall as I would if I were standing next to it. There was a gray and white plush comforter on the bed that felt heavenly against my battered and bruised skin.

"You rest there while I bring in your suitcases. Think about what you want first. Food. Shower. Bed. Though my vote is food first because I heard your belly growl and I'm so hungry I could eat a horse."

I scrunched up my nose as he made his way to the bedroom door.

"You would not eat a horse!" I fired back and gloried in hearing his deep laughter fade as he left the apartment to get my bags.

I reached down and removed my one shoe and then unstrapped the boot, setting it next to my shoe by his nightstand. The second it was off, I let out a long sign of relief and wiggled my toes just a little. Too much and the pain would soar up my leg.

Glancing around Omar's room, I noted he had one long dresser that was made of black painted wood. Above it was a flat screen TV. On top of the dresser, I saw several picture frames. The largest one in the center had what I assumed was his entire family standing in front of a restaurant. It must have been taken a while ago because Omar looked like a very young man. Maybe only twenty or so. His arm was around the same woman I'd seen in the church, though her hair was much shorter and she also looked a lot younger. There was a beautiful woman with thick black hair standing wedged against who I guessed was his father. A younger boy, maybe around fifteen or so, stood on his father's opposite side. There was a sign above the restaurant behind them that said, "Grand Opening."

"That was the day my parents opened their restaurant downtown. *Casa de Alvarado* was the dream of *mi padre*."

"What happened to him?" I took in his father's handsome features. Omar was the spitting image of him.

"Heart attack," he said, a frown slipping across his handsome features. I wanted to kiss that frown away. Make it disappear forever.

"No! I'm so sorry."

"Happened at work. One minute he was cooking up a feast for a huge party of people, the next he was on the floor clutching his chest. He passed before the paramedics arrived."

I reached my hand out, and he came to the bed, took my hand, and sat next to me. "It was the hardest year of my life. I'd just turned twenty-one and all of a sudden, I was the man of the family. Responsible for looking out for everyone, including the restaurant."

"That must have been really hard," I surmised.

Omar nodded, sighed, and sat up straighter. "Speaking of food, let's get you to the kitchen."

He scooped me up as though it were nothing. "Omar!" I cried out. "You're going to tear your stitches. I think you've forgotten you were shot a few days ago."

"Nah, it's a flesh wound." He placed a warm kiss to my neck. "Don't worry about me, baby. As long as you are okay, I'm going to be fine."

He set me down on a padded dining chair. I sat and watched as he opened the oven that I now realized was whirring because it had been left on.

"Oh, *mi amor*, you are in for a treat tonight. Mama brought some of her fresh made pork and jalapeno cheese tamales smothered in her special green sauce."

"Seriously? My mouth is watering. Just bring over the whole pan and a fork," I begged.

He chuckled and shook his head, grabbing a couple plates and setting them on the counter. He dished out three tamales for me and I almost asked him for another when I watched in shock as he brought out a second metal holder that included fresh rice and beans.

"I'm dying over here!" I called out. "Gimmie!"

That time he laughed harder. "You want salsa?"

"Is that a real question?" I cocked an eyebrow.

He went to the fridge and pulled out a trio of ready-made sides. Sour cream, salsa, and cabbage. He brought those over to the table, then got the two steaming hot plates and put one loaded with tamales, rice, and beans in front of me, and the other next to his seat. Then he grabbed silverware, two chilled beers, and two waters.

He set everything down and I looked on in awe, not sure where to start first.

"This is literally Heaven to me. Thank you, Omar." I leaned over, and he met me halfway, allowing me the opportunity to kiss him for the first time. It didn't get heated, but I let my lips linger against his succulent ones and then pecked him twice in quick succession before sighing and picking up my utensils.

I dug into one of the tamales and noted it was a pork one. Once I added a fat dollop of salsa to my plate, I dunked it in, and shoveled the entire bite into my mouth.

Pure bliss.

I moaned around the food. His *madre* could cook. After tasting this, I knew I'd be a regular at their family restaurant in the future. I couldn't wait to bring my family for dinner there. They loved my cooking, but this was superb.

For a long while we both sat in silence and stuffed our faces.

Omar washed down the first two tamales out of the four he plated for himself with a beer. I clinked his glass with my own and swallowed down the crisp, hoppy beer.

I let out a satisfied, "Aaaaaahhhh."

"Good?" He grinned, fishing for compliments.

"You see this face?" I gestured in a circular motion. "This is what true happiness looks like." I smiled wide.

"Love seeing it, *mi lirio.* I always want to make you smile," he added, his gaze going from me back to his food.

"I'm usually pretty easy to please. Good food. Family. Sunshine. Laughter. That's about all I could want outta life."

"Do you want kids?" he asked out of the blue.

I chuckled. "Right now? I have two hundred of them. I teach high school Spanish."

He frowned. "Are you saying you don't want a family of your own one day?"

I shook my head and took a drink of my beer. "No, that's not it. I just wouldn't want to do it alone. Even though my niece Rory is sweet, raising a child on your own is incredibly difficult and I honestly don't want to ever be in that position. I admire Genesis for taking on that responsibility with grace, but if I'm going to have a family, it's going to be with a man who wants it as much as I do."

He nodded. "That's fair. Ophelia is doing it on her own too and it burns me up inside. She won't tell us who the father is and she's not getting any assistance from whoever it is. The entire situation is infuriating. If I knew who the father was, I'd whip his ass into shape. Leaving my sister high and dry with a baby." He shook his head. "That's not a man. A man takes care of his family as well as the responsibility for his actions."

I scooped up more rice and beans together and held it aloft. "Do you think she hasn't told the father?"

"I don't know. Like I said, she isn't sharing. Her response is to drop it. Said the baby's father is not in her life and he wouldn't be in Francisco's."

"Your nephew's name is Francisco?" I smiled.

He nodded and lifted his chest as though pride were running through him. "It was my father's name. It is my middle name, as is Arturo's."

"Rory is a family name too. As you know, her real name is Aurora after Mama Kerri."

"And you and your foster sisters all took the Kerrighan name?" he asked, though I'm sure he already knew that answer from when he was assigned to protect us.

"When we were placed in Kerrighan House, Mama Kerri was alone. The state wouldn't let a single, widowed woman adopt eight children. So, when we were eighteen, each of us went down to the courthouse and filed for a name change. It's a gift we have chosen to honor her with."

He nodded. "It's a beautiful gift. She is important to all of you, and I can see that she's a good woman. Loves you all like she gave birth to you. Loves that grandchild as though the sun wouldn't rise if she didn't have her in her life."

"Exactly. And we love her the same."

"My family is close too. We became even closer when *mi padre* passed. We each had to take on more responsibility for one another and at the restaurant."

"Do you work the restaurant regularly?"

He shook his head. "I make more with Holt Security, but I pitch in a day or two a week as time provides. After *mi padre* died, I worked the late shift or weekends. Whatever it took to keep the business going. Then I secured good people to help. We ended up being able to hire mostly family. Cousins and nieces and nephews from my mother's and father's side."

"That's really cool." I yawned and pushed back my mostly empty plate.

Omar took a final bite and rubbed his hands over his eyes. "You look as tired as I feel."

"I am. I haven't slept much in the past few days. Only quick cat naps in between leads as we searched for you."

I reached out my hand and took his. "I'm so glad you found me."

He brought my hand to his mouth and kissed my fingertips. "We didn't, *mi amor.* Sonia's hotline got a call confirming your whereabouts. I happened to be with Jonah. We'd been chasing a lead to the harbor when we got a panicked call from a member of Sonia's staff."

"Either way, you looked for me. And you were there when I was found."

"And you're here now." He pushed a lock of my hair behind my ear.

"I'm here now."

He closed his eyes when I pressed my hand to his scruffy cheek. He reacted as though he were cementing my presence in his home, at his table, sitting in front of him, in that moment.

"You ready to shower? Or straight to bed?" he asked.

"Shower. I need to get the sea water off my skin from my last escape. And my hair feels as though it's glued to my scalp." I scrunched up my nose and he reached out and tapped it playfully.

"Come now, stand," he said, and I braced my good hand on the table and stood up.

Once again he lifted me up princess-style and took me through his bedroom to the master bath, then set me carefully on the vanity.

"You have two choices. Sponge bath leaving your bandages on, or fully washed and I wrap you back up."

I slumped where I sat. I really needed to be washed completely. I frowned and could feel a full-body pout brewing at the lack of options.

He cupped my cheeks. "No sad eyes. I watched the nurse wrap your foot carefully. I'm a novice but I think we can manage. The sling can go back on right after you're dried off and in your clean clothes."

"I want to be completely clean. I need it to feel human again."

He kissed my lips softly. "Then that's what you'll have."

My God. How could I have believed this man was an overbearing, hard to manage, alpha-male who wouldn't listen to reason. Since my return, he'd deferred to my needs and desires with very little thought for his own. He took on my care as though I'd been in his life for five years, not a day. Well, six months, if you go back to when we first met. I'd been incredibly wrong about him.

"Thank you, Omar, for everything. I know you've wanted something more between us for a long time, and I kept pushing you away…"

He listened and unraveled the bandage on my foot and ankle.

"I just want to say I'm sorry. I was scared. Heck, if I'm being honest, I'm *still* scared. Scared of how much I feel for you. Scared that this situation is going to ruin what could be between us. Scared of being harmed again by those criminals. I'm scared of everything."

He finished removing the bandage and winced as he saw the black bruise from the cleat on the bottom of my foot, not to mention how swollen it was.

"Liliana, most things that are worth having are scary. Nothing in life is ever easy. I think that's what makes it worth it the end. The struggle. The journey. The give and take. The good and bad. All of those things change us. We just have to choose how we're going to let it move us forward. And there is very little I wouldn't risk to move forward with you."

I placed my hands on his neck and tugged him forward. "It's been a day and you're charming the pants off me," I teased.

He grinned and waggled his brows as he tugged at the pajama pants he lent me and tugged them under my butt and off my legs.

"Whoops! Looks like I already charmed them off." He smiled so huge I leaned forward and kissed that smile right off his face.

It got heated quickly, our tongues tangling while his hands ran up and down my bare thighs. Eventually, I pulled away, completely drunk on his kisses.

"Are you going to shower with me?" I asked on a hushed whisper.

He removed my sling carefully and glanced at my face. "Are you capable of showering alone?"

I shook my head. "Nope."

"Then you have your answer, don't you?" He lifted the black T-shirt over my good arm and my head and eased it past the bum shoulder, leaving me sitting completely buck-assed naked.

"Are you going to be naked?" I asked in a voice so low it sounded like a prayer.

"Do you want me to be?" He cupped my jaw and lifted my chin, so I'd have to look him in the eyes.

"Yes."

"Then it's decided. I'll wash your back, you wash mine." He winked then stood back and removed his shirt.

A wall of jam-packed muscle hit my vision.

"*Jesucristo*, do you do anything but work out?" I scoffed, my eyes scanning nothing but beautifully honed muscles and skin the color of brown sugar. His abdomen was an eight pack with such delicious dents I wanted nothing more than to run my tongue and fingers down each one. Maybe play a game of tic-tac-toe.

He grinned. "You like?" he teased, knowing I liked what I saw very much.

I rolled my eyes. "Are you kidding? Every human—gay, straight, bi, pan, and gender-neutral—can appreciate a beautiful body like yours. You're like a living, breathing superhero. That's it!" I held up my hand and made my demands clear. "New rule. You go shirtless at all times. It's only fair that we get to feast on such beauty regularly, instead of you hiding it behind those blasphemous T-shirts."

He laughed good-naturedly and scanned my form from chest to feet.

"And you look good enough to eat, *mi amor*. If you weren't wounded, I'd be fucking you where you sit." He reached out and cupped both of my breasts, running his thumbs across the erect tips.

I arched into his touch but then hissed in pain as my shoulder smarted without the sling.

He stepped back, his nostrils flaring. "I can be good," he grumbled, and I wasn't sure if it was to me, or as a reminder to keep himself in check.

Then I watched as he undid the button on his cargo pants, brought down the zipper, and shoved his pants and underwear off in one move.

His cock bobbed free, and my mouth went dry.

"What the…" I blinked several times and then looked again. Nope still there. I closed my eyes and then opened them quickly to ensure I wasn't seeing things.

"Liliana, do not look at a man's cock and open and close your mouth without saying anything."

"I-I…" I swallowed again unable to form coherent words.

His cock was *huge*.

Huge, huge. Not like, oh, my man is above average. No, it was more like, I'm not sure that thing is going to fit inside my tiny va-jay-jay.

"We have to break up," I whispered, staring in complete and utter shock at the giant appendage standing proudly at his pelvis.

"We just got together, *mi amor*." He came closer and stood with his hands clutching my thighs.

I shook my head. "It won't work."

"What won't work?"

"That." I pointed at his beautifully hard, thick, long, and girthy cock. "It will not fit inside me. No way. It defies the laws of physics."

217

My response had Omar pressing his forehead to mine. He burst out laughing so hard, his abdominals flexed sexily, and that giant cock bobbed with each guffaw.

"Baby, it will fit," he murmured against my temple then placed a kiss there.

I shook my head. "It's as big as a baby's arm! Do you see me? I'm fun-sized, not king-sized."

He laughed so hard he had me giggling with him.

"Omar, I'm not kidding." I pressed at his chest to get another gander. "I've never seen anything that size in my life!"

He kissed me fast and hard. "Good. Then it will feel like your first time."

I groaned and closed my eyes for a second but only a second because I simply could not stop looking at his package. Even the twin balls hanging down between his thighs seemed large.

He went over to the shower to turn on the water, gifting me an unencumbered view of his toned butt. I couldn't help but whistle at his tight buns. The man was the epitome of perfection. How did I, Liliana Ramírez-Kerrighan, score such a beefcake who was also kind, loving, and gentle, not to mention a good man?

"I think I'm dreaming," I murmured. "The lack of real sleep has caught up with me and I'm dreaming. No man has a package that size and a body that fine."

Omar grinned that panty-melting smile that would have taken my panties off if they weren't already gone.

"Time to get clean." He tugged me off the vanity and brought me into the shower. Thankfully, there was a bench seat at the back of the freestanding shower where he placed me.

"I'm going to start with your hair, *mi amor*," he instructed, but I was too dumbstruck by his body and the size of his cock. I couldn't speak. I just stared like a creeper at every inch of skin I could take in. His pecks were tightly squared off with small, flat, brown nipples. His shoulders were wide and fed into bulging, rock-hard biceps. Without realizing it, as he washed and scrubbed my filthy hair, I ran the fingers of my good hand all over his magnificent chest. Whatever I could reach, I touched. Save his eager cock. I didn't want to start something I could not finish, and Omar wasn't making suggestive overtures. I think we were both so beyond tired that we could only look at and feel one another. Giving comfort and intimacy in a way couples who had been together a long time take for granted.

I never wanted to take Omar for granted.

He rinsed my hair and then added conditioner, combing through my curls as he did.

"I love your curls," he murmured.

"I love your body." I flat out admitted it because it had to be said another one million times. "It's a work of art," I admitted in awe.

"Before my father died, I wasn't like this. Now I take excellent care of my body and heart to ensure I'll always be around for *mi familia*."

I frowned. "Now I feel bad. Here I am ogling your awesome bod when you've done it out of selflessness."

He lifted my chin in a way that was becoming very familiar when he wanted me to not only *see* his response but *hear* it. "I like that you can't look away. It turns me on. You see how hard I am? I've been that way since I first saw you in that flirty dress six months ago. That night I went home and jerked off several times to the fantasy of running my hand up that dress, touching those luscious thighs, and pounding inside your sexy little body."

Arousal roared through my body, and I squeezed said thighs together. "Omar," I whined, then wrapped my hand around his huge cock and jacked him once, twice, and a third time, before he gripped my wrist.

"Not until we can play together, *mi amor*."

"But I want to and you're so ready." I licked my lips and stared at the appendage that held all of my attention.

"Tomorrow. After a full night's rest."

I begrudgingly looked away from his sex. "Swear it." I blinked up at him.

He smirked. "I swear."

I sighed and let out a long breath.

"Tip your head back," he instructed, and I did as ask, humming in appreciation as he rinsed out the conditioner.

Then with slow, even movements, he lathered up the soap in a clean washrag and then washed every inch of my body before his own. When he ran his fingers over my breasts, they ached. I could imagine him doing a hundred other even more pleasurable things with them than simply washing the girls, but he was committed to his task.

Eventually he washed most of his own body and then helped me to balance on one foot as we did one another's backs. I took a lot longer on his back and tight buns, then dropped the rag, reached around his body, and just pressed my naked skin to his.

He groaned and lifted his head to the ceiling. "I will not survive this night if you keep that up, Liliana."

"I just want to feel you against me." I ran my good hand

up and down his muscular chest and abdominals and down to his cock which had not gone down. I wrapped what I could of my hand around him and smoothed the soap up and down his rock-hard length.

"Fuck!" He balanced himself against the wall with one hand and reached behind him to hold me to him so I wouldn't fall.

He let me play for a couple minutes. I kissed his back as I ran my hand over him. I thought he might let me finish him off, but at the last second, he grunted and spun around, taking my mouth in a heated, deep kiss. We kissed and touched like new lovers learning one another's bodies until the water ran cold.

"Let's go to bed," he said.

I grinned. "Yes, let's."

"To sleep." He reiterated the plan.

"Yes, to eventually sleep. After I put my hands and mouth all over that body." I grinned, then immediately followed it up with a loud yawn, ruining my plan entirely.

Omar dried us both off, sat me on top of a towel on the vanity, and rewrapped my ankle with extreme care. Then he took me naked into the bedroom where he opened my suitcases. I pointed to a tank and pair of panties. He helped me put on the panties first, then the tank, all while I stared at his gorgeous body naked as a jaybird.

Once I was dressed and was back in the sling, he went to his wardrobe and put on a pair of blue boxer briefs. They were a ten out of ten on the sexy scale, not that he'd let me have my fun. And the truth was, as much as I wanted to be intimate with Omar, we were both delirious in our exhaustion.

He got me under the covers and entered behind me. I

rested on my good side as he paired our bodies from behind, pulling my bottom against his still-hard cock.

"Is that a baseball bat in your pants, or are you happy to see me?" I joked stupidly.

He snuffled against my neck and pressed closer. "Go to sleep, Liliana."

I yawned again and then snuggled into him and the comfortable bed linens. "Have you ever had problems in the sex department with that giant pipe you've got in your pants?" I was genuinely curious.

"Be quiet, Liliana," he admonished.

"I'm being real here. It's abnormally big. Have you gotten complaints?" I mean, it *could* be possible.

"Maybe you just had small men in the past. I'm sorry to hear it, baby, but those problems are no longer yours." He tugged my bottom half closer, wedging the length of his erection between my cheeks. I wanted to rub against it, but frankly I was too tired to move.

My mind finally wrapped around what he suggested. "Damn, maybe you have a point." I thought about the men I'd been with. He could be right. "Do you think you're above average in size? I think you are." I answered for him because honestly in my sleep-deprived brain, I couldn't think about anything else.

"*Mi amor*, close your eyes, stop thinking about my dick, and go to sleep." He groaned under his breath.

"But it's sooooooo big. I really don't think it's gonna fit." I sighed.

"Baby, you were meant for me. It's gonna fit. Now go to sleep and stop worrying about it."

"But…"

"Liliana! I'm going to go sleep on the couch if you don't quiet down."

Him sleeping away from me was the absolute last thing I wanted or needed. "Okay, okay. Goodnight, handsome."

I could feel him smile against my neck and it made my heart skip a beat. Tomorrow we'd find out if size really did matter.

Chapter
SIXTEEN

THE SOUND OF BIRDS CHIRPING WOKE ME FROM A DEEP SLEEP. I started to wake slowly, my eyes opening while I took stock of my body aches. Ankle still throbbed but not nearly as painfully as yesterday. The shoulder, however, felt a lot better. My head was no longer fuzzy from lack of sleep and my emotions were surprisingly serene.

I felt Omar's arm grip me tighter around the waist, his breath heavy against the back of my neck. We didn't move much in the night it seemed, both of us conking out straightaway, locked within the comfort of the other's embrace.

His cock was either still hard, or he was a morning wood kind of guy. Either way, arousal simmered low in my belly and seeped over my lower half as I wiggled my *culo* against that hardened appendage.

Omar groaned against my neck and bit down. "Hmmm. Good morning, *mi amor*." He ran his nose along the column of my neck. I sighed, enjoying the pleasant caress.

I continued to slowly circle my hips, feeling satisfied when he ground against me in return. I grinned wickedly, knowing exactly what I wanted to happen. "Good morning, handsome." I let out a yawn and stretched against his long body, glorying in how his warm skin teased along mine.

"How are you feeling?" He ran his hand up and down my

bare thigh, teasing the fabric of my panties at the top of my hip with a single finger.

"Horny. You?"

Omar burst into surprised laughter against my neck, which sent tendrils of excitement skittering across the surface of my bare skin.

"You have a one-track mind, *mi amor.*" He shifted his body so that I came down flat against the mattress, and he hovered over me. His eyes were a dark brown this morning and blazing with desire. "I like it." He licked his bottom lip, and I reached out my good arm, cupping him around his neck.

"So, what are you going to do about it?" I taunted, my heartbeat banging against my chest with anticipation.

He traced the sling with one finger and then unclipped it, slowly removing it and setting it beside the bed. "Okay?" he asked when it was removed.

I nodded. "It's fine."

"You'd tell me if it hurt?" He cocked a brow.

"No," I admitted. "But I promise to be careful with the shoulder if you do."

He leaned forward and pressed light kisses all around my bare shoulder. Then his lips moved over my chest, kissing my breasts through the thin fabric of my sleep tank. I arched toward his kiss, but he pressed a heavy hand to my sternum and shook his head. "If you want this, you'll have to just lie there and take it, *chica.* Every time you move toward my kiss, you wince in pain. I won't play with these..." He sat up and cupped my breasts through my shirt and pinched at the tips. I moaned deeply in response. "...if you won't be still."

I swallowed and nodded. "Don't stop." I heard the begging note in my tone, but I no longer cared. I wanted Omar so badly it would physically and emotionally *hurt* if he stopped. "I'll be good."

He shifted so that he was straddling my body completely, his bulk a feast for my eyes.

I lifted my hand and ran it down all those slabs of finely honed muscle. "You are magnificent, Omar. I want so badly to touch and kiss you *everywhere,* but know I can't." I grinned as I dragged my hand down to the package tenting his boxers. I rubbed my palm over the length of him and watched his muscles flex deliciously. "Means you're going to have to do all the work for a while, baby, but don't worry. When I'm all better, with full mobility, I will rock your world." I tugged at the edge of boxer briefs allowing the head of his enormous cock to make an appearance. The tip was glistening, and I ached to have a taste.

I licked my lips. "Come here," I whispered. "Let me taste you."

He didn't say a word as he slowly shuffled closer to where I rested my head against the pillows at the perfect height for his hips.

"Show me *la bestia,*" I requested, my tone sultry and intoxicated by the sheer beauty before me.

Omar shoved down his briefs until the fabric bit into the brown skin of his thick thighs. His "beast" as I called it, bobbed near my face.

"You ask, you shall receive, *mi amor,*" Omar said, then hissed as I ran my hand up his thigh and over to the base of his cock, encircling my fingers around the thick root. I stroked up and back a couple times, then urged him to come closer by tugging his length toward me. He did so, and when he was exactly where I wanted him, I wrapped my lips around the bulbous crown and hummed in appreciation as the salty rich taste of him hit my tongue.

He hissed between his teeth and gripped onto the headboard. His hips started to move just a little, more of a swaying motion that took him in and out of my mouth in a slow and gentle rhythm.

I closed my eyes, my other hand stroking along with his movements as I lost myself in all that was Omar. It was a tight fit and I could only take a few inches this way but Omar didn't seem to mind. His constant pleasurable moans and grunts as I ramped up my speed confirmed he was also lost in the moment.

"Fuck, Liliana. I could come down your throat so easily. Your touch, *chica*..." His body strained, his muscles flexing and moving as though he were fighting against the pleasure. "*Tu boca es la perfección.*" He switched to Spanish, telling me my mouth was perfection as his hips continued in a sloppy yet slow pace. More of his seed slid over my tongue, and just when I thought he was going to do as he said and let go, he slipped his body from my mouth, scrambled down my form, and yanked down my panties. Once I got my unhurt leg out, he left the fabric dangling on my other leg. Instead of removing them, he spread my legs wide, planted both hands against my inner thighs framing my sex, and covered me with his mouth.

I cried out at the intense sensation of his tongue delving straight inside my core. He took me from zero to sixty in no time, sucking, licking, and teasing the tight bundle of nerves with his masterful tongue.

He groaned against my flesh, his hips fucking the mattress as he took me to the highest peak and then shoved me off when he inserted two thick fingers and pleasured me with them. The orgasm felt like it went on and on. Omar did not stop. When he'd rung one orgasm out of me, he doubled his efforts. One hand slid up my stomach and under my tank to tweak and tease my nipple while he sucked that tight, throbbing knot that made me scream in total ecstasy.

Another orgasm was barreling through my body, but I wanted it to be with *him*. Together.

"*Dame la bestia,*" I begged. Give me the beast.

I fisted the top of his thick, dark hair, forcing his face from my sex so that he could look into my eyes. His lips and chin were soaked with my essence and his eyes wild with lust. "Omar, baby, make love to me," I pleaded.

He licked his lips and stared into my eyes as though I were the most beautiful creature he'd ever laid eyes on. In that moment, I believed I was.

Slowly he eased over my body, like a panther ready to take down its prey. With one hand he eased up my tank until the fabric rested above my breasts, then traced his fingers over the tips of each teasingly. "You have the most beautiful body, *mi amor*. I want to touch and taste you *everywhere*." He continued to tease as I circled my hips, trying to get his beast to rub against my sensitive flesh. Still, Omar took his time, touching my breasts, my clavicle, and the hollow at my throat before moving down to my ribcage, belly, and then finally cupping between my thighs. He pushed two fingers inside and crooked them perfectly against the wall of my sex until I gasped and clenched around him. "Especially *here*. You taste like the finest honey on my tongue. I could lick you for days, baby."

"Omar, please," I begged, delirious in my need to have him inside me.

He removed his fingers and put them into his mouth. He closed his eyes and hummed.

"Baby…"

He opened his eyes, wrapped a beefy hand around his thick cock, and stroked it. "Are you on birth control?" he asked suddenly.

I blinked stupidly for a moment, content to watch his hand on that insane cock.

He chuckled. "*Mi lirio*, are you protected from getting pregnant?"

I shook my head. I hadn't had a man in a while, and I didn't believe in putting something unnecessary into my body when I wasn't actively having sex. I'd be making an appointment in the near future, that was for sure.

Omar leaned over me, pulled open his bedside drawer, and pulled out a foil package. "I bought these not long after we met. I'd hoped to have you naked in my bed months ago." He smirked, removing the condom and rolling it over his beast.

I swooned and widened my thighs instinctively.

With his eyes on me, he rubbed the tip over the wetness at my center, teasing me.

"Omar," I warned on a groan.

He smiled, shifted his body to hover more fully over me, and then pushed his tip where I wanted him most. "Breathe, *mi amor*. Let your man in." He whispered against my lips and eased the head inside. I gasped at the pressure of his sheer size spreading my oversensitive walls. I clung to his back with my good hand, digging my nails in.

He took my lips in a deep kiss, our tongues sliding tantalizingly over one another as he continued to inch his beast within me.

I knew he was only halfway in when I gulped and pressed my head into the pillow, trying to spread my legs open further to take more of him.

"You're too big." I dug my nails in, the pressure between my thighs immense.

He nipped at my neck then curved his beautiful body over me to flick and tease my nipple with his mouth. I threaded my fingers through his hair and let it all go. Focused entirely on the sensations he brought to my body.

When he shoved one of his hands between us and encircled that small bundle of nerves, electric pleasure shot through my form. My body finally gave way to his beast, allowing him to sink fully inside me.

I was filled to the brim with my man.

Complete.

Finally.

His body lie against mine, and I lifted my legs, bringing my knees to his sides and forcing his length to sink even deeper.

"*¡Dios mío!*" I cried out, which was when he finally decided to move.

In and out.

Heaven and hell.

The feeling was indescribable. Life-altering. Earth-shattering.

For an eternity, my mind, heart, and body swirled in a haze of extreme bliss, the likes I'd never felt before. It was as though our bodies were *made* for one another.

I wrapped my limbs the best I could around his massive form and let him merge with me.

"Look at me, *mi amor*," Omar demanded in a gruff growly tone he'd not used with me before.

My eyes snapped open, and I stared at the only man I wanted to be this vulnerable with. I gave him all of my fear, my anxiety, my joy and yes, even my heart. In that one look I gave him me.

"I'm falling in love with you, Liliana," he admitted as though it was torn straight from his very soul.

Tears filled my eyes as the gargantuan feeling of rightness flowed through my body.

"Me too," I confessed, no longer scared to be vulnerable with this man. He wouldn't hurt me. He'd already proven that with his actions and words.

Omar quickened his pace, thrusting his beast inside my body, hitting my G-spot over and over until I saw stars. I arched just my head, giving him my throat as everything within me locked down around him. I dug my nails into his flesh. My sex throbbed and tightened around his length, and he roared in response. His hips moved faster, pressed deeper, harder, until there was no me and Omar, just us. One unit, taking and giving pleasure.

My orgasm crested and he wrapped me up in his arms, tunneling his cock deep as I shook in his arms. His powerful frame bowed with the effort as his orgasm shredded through him. And yet, he kept his body from putting weight or pressure on my upper half, ensuring my shoulder was safe as the rest of me broke into a million pieces of light.

I clung to what I could of his frame, my sex fluttering against his softening cock.

For a long time, Omar simply breathed against my chest, his breath teasing my erect nipples with the heavy bursts of air. I let myself take the time to catch my breath, my fingers threading through the layers of hair at the crown of his head, wanting to touch him and continue the intimacy of such a momentous change in our relationship.

Eventually Omar came back to the present and pressed his fists into the mattress to hover his stunning body over me.

"If that's what it's like when you're hurt and incapacitated, *mi amor*, I can only imagine what it will be like when you're fully functioning." He grinned wickedly.

I smiled wide in return and petted what I could reach of his fabulous chest. "You'll just have to wait and find out," I joked.

He leaned down and took my mouth in a slow, wet, kiss.

When we'd kissed until our lips were bruised and swollen, he got up and took care of the condom then came back to bed. He turned us over and put me half on top of his naked body, my bad arm lying gently across his beautiful chest. We snoozed for a while until I was awakened from my sex daze by the scent of bacon.

I sniffed the air and then leaned up into a seated position, tugging the sheet up to cover my breasts.

Omar playfully tried to pull down the sheet to get to my tits.

"Do you smell that?" I asked.

Just as Omar sniffed audibly, the smell was followed by the sound of a baby's cry.

My eyebrows rose up toward my hairline. "Someone's here?" I shivered.

Omar smiled and shook his head. "Fucking nosy brat." He grumbled but did so with a grin. "It's Ophelia." He sighed and then sat up, kissed me quickly and cupped my cheek. "One thing you're going to have to get used to very quickly, Liliana, is that my family is very intrusive."

"You mean your sister is here? Right now?" I pointed down to the bed that was a mess from our lovemaking.

He nodded. The sound of pans clanging into one another came from the other room.

"I'll get rid of her and come back to bed." He moved to get up.

I scrambled to my knees with the sheet clutched to my chest. "You'll do no such thing," I whispered with acid in my tone. "I'm not going to be the girlfriend that hates family visits. Just get me a dress from over there." I pointed to a spaghetti-strapped yellow number that I'd picked up at Target last month. "And a new pair of panties."

He smiled sweetly and dug through my open case and brought the two items over to me. I shifted the best I could toward the edge of the bed. He helped me slip on the lacy panties and then gave me an arm to brace so I could stand. Then he removed the tank I'd worn to bed and helped me get into the simple summer dress. It fluttered down to mid-thigh and was slinky against my curves. It had a shelf-bra in the top that gave my boobs a bit of support but mostly the light padding helped to hide my straining nipples.

"Can you get the sling?" I asked.

He nodded and brazenly walked around the bed naked to where he'd tossed the item.

After he got it back on me, I hopped on one foot into the bathroom. There was no way I was going to meet his sister with sex-hair.

"You could have let me carry you," he called out, but I ignored him and assessed myself in the mirror.

Things weren't too bad. Since Omar had washed and conditioned my curls last night, they were wild but almost looked as if I'd styled them that way. I wet my fingers and teased a few wonky locks into place, then grabbed Omar's toothbrush and paste and went to town on my teeth.

He came back into the bathroom wearing a pair of loose athletic shorts and a white T-shirt. His gaze went to his toothbrush which was sticking out of my mouth.

"You're using my toothbrush?" He scoffed as though offended.

I leaned over the sink, spit, and rinsed out my mouth. "You've had your tongue in my mouth and my cunt and you're worried about your toothbrush?"

He wrapped his arms around me from behind. "It's kinda gross, *mi amor*."

I scrunched up my nose. "Let me repeat in case you missed it the first time. Your *tongue* has been in my mouth and my va-jay-jay. You put your fingers inside me and then sucked them." His eyes lit with a renewed fire. "*Cállate* about the toothbrush."

He chuckled and then kissed my neck on one side and then the other. "You ready to meet *mi hermana y mi sobrino?*" he asked, referring to his sister and nephew.

I inhaled deeply, pinched one cheek, and then the other to give my face a little color, and then I nodded. "As ready as I can be."

He completely wrapped his arms around me and rested his chin against my good shoulder. "Baby, she's going to love you. I promise."

I bit down on my bottom lip and nodded.

Then before I could I try another stalling tactic, he swooped me up and into his arms and brought me out into the kitchen.

My mouth watered at the smell of bacon and fried potatoes.

"Good morning, *mocosa*." Omar greeted them, then put me into the same chair I'd used last night.

The stunning woman spun around, her long ponytail flying over her shoulder.

She smiled wide and I was once more shocked at just how lovely she was. The woman bounced on her feet and put her hands together as she approached, ignoring her brother completely.

"Wow! You are so beautiful!" She gushed as her eyes set on me. "She's gorgeous, Omar. You said she was pretty but wow!" she said again and held out her hand in greeting.

I smiled and shook her hand. "Thank you, and the feeling is mutual. I'm Liliana."

"Lily, I know! I'm Ophelia, Omar's twin sister." Her eyes alighted with happiness.

"Yes, he told me about you as well."

Her eyes widened. "Did he? Well, don't believe everything you hear from my brother."

"All good things," I confirmed.

In the center of the table was a baby bouncer that had a sweet baby boy clipped into it. "This is Francisco, *mi niño.*" She reached for his foot and tickled his toes.

The baby kicked his feet and smiled.

"How old is he?" I asked.

"Two months today." She looked at her son with pride in her expression.

"He seems to be a very good baby."

She nodded. "Oh, he is. The love of my life." She caressed his cheek with her finger. "The food!" She chirped suddenly and spun around to find that Omar was already tending to what was on the stove. Ophelia went over to him and batted his arm away. "I'm making you guys breakfast!"

"Woman, you couldn't make breakfast to save your life! You're overcooking the bacon and the potatoes need to be turned repeatedly so you don't burn them. Go sit down. I'll finish this up."

She put her hands on her hips and her spine went ramrod straight as she got in Omar's face. "Don't tell me what to do. This was my welcome to the family gift to Lily!"

Welcome to the family?

What the hell did Omar tell his family about our relationship?

"You want to welcome my girlfriend, then get her a cup of coffee," he advised.

She glared at him. "Fine! But only because I'm good at making coffee."

"The only thing you're good at in the kitchen," he mumbled though it was loud enough for me to hear even across the room.

"I heard that!" she fired off.

"I wasn't trying to be quiet. You're a mess in the kitchen. You know that." He cracked not one, but two eggs into a sizzling frying pan with only one hand. It was amazing.

She got a coffee cup from the cupboard above the pot and filled it with the heavenly brew. I could smell the incredible energy-giving source from here.

"I'm learning, you know! I have a child now. I need to learn how to cook," she huffed.

"Your brother lives next door, and your family owns a restaurant you work in. Leave the cooking to the professionals.

And don't you dare feed Cisco any of your attempts at cooking. The poor kid will go hungry!" he added.

"How am I ever going to get it right if none of you will let me try!" She continued their battle while making me coffee. Something she didn't ask how I liked, but I'd take it how it came. At that point I was not picky. I just needed caffeine.

"Liliana likes her coffee with cream and no sugar. Did you think to ask her?" He shook his head.

She looked down at the cup, frowned, and then snapped her gaze to me. "I'm so sorry! I should have asked."

I shook my head. "It's fine. I'm happy with how you serve it."

"She's sooooooo much cooler than you." She bumped her brother's hip as she went back to the cupboard and got a new cup.

"You really don't have to make another," I said but she poured a new cup anyway.

"No, no, it's no trouble at all. I'm sure I'll learn your likes and dislikes soon enough." She prepared my coffee the way I liked it and brought it over to me. I took the cup and sipped as she checked on Francisco who was already closing his eyes sleepily.

"He really is a good-looking boy." I took in his cheery rounded cheeks, little cherub-shaped lips, and wide, knowing eyes.

"Takes after his *tío* Omar," she whispered. "Not that I'd ever admit it to the punk!" She glared at Omar's back but smiled playfully at me.

These two fought the same way me and my sisters did, making the situation even more endearing.

Ophelia grabbed the first coffee she made and sat down

next to me. "Tell me everything there is to know about you. I'm so happy to finally meet you in person."

"Um, well, to start, I have seven foster sisters, one who passed a little over six months ago." I clenched my jaw and took a breath, allowing the pain to race through me.

She covered her mouth. "Oh, I'm so sorry, Lily. To lose a sister so young." She frowned.

I nodded and cleared my throat pushing down the sorrow that threatened to rise to the surface at the thought of my sister Tabby.

"Like you and your brother, my sisters and I are very close. Bicker all the time."

"All good families bicker. We care about each other's lives. If we didn't care, we wouldn't fight. Right, punk?" she called out.

"That's right, ¡mocosa!" *Brat* he called her in return.

"Omar tells me one of your sisters is a fashion designer and one is a model. Oh! And one is a senator! It must be amazing having so many famous people in your family," she gushed, resting her chin in her hand, settling into the conversation.

I chuckled. "I guess they are famous, but it's not something that we ever really talk about. It kind of just happened over time so we all got used to it. Mama Kerri always taught us that our jobs are what we do, not who we are. So, to me, they're just my sisters."

She nodded. "Fascinating."

"Not really." I shrugged and then hissed at the pain of the sudden movement.

Omar took that moment to set two plates of food in front of us. "I'll get your pain meds," he announced.

I shook my head. "I'd rather not. If I can go without them, I'd prefer to do so. I don't like the floaty, sleepy feeling."

He tilted his head and looked at me with a serious expression plastered to his face. "How about today you take your meds, eat, sleep, and rest? Then tomorrow we start to wean you off and only do before bed. There's no need for you to be in pain unnecessarily when you need the rest."

I nodded. He was right. If Mama Kerri were here, she'd be saying the same thing.

"Okay, thank you." I lifted my chin, and he took my lips in a sweet, lingering, kiss.

"God, you guys are so sweet together. Mama is going to lose her mind. She'll be pushing you to get married and give her more grandbabies within a day. Mark my words." She poked a fried potato with her fork and plopped it into her mouth, grinning.

Omar chuckled. "She is not exaggerating, *mi amor*. I suggest you get your force field ready. My guess, we have until this evening before she is banging the door down. And once she gets a look at you and me together, she'll be planning the wedding."

"Hey, Mama Kerri has been bugging us for the past four years for one of us to give her another grandchild. I think I can handle your mother," I stated with confidence as I bit into a perfectly cooked piece of crispy bacon.

Ophelia snorted and hid her laughter behind her hand. "Good luck with that. You'll need it."

"Really?" I asked as I continued to eat.

"When Mama gets a load of all that's you," she ran her fork up and down in the air gesturing to my entire form, "she'll have wedding colors picked out, the reception menu planned, and a date in her mind within moments."

"*Jesús, María y José*," I whispered.

"That's a good idea. Pray now," she warned.

Omar entered the room once more with my meds. "Stop scaring my girlfriend, Ophelia. Mama's harmless. Mostly." He looked at Ophelia and then at me. "I'll make sure she lays off the future talk."

"Like I said." Ophelia smiled a cat-that-ate-the-canary grin. "Good luck."

Chapter
SEVENTEEN

THE REST OF THE DAY PASSED IN A PAIN-MEDICATION-INDUCED haze. Omar was able to ward off his mother and sister from barging in again that evening. We had another homemade meal Omar's brother Arturo dropped off while I slept. It was shredded chicken enchiladas that rivaled my own recipe. We ended the night making love and falling into an easy sleep.

Day two at Omar's, however, ended up much like the first. After waking and showering, Omar set me up on his cushy leather couch and went to retrieve our coffee. Then he was planning to wrap my foot. I had the shoulder sling on and was thrilled to find I felt a lot better. Even the swelling in my foot had gone down from having it propped up on pillows most of yesterday while Omar played nurse while we watched movies as I slept on and off.

However, our little bubble of quiet relaxation ended with a rapping knock at the door.

He looked through the peep hole and frowned, then opened it enough so he could speak to whomever was out there.

"She wouldn't take no for an answer." I heard Sylvester Holt's low growl as the door propped open and Mama Kerri came bustling in. Her arms were filled with grocery bags and a vase of fresh-cut flowers. I knew, based on the flowers, they had come from her yard.

"Chicklet!" She smiled warmly.

"Hi, Mama!" I waved and smiled, genuinely happy to see her. "What are you doing here?"

She moseyed in as though she'd been to Omar's a hundred times, when she'd never even set foot here. I watched as she placed the bags on the small kitchen table. Then she brought over the flower vase until they were close enough for me to smell.

"Blooms just for you, sweetheart."

I inhaled the scent deeply, allowing that feeling of home to settle into my lungs and heart. She cupped my cheek and did the mom assessment. "You look lovely today. I knew a full day of rest and recuperation with your beau was exactly what you needed."

I chanced a glance at Omar and gave him a cheesy smile. "Look, honey, my mama is here." I chuckled.

He was worried about his overbearing mother popping in, but it was mine who weaseled her way over without a heads-up.

Omar let in Holt and gestured for him to have a seat.

"Wants some coffee?" Omar asked.

Mami Kerri waved her hands. "Oh, I'll handle the coffee and breakfast, dear. I've got enough to feed an army."

Of course she did. I watched as she set the vase on the center of the kitchen table and moved herself right into my new man's kitchen as if she owned the place. I closed my eyes and snickered, leaning against the couch.

"*Gracias*, Ms. Kerrighan. I need to wrap Liliana's foot."

"Oh, call me Mama Kerri, sweetheart. Now you go on.

Take care of our girl. I'll find my way around. Don't mind me." Mama Kerri tittered and went about unloading whatever it was she'd brought for breakfast.

Just as Holt had secured a cup of coffee, the doorbell went off.

I snorted and covered my mouth as Omar groaned and went to the door. He looked through the peep hole, pressed his palm to the flat wooden surface, and then set his forehead to it defeated.

"Hope you're ready to meet my mother," he announced before opening the door.

Without even so much as a "hello" the door pushed open and a curvy woman with long black hair the same as Ophelia's entered. She also was carrying a couple grocery bags.

"I waited an entire day, *mi hijo*. I will wait no longer to meet my future daughter-in-law," she grouched, and then looked around the room until her gaze landed on mine.

Daughter-in-law?

Again, what the heck did Omar tell his family about me? We'd be talking tonight, that's for sure.

"*¡Jesucristo!* She's an *ángel* come alive!" She gasped and her hands moved toward her face as though she'd forgotten the bags she held in her arms.

My man was fast and caught the bags before she could drop them on the floor. He took both and put them on the table that had just been cleared of the items Mama Kerri brought over.

The woman tiptoed over to me slowly as though she were approaching a foreign creature. "Liliana, *ángel*, how are you feeling?" Her cheeks were high and rounded, much like my own. Her face was lightly enhanced by black kohl around her dark eyes, with the best eyelashes I'd ever seen. She had a pink hue at her cheeks that accentuated those cheeks perfectly. She wore a shimmery mauve lipstick that suited her features well. Overall, the woman was a beauty.

My heart squeezed as she referred to me as an angel. I actually couldn't wait to tell my sisters that. They called me the fiery, wild-spirited one with good reason.

"I'm good. On the mend. Thank you for asking."

"*¿Mi hijo te está cuidando bien?*" *Is my son taking good care of you?* she asked in Spanish.

Since she asked in Spanish, I thought it appropriate to respond in kind. "*Sí. Él me está cuidando excelentemente.*" Which translated to, "Yes, he's taking excellent care of me."

"*Muy bien.*" *Very good,* she said as brought her hands to her chest in prayer position. "And she speaks excellent *español*! Omar, she is the one!" She hollered out loud enough for everyone to hear.

"Mama, I know. Lay off already," he warned but his tone seemed playful.

She pranced around adjusting the couch pillows then asked, "What can I get for you, *ángel*? Do you need food? Drink?"

"I think *mi madre* has it covered in the kitchen." I lifted my chin toward the kitchen area just as Mama Kerri came into the living room with a steaming cup of coffee and a plate of small pastries to nibble on.

"*¿Tu madre?*" She spun around and reached out her hands to Mama Kerri once she'd set the plate and hot coffee on the table before me.

Mama Kerri was promptly pulled into the strange woman's arms in a big hug. I watched as Mama Kerri hugged her back. "Hello, I'm Aurora Kerrighan, Liliana's mother. And you are?"

"I am Renata Alvarado, *la madre de* Omar. We are all so excited to have your Liliana with our boy. He has been chasing her for months!" She chuckled. "She's slippery!" Then she pointed to her temple. "Smart one. Made him work to catch her. I approve of this." She boasted.

Mama Kerri gave me the side eye and grinned. "I approve as well." She hooked her arm with Renata's. "Would you like to help me make them breakfast?"

"*¡Sí, sí!* She must eat to be well again," Renata stated emphatically.

"I don't think eating is going to heal my bum foot and shoulder," I called out, but was certain the comment fell on selectively deaf ears.

Omar shook his head where he stood, leaning against the front door with his massive arms crossed over one another while he took in the scene unfolding in his home. "*Mi madre* believes food heals all ailments, *mi amor*."

I hummed. "Maybe that's why Mama Kerri always makes tea and cookies when we have a problem or concern in the Kerrighan household?"

Omar sighed and came over to the table and grabbed the Ace bandage and proceeded to wrap my foot while Holt sat at the table on his phone, drinking coffee while our two mothers became best friends and cooked for us.

"Anyone else planning to pop over, Mama Kerri?" I asked as I watched her set the table.

She shrugged and fluttered around the kitchen. "I know your sisters are eager to see you again, but I do know that

Jonah and Ryan have been chasing down some leads and plan to notify you of their progress."

Once Omar finished wrapping my foot, he placed a kiss to the top of it. "I'm going to go call the guys from the balcony. Will you be okay with our mothers?" He grinned.

I rolled my eyes. "I'll be fine. Go on. I hope you get good news."

He bent over in half, took my mouth in a small kiss and whispered, "I hope so too."

I watched his body move as he walked. His frame was so powerful, it made the room feel smaller, but he maneuvered it with grace and ease. Reminded me of how he moved over me just last night. Smooth easy strokes, long, drawn-out drugging kisses.

My temperature rose as my cheeks heated.

Mama came in and frowned. "Are you feeling feverish, chicklet?" She put her hand to my forehead. "No, you feel cool enough. I think you need to eat and go back to bed."

I groaned. "All I've done the last two days is sleep. I need to get back up and around. I missed the last fitting for the bridesmaids dresses which has to be worrying Blessing and her timeline to get everything done. I'm just lucky we're out of school for the summer."

The term bridesmaid dresses must have hit Renata's "wedding" sensors because she said, "Bridesmaids? Who's getting married, *ángel?*"

"My sister Simone. And actually, not long after that my sister Addison will be getting married."

"You are a lucky woman, *mi amiga!*" She bounced her shoulder against Mama Kerri's.

She laughed in response. "I thank the Lord every day for

my blessings. My girls are my life." Her voice cracked as her gaze slid to mine.

"Mama." I felt a wave of emotion filter over me seeing her sudden stress. The last few days must have been horrible for her. A mother having had such extreme traumatic situations with her children so close to one another. Me being kidnapped, after going through it with Simone and Addy, and losing Tabby, that wound still so fresh…

I reached out my hand and Mama Kerri came over and took it, sitting next to me. "I was so worried you'd not make it back." Mama's eyes filled with tears and fell down her cheeks. "They had you for *days*." She let out a tortured sob.

"I'm sorry," I choked out, trying to comfort her the best I could.

She shook her head. "It wasn't your fault. You were in the wrong place at the wrong time." She sniffed and wiped at her eyes with a handkerchief she pulled from her bra. "I'll be okay. If you're okay, I'm okay." She lifted her upper body and took a deep breath. I ran my hand up and down her back, seeing how my disappearance had really taken a toll on her.

"I love you, Mama," I whispered, staring into her comforting green-blue eyes, wanting her to know it down to her bones.

"I love you too, Liliana. Always and forever, chicklet." She cupped my cheek.

I nodded. "I know you do. We all know. You tell us all the time." I wanted her to know we never took her love for granted. It was such a gift to our lives.

"Don't ever forget how much you are loved, child." She needn't remind me.

I shook my head. "Mama, I won't. I feel it every time I look at you. Every time I think of you."

She patted my hand then squeezed it. "Good. Now, let's get you some strawberry waffles and whipped cream."

I groaned. "Yaaaaasssss. I'm so hungry for your home-made waffles." I licked my lips, my stomach perking up, ready for some amazing food. We'd talk more later when it was just us, but now I understood how badly she'd needed to come over this morning.

"Holt, be a dear and help Liliana to the table, will you?" She got up and pointed at me.

"Anything for you, Ms. Kerrighan. You keep feeding me and my team all your homemade goods, we're never going to want to guard anyone else."

She smiled and waved her hand as Holt helped me stand and then scooped me up just like Omar did, instead of help-ing me hobble over to the table.

The second I sat down, a steaming plate of strawberry waffles loaded with butter, syrup, and whipped cream was set in front of me. Renata must have been at the waffle iron while we chatted. "Eat, *mi hija*. You need your strength." She lifted her arm and made her muscle flex. Not for nothing—the woman had some guns on her.

I picked up my fork and dug in. Which is also when Omar came back from his phone call and accepted a plate from his mom then sat down next to me. Mama Kerri served Holt a plate and then she and Renata took their own plates and went into the living room chatting like old best friends.

"What's going on with the FBI? Did they find the MacCreedys?" I asked shoveling in a huge bite.

Omar did the same, chewing and then wiping his mouth

before responding. "No. The last thing they found is the totaled car left not far from where the storage unit was. There've been a series of stolen cars since then that they believe may be attributed to the duo. They're on the hunt and they feel confident they'll wrangle them up soon. A BOLO was put out to all the authorities within a two-hundred-mile radius detailing who they are, their names, faces, and the last car they stole. Someone's going to lay eyes on them. They can't run forever," he surmised and took another bite of his food.

"Means we're on the job until they're found," Holt added.

Omar nodded. "I'm sure you'll get the official request from the FBI shortly."

Holt shrugged one shoulder. "This family has been through enough. We'll keep 'em safe."

"Absolutely, boss." Omar lifted his fist and Holt bumped it.

The next day I finally felt human. My shoulder was even better than before and the swelling in my foot was gone. With the boot on, I could actually bear a bit of weight without too much pain. Which meant I needed to get my butt to Blessing's for the final fitting. The girls had shifted it to today and there was no getting out of it. Besides, I wanted to see my sisters. They'd been good, texting and calling when they needed to connect, instead of storming Omar's apartment. Something neither of our mothers were content with.

His mother had finally gone too far. Just this morning Omar was going down on me in the shower. While I sat on the bench, legs spread wide and close to screaming out to the

Heavens, we were interrupted by the sound of knocking. On the *bathroom* door with a screamed, *"¡Hola, buenos días!"*

Nothing takes away an orgasm quicker than a visit from your man's mother.

Omar had his tongue *inside me* when this occurred.

Talk about embarrassing.

Words couldn't describe how humiliated I was that she not only knew we were in the shower, naked, together, but what if she'd heard me moaning? I was not quiet in the bedroom, and neither was Omar for that matter. My man went down on me as though he hadn't had a meal in years, groaning, moaning, grunting. You name every sexy sound one could think of that would turn you way the fuck on while getting busy, and my man made it.

Eventually, Omar went into the main room, wrapped in a towel, and shooed her away. There was not a chance in Hell I was coming out to see her, after she knew I'd been in the shower with her son. I couldn't handle it. No way. No how.

Instead, I got ready for my afternoon with the girls. Since my sister Addy lived with her fiancé Killian in a guarded, secure building with a big ass scary Rottweiler named Brutus, the group decided to meet there. Plus, the loft was spacious and provided a lot of space for Blessing to work.

Omar brought me to Killian and Addy's, and the two men went up onto the roof to discuss man things while I was stationed on the comfy teal couch with my sisters all around me.

"I can't believe the wedding is in two weeks!" Genesis held up her finished bridesmaid's dress. It was a shimmery peach that looked incredible against her mocha-colored skin tone.

Simone pointed to a booklet that had a bunch of cakes

on it. "I know, right? It crept up on us." She smiled. "What do you think of this one?"

I looked at the tiered cake she referenced. It had pretty pink and peach carnations around the edge of each of their tiers.

"Do you need something that large?" I asked scanning the details of the cake.

"Oh yeah, I didn't really think about it. We're only having fifty people," Simone stated.

I looked at the number of slices under the three-tiered cake and noted it said 100 to 150 guests. "It's three times the size you need."

"Do you have a budget for the cake?" Addy questioned.

Simone shook her head. "Not really, but we do have a mortgage, a dog, and already Jonah is yapping about getting me pregnant right away. So we don't have money to burn if that's what you're asking."

"Shut up!" Charlie gasped at what Simone slyly slipped in the middle.

"Say what, boo?" Blessing stopped working on taking in my dress, since I'd lost weight since the last fitting.

Simone nodded and smiled shyly. "I don't know, though. I've finally got a great job, a man, a house, and a dog. I have everything I could ever want..."

"Except a baby," Genesis added. "And Rory could sure use some cousins."

"Guilting me into having a baby is uncool, Gen." Simone narrowed her gaze.

Gen smiled. "Sorry, not sorry. I can't wait for all of you to start pushing out nieces and nephews for me to spoil rotten.

It will serve you right for years of giving Rory everything she wants."

Blessing made a "Pssshhttt" noise. "What the Queen demands, the Queen gets. It's as simple as that. Rory asserted her dominance over all of us before the age of one years old. By two, we were long gone to her rule. At three, we were devoted citizens. At four, she runs a smooth kingdom. You can't blame us for that."

I laughed out loud because Blessing was so right. Little Rory did have every one of us wrapped around her sweet little finger.

"I don't want to live in a world where Rory isn't the Queen, so I'm okay with my lot in life," I announced.

Charlie snorted. "Here, here."

Blessing added. "I heard that!"

Addison giggled and nodded while Simone and Sonia got lost in a discussion about cake.

"Why don't you just have cupcakes, Simone? You love cupcakes," Charlie suggested.

Simone stopped scanning the pages and looked at Charlie. "I could do that?"

"It's your wedding, Si. You can do whatever you want," Sonia agreed. "And you do love cupcakes."

"I totally want cupcakes then. Peach frosting with edible glitter!" She closed her eyes as if she was already tasting the glittery frosting on her tongue.

"I'll call Mama, tell her what you want. She has the hookup." Sonia stood and pulled her trusty phone out of her back pocket. No matter what she was doing, that woman always had her phone nearby.

Blessing held up my dress and shook it out. "Okay, stand up, strip, and let's see if this baby fits."

Genesis and Charlie helped me stand. Blessing removed my T-shirt dress and slid the shimmery fabric over my body. The top was a halter style with ruching up the ribcage covering the breasts. It pressed your boobs together making all of us look like busty betty's. I spun around carefully while I balanced, and the back came into view in the mirror that Addy had brought out for us to size up our dresses.

A loud whistle cut through the air from across the room as the guys descended from upstairs.

"*Chica*, you will not be going far from me in that dress. *Jesús, mi amor.*" He came over and took my hand from Charlie as he tilted his head and scanned my bare back with his gaze. The dress went around the neck and left a huge open oval, the end falling just above our assess. Each was tailored to fit our bodies to perfection. There would be no booty or booby slips as Blessing did not do half-assed designs. She'd make sure we felt as good in the dresses as if we were walking naked.

"Simone wanted sexy bridesmaids dresses so we would all feel pretty on her wedding day. You like?" I dropped my voice blatantly flirting with him.

He licked his bottom lip and then sucked it into his mouth as he trailed his fingers along my spine. I shivered as he made it to the end of the dress and brazenly cupped one of my ass cheeks. "Liliana, you are on fire in this dress. I'm a lucky man."

"Yes, you are, brother. Glad you know it." Blessing pressed her lips together and nodded in appreciation. "You look fine as wine, sister. Now take it off so I can place those last stitches, then have them all pressed."

"Um, can you guys turn around?" I asked Omar and Killian.

Omar looked directly into my face, then let his gaze trail all down my body and then back up when he shook his head and said, "No."

All of my sisters cracked up laughing and I put my hands to my hips, getting ready for a battle.

"Are you for real, pulling this macho man attitude in front of my sisters!" I grouched.

He chuckled. "How's about everyone else turn around and I'll help you get that dress off. We'll call it a practice round." He dipped his head and rubbed his nose along my neck.

I sighed at the dreamy feeling of my man being so close and saying overtly sexy things in order to tease me.

"Oh girl, he told you!" Charlie cackled and promptly turned around, even though she'd seen me naked a thousand times. None of us were shy. We grew up in a house full of nine women with one upstairs bathroom. There wasn't room for modesty in a household like ours.

I groaned under my breath. "Fine, but no sneaking grabs!" I threatened.

The rest of my sisters and Killian turned around, each having their own little chuckle at my expense.

"No promises, *mi amor.*"

I growled under my breath as he helped me remove the dress. I pointed to my previous clothing, and he grabbed it off the couch and put it over my head while I used him to balance.

Once I was back in my own dress, he helped me sit down.

"I'm clothed," I announced, and the rest of the girls and Killian got back into the fray.

While Omar sat there touching me and Killian plopped down on a chair, pulling Addy to sit in his lap, we finished up all the remaining items Simone needed our help with. The dresses were almost ready, flowers, music, dessert, and everything in between had been handled. Mama Kerri was on top of it all.

The last thing that remained was Simone's final fitting.

Blessing made a show of taking Simone into the bathroom across the room with a black zippered dress bag. All of us sisters, Killian, and Omar waited patiently for them to return. Even Brutus was snoozing on a bed in this section of the loft. We'd tuckered the boy out playing with him when we first got there and now, he was wiped. Still, his doggie booty was next to the door which was the most likely entrance for a predator.

Omar played with my curls as we heard Blessing call out to all of us from across the room. "Close your eyes! I want to do a mini-reveal."

My heart sped up in excitement as I closed my eyes along with everyone else. I could hear the sound of fabric swishing across the floor and heeled feet clunking on the wooden surface.

"Okay, open your eyes!" Blessing said excitedly.

When I opened them, Simone stood in front of us. Each person shocked into silence as awe pierced the entire group.

Simone wore a strapless, cream-colored gown that curved around her large breasts and dipped in at her ribcage and waist, then flared back out around her generous hips and out again at the knee. The material was made mostly of a wispy chiffon that glided over her body into a sweeping wave of bustled fabric at the bottom. Imagine a wine glass upside down. The bottom even looked like glimmering crystal tiny bubbles that coasted over the shimmering ruffles, catching the light as she moved from side to side.

Tears of joy and love poured over my cheeks as I looked at the most beautiful bride I'd ever seen in my life.

Sonia broke down into sobs. Covering her face to hide her feelings. Genesis pulled her into her arms, her own eyes teary as each of us took in all that was Simone.

She was the first of us to get married and it had every last one of us extremely emotional.

"Do you not like it?" Simone asked Sonia because Sonia was her big sister. The one person in the entire world she'd known her entire life. Their bond was unbreakable and cemented in the deepest sense of loyalty and love.

Sonia nodded avidly. She wiped her tears and then cleared her throat. "Our mother would have been so moved by your beauty today."

Simone's lips trembled and she held back her tears. She wasn't talking about Mama Kerri. She was referring to the woman who'd given them life.

"She would have been so proud and given anything to see you marry the man of your dreams. Even though she's not here, it's like I can *feel* her." Sonia sniffed and wiped at more tears that fell.

Sonia and Simone's biological parents died in a house fire over twenty years ago, but like my own family that died in a car accident, we still loved and missed them being in our lives. Especially for things such as a wedding.

"Me too. And Tabby as well. It's like the wedding is all falling together so easily because it was meant to be. Like maybe we have them in the background helping out." Simone wiped at her own teary eyes.

I liked to think of Tabby in Heaven plotting to make sure Simone's day was just right. She'd do that too. Tabby may have had a hard time with other people, and never lived what some would consider a "normal" life, but her foster sisters had meant everything to her. It's why she gave up her life. To save Simone and Addy. She'd absolutely want Simone to have everything her heart desired on such an important day. And to think that Simone chose Tabby's birthday to have her wedding, to honor her, it brought more tears to my eyes.

"You okay, *mi amor?*" Omar turned my head and wiped each of my tears while he stared into my eyes.

I nodded. "Just happy to be here with you and my sisters. It's a good day," I swallowed down the heavy emotion and snuggled against his chest, staring at Simone in her stunning dress. "The dress is absolutely perfect," I said.

"Freakin' amazing!" Addison noted.

"Jonah is gonna shit when he sees you!" Charlie gushed.

"You make a gorgeous bride, sister," Genesis said with a smile.

"What am I? Designs-R-Us? You say nothing about my mad skillz?" Blessing harumphed even though she knew we were blown away, or we wouldn't have said how perfect Simone looked.

"It's a one-of-a-kind design, what could we say?" I blurted.

"Yeah, we already know you're going to kick some serious fashion ass. Just wait until the paparazzi get a gander at it. You'll end up with tons of orders for wedding gowns!" Charlie noted.

Simone frowned. "I hope they don't break in. Jonah assured me that between Holt Security and the FBI, no one would be getting any pictures."

I watched Sonia shrug. "You know how they are. Where there's a will, there's a way."

I petted Omar on his chest. "Do you think you guys will be able to keep everyone away?"

Omar sighed deeply. "We're gonna try, baby. That's all we can promise at this point."

"Try hard." I trembled in his hold, worrying about such a public event happening at a now very public location. The paparazzi had been crawling all over Kerrighan House for months.

Omar lifted my chin so he could get my attention, in the way I'd already become accustomed and secretly liked.

"I will keep you safe," he promised.

I traced his lips. "Keep my family safe. They're all that matters," I whispered and kissed his lips.

He took my kiss, and then pulled back. "And you're all that matters to me."

"Then you better work really hard because I wouldn't be me without them. Remember that when you talk to Holt and Jonah about their plans."

"Okay, *mi amor*. I will keep you and your family safe."

I snuggled back against his chest, happy in the knowledge that Omar would do everything in his power to keep us all protected.

I hoped it would be enough.

Chapter
EIGHTEEN

Two weeks later...

"FUCK, LILIANA. DAMN." OMAR BIT BACK ANOTHER CURSE as I held on to the top of the headboard and rode my man *hard*. His beast hammered at the perfect angle, hitting me right where I needed it over and over.

"Come, baby," I whined, arching against the indescribable pleasure, glorying in the fact that I no longer felt pain from my shoulder or foot as both had completely healed.

"Harder, *mi amor*." Omar grunted, curling his hands around the fleshy part of my hips and thrusting up into me wildly.

"Goooooddddd!" I cried out. Everything was misted in sweat, my heart pounding a mile a minute as my lady bits throbbed in desperate need for release.

At the first tingle an orgasm was about to hit, Omar sat up, crossed his arms around my back, and flipped us around so that my back was now flat to the bed.

"Hey! No fair!" I griped. He never let me ride until completion, always taking control in the end.

He lifted my thighs up toward my head and spread them wide before pounding against my sex. His balls slapped my ass, and I lost my ability to breathe, too lost in the pleasure to continuing complaining.

259

"Baby," I whimpered as he ground his pelvis down on that hot button of nerves and sent me soaring. "Yaaaaassssss," I screamed as he kept going, lost to his own desire.

"Every day I'm inside of you is the best day of my life, *mi amor*! Take me. Take it hard, baby." He growled through his teeth, plowing me right into a second orgasm that spasmed around his beast.

"So good." Omar sucked at my neck, grinding against me.

He moaned low and deep against my skin as his hips thrust home and finally, masterfully, stilled. His body convulsed around me, trembling with his release until each aftershock slowly abated.

I noticed the pulsating tingle of pain at my neck, and I realized what he was doing. "Don't you dare give me a hickey, Omar Francisco Alvarado! The wedding is today!"

He hummed against my neck and kissed me lightly there as if he were physically apologizing.

"Woman, I lose my damn mind when I'm inside you," he grumbled, then ran his tongue from my neck, across my clavicle, and between both my breasts which he gently palmed and pushed together. He sipped at each peak he'd already tortured this morning until the brown numbs looked like ripe raspberries.

I lie there breathing, attempting to allow my body to come back to something akin to normal.

Once I had started to feel better from my injuries and could fully contribute to our activities in the bedroom, Omar had ramped things up quite a bit. The man was *insatiable*. Wanted me morning and night like clockwork. And because he didn't like to be far away from where Ophelia lived, in the event she needed her big brother, we spent our nights in his bed.

I didn't care. My apartment was nice, but no better or worse than his. And if it gave my man peace of mind to be close to where his sister was singlehandedly raising a baby on her own, I'd happily sleep in his comfy bed. Besides, most days I woke to his hands or mouth on me, which made my mornings very nice indeed.

"We have to be at Kerrighan House early," I reminded him.

Omar snuffled against my breasts and then kept moving down, kissing my sternum, around my belly button, and just above the thin triangle of hair I kept down below.

He inhaled against my skin there. "I love how you smell like us after we've made love. Makes me hard, baby," he warned and then bit where my thigh and hip met.

I moaned and tried to shake off the arousal he was building up. I reached down to grip his head, knowing he was going for round two even though we had to get ready to go. He was already going lower, humming against my flesh as he took a long, luxurious lick of my oversensitive clit, sucking it into his mouth and teasing it mercilessly.

My legs slammed around his ears, and he moaned deeper, bringing his hands up to clutch onto my butt cheeks for leverage.

"Omar, we need to get ready…" I sighed, but also wantonly lifted my hips so he'd have better access.

The man was so good at going down on me. He could get me off in minutes if he wanted to.

"Five more minutes," he murmured against my flesh, licking along my slit.

"Jesus, baby. I'm not going to be able to walk down the aisle," I gasped as he sunk his tongue deep.

He licked and kissed along my already overworked sex. "Then I'll carry you, *mi amor*. Now give your man what he wants," he asked in that sexy tone I couldn't deny. It was downright sinful, needy, and shameless.

"Five more minutes? Can you get me off that quick?" I taunted, knowing he could.

He lifted his head, licked his already wet lips, and smirked.

I sighed, cocked a brow, and boldly butterflied my legs wide open. Unembarrassed and unashamed. It was exactly what he wanted.

His eyes darkened, his nostrils flared, and he gifted me the tiniest smile.

It took him less than five minutes.

Omar and I pulled up to the front of Kerrighan House to find not only the press circling the grounds but other media outlets sent entire crews to scope out the event.

"What is going on?" I scanned the many media vans. There were the standard local news, but also the crazy gossip rags that made up things about people to suit whatever picture they happened to capture. Those were the ones that freaked me out. Usually, the news stations reported news. The gossip hounds however liked to post things about Addison, my model sister, that were not nice. Usually about her weight, her kidnapping, or her money. Recently they'd been all over Sonia too, because she's being scouted to serve as a primary candidate for the Independent Party in the next Presidential election. Something she didn't seek out and has made a point not to discuss with any media outlets. Much to their determined prodding.

The press immediately barked out questions like they always did.

"Are you upset the MacCreedys got away after hurting you?"

"Do the FBI have any new leads on the MacCreedys?"

"What was it like being kidnapped?"

"Back off, guys!" Omar barked as one of the gossip reporters approached.

Omar opened my door while both Ryan and Holt bolted down the steps of the house and onto the sidewalk to meet us. Ryan was in a tux and Holt in a nice suit, both looking dashing but deadly as they approached.

"Get Liliana inside. I'll get her stuff," Ryan ordered, heading to the back of Omar's SUV.

Both Omar and Holt led me inside my own home as I clutched my dress bag to my chest. Once I was safely behind locked doors, the crazy didn't stop.

People were running around, in and out of the kitchen, backyard, and up the stairs. Servers, friends of both families, and of course Aunt Delores, who I'm sure Mama Kerri coined the "leader" who was currently barking out orders.

"I'm gonna see what's going on up there." I pointed to the stairs where I knew the rest of my sisters would be.

Omar nodded. "I'm going to get the lay of the land."

I pressed my palms flat to his hard chest. "Hey, you look incredibly handsome today." I smiled up at him.

His chest lifted and he grinned. "You like the suit, eh?"

"I'm going to like stripping it off you later even more." I batted my eyelashes.

263

He dipped his head close enough so only I could hear him. "I fucked you hard this morning, got you off two more times, and you're already ready for another round?"

I cocked my brow. "Is that a problem?"

"Not even close. I'm wondering when I should get down on one knee and pop the question. Make you *and* that sex drive mine forever."

I grinned wide, lifted on my toes, and kissed him deeply. "We've got all the time in the world."

"What if I don't want to wait?" he asked, sounding more serious than ever.

I frowned. "Baby, we've only been together a short time."

He cupped my cheeks. "Why wait when we're in love? You think that's going to change any time soon?"

My heartbeat banged against my chest. "No, I don't think I'll ever stop loving you."

"Then make me the happiest man alive and think about marrying me. Okay?"

Pure joy spread through my veins. I was happier than I'd ever been in my entire life. "I will. But today is about Simone. And a few months from now, it will be about Addy."

He looped his arms around me. "And when will it be about us?"

I glanced off to the side and made a humming sound. "Spring?"

He chuckled. "Spring it is."

I kissed him hard and fast. "You better think up an amazing proposal. Your mama will never let you live it down if you don't."

He groaned. "True. My father spoiled her."

I shrugged and was glad to note it didn't hurt. "I'm sure

my man will think of something." I cupped his cheek. "Gotta go check on Simone."

He kissed me once more. "We'll be continuing this conversation. No getting out of it, *mi amor.*"

I crossed my finger over my heart. "I swear. Now go." I shooed him away and took my time going up the stairs. I wanted desperately to wear my heels with my dress, but I didn't want to overdo it before the wedding even started.

Once I got to the master bedroom, I knocked on the door.

It opened an inch and then Charlie's hand darted out. She opened the door just enough for me to fit and pulled me in before slamming the door shut again.

Simone stood in the corner in front of a tall oval mirror. Her dress sparkled against the light streaming in and she looked like a glowing goddess. Even her skin shimmered. Her hair was down around her shoulders in big beachy waves that were styled to perfection. Her makeup was peachy pink and accentuated her natural beauty without being caked on.

"Simone…" I swallowed. "You are enchanting. Like a goddess," I breathed in awe.

"Thanks, Lil." She swished her skirt from side to side.

"She looks like a fairy princess! And look at me! We match!" Rory spun around in a circle letting her own dress made of cream-colored tulle and chiffon spin up into the air. It truly was a mini version of Simone's dress, only it had one-inch straps at each shoulder holding it up, while Simone's dress was strapless. Rory even had a matching bow like Simone's.

"You look like a true queen!" I hunched down and scooped my niece into my arms, giving her a snuggle.

"You are not dressed." Rory scrunched up her face.

"I didn't want to wrinkle it or get it dirty at *la casa del tío* Omar."

Her little mouth opened into a big "O."

"Come on over here, Sprite. I'm doing your hair and makeup!" Addison waved me over as Charlie pushed me toward Mama Kerri's vanity.

Sonia of course was pacing the floor with her phone pressed to her ear. "Tell them I have no damn comment about the Presidential election. Frankly, I'm tired of hearing about it, Quinn. Handle this. I'm at my sister's *wedding*. Which you better not miss, by the way." She put her phone out in front of her. "Starts in an hour in case you didn't notice." Her brows pinched together and then huffed. "Oh, you're both downstairs at the bar?" She smiled. "Then never mind. Tell them all to suck on a box of rocks. My sister is getting married! See you down there!" She groaned at her phone and then tossed it on the bed. "I hate that thing."

Simone snorted. "That phone is your life."

Sonia walked over to her sister and put her hands to her biceps and looked at Simone and her reflection in the mirror. "No, *you* and this *family* are my life. And today you're going to start a family of your own by marrying Jonah. How do you feel, sis?"

Simone swallowed and lifted her chin. "I feel like it's the first day of the rest of my life. And I'm happy. So damn happy. And I'm finally looking forward to every new day because Jonah's in my life."

"That's all I could have ever hoped for you." Sonia hugged her from behind.

Mama Kerri approached the two sisters. In her hand was a pair of diamond drop earrings. "I wore these when I married the love of my life. Today, I'd like for you to wear them, if you want to."

"Oh my God, Mama Kerri, I'd be honored." Simone breathed, emotion filling her words.

Mama Kerri held Simone's hair back as she put one earring in and then the next. "They look perfect."

"They're beautiful, Mama." Simone wiped a tear away.

"They were a wedding gift from my husband."

"I'll keep them safe." She held onto Mama Kerri's hand as all of us watched the display with our hearts in our throats. This woman was everything to us. She'd given us a home, a family, a good life, but most importantly, she'd given us *her*. A mother who truly loved us unconditionally.

"I know you will, chicklet. I love you so much. All of you." She patted her eyes with her handkerchief. "You have brought unending joy into my life. I'm so blessed to have all my girls. And today, on our Tabby's birthday, we will honor her with love. Every year we will celebrate her love and the love you and Jonah have for one another. She would love that, chicklet. So much."

Blessing took that moment to break the tension while holding a tray of bubbling champagne. Each of us took a glass and held it aloft.

"To Simone and Jonah, to my girls, to Tabitha, may she smile down on us this day, and to each and every one of us having a long and beautiful life!" Mama Kerri lifted her glass.

All of my sisters clapped, drank, and cheered as we wiped the tears from our eyes.

267

"You may now kiss the bride," the officiant announced.

Jonah wrapped one arm around Simone's waist, the other around her back, and lifted her in the air. He spun her around like a knight in a fairytale. Then he let her slide down his body where he laid his lips over hers. He kissed her for a solid thirty seconds with the entire party hooting and hollering like wild animals.

When he was done kissing her, he pressed his forehead to hers and whispered something none of us could hear. Her cheeks pinked beautifully and then she smiled wide as he interlaced their fingers and held their hands up in the air.

"Mr. and Mrs. Fontaine, everybody!" the officiant stated loudly over everyone's cheers.

The music picked up and the couple danced their way down the petal-covered aisle. All six of us sisters did the same with the groomsman we were assigned. The wedding party danced our way deeper into the garden to take pictures, while the attendees got to feast on appetizers on the deck.

When we were done, Omar met me with a glass of bubbling champagne.

"For *mi lirio*." He handed it to me. I took a sip, then kissed him deeply, wanting him to taste the champagne and my happiness on his tongue.

He hummed against my mouth. "You taste good, Liliana. Good enough to eat." He nipped at my lips playfully.

I grinned and looped my arms around him. "Wasn't the wedding perfect?"

He nodded. "Gorgeous. You in that dress was the highlight," he teased.

I batted at his chest playfully. "Stop it. Simone was stunning."

"She was, *mi amor*. And Jonah could not take his eyes off her." His gaze left me as he watched his mother parade around with her arm hooked to Arturo's. "We need to thank Simone and Jonah for inviting *mi familia*. Mama is losing her mind over how many sisters you have. She's being choosy trying to decide which one should marry Arturo."

I grinned. "Well, she better hurry up. Simone and Addy are taken. That leaves Sonia, Genesis, Blessing, and Charlie."

"I think she has her eye on Charlie. She made the comment earlier that it would be amazing to have a fire-haired grandchild," he chuckled.

"You think those genes would pass down?" I shook my head. "I'm thinking you Alvarado men will be passing down the dark hair and eyes. Just look at Cisco. He's a mini-Omar."

He grinned and waggled his brows. "I know. Just wait until we have ours one day. You will be busy batting off the *chicas*."

"Definitely." I sipped on my glass and scanned the crowd, enjoying everyone having fun. But out of the corner of my eye I glimpsed a man with long brown hair and searing blue eyes I recognized. A flash of that screaming face as he threatened to cut off my head stole across my mind's eye. My stomach clenched and sank as I gasped. In a single blink, the man was gone.

I stepped around Omar to get a better view across the party. "Did you see that man?" I asked in a panicked tone pointing to where I thought I saw my worst nightmare.

He turned around abruptly, looping an arm around my waist and bringing me close to his chest as if on instinct. His smile slipped away as his gaze burned through the crowd. "No. What did you see?"

"I thought, I…" I shook my head. "It's stupid. I thought I saw MacCreedy. John. Or Mac. Whatever he likes to be called."

"Here?" The single word came out sharp and deadly.

I slumped against Omar's side and rested my head to his chest. "I think I'm seeing things. There's no way he'd be here."

"The last report said they found one of the stolen cars linked to the duo in Ohio, as though they were heading East. They're on the run. That was a little over a week ago." Omar reminded me what we'd been told.

"True. I'm being stupid." I took a full breath in and let it out. "I'm going to go to the bathroom. Freshen up." I pecked him on the lips and handed him my champagne glass.

"I'll go with you." He frowned.

"No, no. I think it's just all the excitement making me see things that aren't there. Don't worry. I'll be right back. We'll get some food. I'm hungry. We haven't eaten much today."

Omar tilted his head. "You sure? I can follow you."

"No, I need a moment."

"Okay. I'll get a plate of appetizers and meet you at the front of the seating area over there." He gestured to the round tables that had already replaced the seats the guests had used for the ceremony.

I nodded. "Thanks, handsome." I smiled weakly, still feeling a little out of sorts. My skin felt clammy as I maneuvered through the guests. I made it to the kitchen and bumped into Mama Kerri.

"Hey, chicklet. You look like you've seen a ghost." She put her hand to my forehead immediately. "You feel clammy, honey."

I waved at my heated face. I couldn't shake the slither

of fear scaling up my spine and pressing into my heart. "I'm gonna go use the bathroom and freshen up."

"Okay, but come back and see me if you're not feeling better."

I nodded and gave a half-hearted smile as I made my way down the back hallway to where the bathroom was. I just stepped one foot inside, when I was shoved hard into the bathroom from behind. My palms hit the opposite wall and I spun around to come face to face with the devil.

John MacCreedy was standing there with his long hair down around his face, those scary blue eyes searing me to where I stood. He wore a waiter's getup—which must have been how he got in.

"We meet again, pretty, pretty princess," he snarled. "You thought you got away scot-free, didn't you?" He pulled a long butcher knife from behind his back.

Unbridled terror pounded in my chest as I tried to breathe against the fear. The light in the bathroom glinted off the shiny metal knife as if foretelling my doom. The blade was at least six inches long and could definitely kill me.

"What do you want?" I lifted my chin trying to stay calm and show I wasn't scared, even though I was petrified.

"We have unfinished business, me and you." He tilted his head like a coyote might right before a lethal strike.

"Look, I'm sorry about what happened at the bank and at the boat. I had no part in that. I was trying to escape just like you did in the end. We're the same, you and me." I tried to find a level playing field with the murdering psycho.

He glared and snarled. "You think you are like me!" He pointed at his own chest as his voice rose. "I walked hundreds of miles through war-torn desert to survive. Killing men, women, and children, just to survive. All because Uncle Sam demanded it. And what did I get for my service? Kicked out. Dishonorable discharge, because I did my job!" He roared in my face, spittle flying against my cheek.

I held up my hands. "I'm sorry that happened to you."

"You're sorry!" He laughed maniacally. "Sorry doesn't cut it, sweetheart! Only blood spilled can wash away your sins!" He sneered in a twisted form of a smile.

He lifted the knife and I screamed at the top of my lungs. Just as it was coming down, the bathroom door went flying open and Omar barreled straight into my attacker from behind. His hand caught the knife hand at the wrist, and he slammed it against the wall right next to my head.

I screeched and pushed to the opposite side of the room, shaking in fear. Then I took a breath and shrieked out, "HELP! HELP!" while Omar and MacCreedy duked it out with their fists.

Jonah and Ryan along with Holt stormed down the hallway in what felt like seconds as Omar beat the ever-loving shit out of MacCreedy. He got him to drop the knife, the thing clanging to the tile floor, then he smashed his fist into the man's ugly face over and over until blood sprayed across the floor. I wedged myself against the small corner of the room between the wall and the freestanding sink, trying to stay out of the way.

Jonah pulled me from the fray and passed me back to Ryan, who passed me back to Holt who tried to pull me away and down the hall, but I wasn't leaving without Omar.

"No!" I fought back as he held my arms to my sides.

Omar was yelling his own profanities, letting his anger fly as he beat up the man that had made my life a living hell.

"You'll never touch her again!" He clocked him in the gut.

"Send you straight to hell, motherfucker!" He punched MacCreedy's already bloody face.

"That's enough, Omar!" Jonah looped Omar around the waist, but he wasn't strong enough to pull my man off his nemesis.

It took both Ryan and Jonah, each grabbing one of Omar's monster arms, in order to get him off my attacker.

"He kidnapped and hurt Liliana! He killed those innocent people!" He spit on MacCreedy as he was pulled off him. "Rot in hell. Rot in hell!" He continued to yell as he was removed from the bathroom and dragged several feet into the hall.

Jonah shoved Omar toward Ryan who brought him into the hallway. "Tend to your woman," Ryan stated looking Omar in the face but Omar wasn't paying any attention. No, his gaze was on the bathroom where the devil lie battered and bleeding. Omar's eyes were white hot fire and his entire body pulsed with his anger. Every muscle in his body was activated to do harm.

I started to cry, whimpers slipping from my lips as I watched Omar fight against Ryan.

"Omar!" Ryan gripped his face and shook the man aggressively. "Tend. To. Your. Woman!" He growled each word.

Omar's gaze shot to mine and he shook Ryan off, stomping toward me. "Let. Her. Go." He warned Holt, his tone scathing. When Holt let me go, I jumped into Omar's arms, pressing my face to his neck where I burst into bone-shattering sobs.

"I've got you." He held me tight. "He can't hurt you anymore. I took care of him, baby. He's going to jail where he belongs."

"D-did you k-kill h-im?" I choked out needing to know.

He shook his head and petted my hair. "No, *mi amor*. He's breathing. Unfortunately. At least he will pay for his crimes. Every one of them."

I nodded into his neck and bucked against him as everything that just happened came over me.

Mama Kerri entered from the edges of the hallway and approached us. "Okay, chicklet. Come now. Let's get you cleaned up and let those boys do their job."

Behind her I could see Simone in her gorgeous wedding dress, clinging to Sonia.

Omar brought me over to Simone who immediately clutched at me and brought me into a full-body hug.

"I'm sorry I ruined your wedding!" I cried against her neck.

She shook her head. "Are you kidding? We got the bad guy and you're safe. We're all safe now! This is the best day ever!" She smiled and squeezed me tight.

Jonah and Ryan, both in beautiful tuxes, hefted up a bloody John MacCreedy who didn't seem to be able to see out of either of his eyes.

"You are right baby, best day ever!" Jonah grinned wide as he passed by our group. "Let me put this piece of shit in the squad car and we'll party on, yeah?"

Simone lifted her arm and fist pumped the air. "Go get 'em, baby!" Then her voice dipped low. "God, he's so hot when he catches bad guys." She sighed in a dreamy tone that really proved she was not upset.

I sniffed and pulled from her arms wiping at my eyes. Mama Kerri handed me her handkerchief and I blotted at my face. "You really aren't mad?" I asked Simone.

Simone shook her head. "You think anyone is ever gonna forget my wedding?" She laughed.

Sonia sighed. "Only you would think capturing a criminal at your wedding would be cool."

She shrugged. "My husband is a hot guy FBI agent? What do you expect?"

Omar came back without his suit jacket and tie on, probably because they were coated in MacCreedy's blood. He'd washed his hands and there was no longer any hint that he'd been in a fistfight other than his swollen and split knuckles.

"You okay, Liliana?" he asked solemnly.

My heart broke at the defeated note in his voice.

"Thank you for saving me." I swallowed down the desire to start crying again. I needed to be strong. Not only for me, but for him and my family.

"Come here, *mi amor*. Let me hold you." He gestured with his hands, and I went willingly into his arms.

He wrapped those massive arms around me, and I pressed my ear to his chest and listened to his heartbeat. I let everything else disappear as the rightness of being in his arms spread through my heart, mind, and body, bringing nothing but a true sense of peace.

I could handle anything if I was in this man's arms.

Chapter
NINETEEN

A few days later…

AFTER CATCHING JOHN MACCREEDY IN THE MIDDLE OF Simone's wedding, shockingly or maybe not so shockingly with it being *Simone's* wedding, the party continued. As much as I'd wanted to leave and hide away in Omar's apartment, under his covers, with my man's arms around me, I was determined not to let the MacCreedys steal any more of my time with my family. So, we stayed, watched the first dance, the speeches, and the cupcake smash where Simone nailed Jonah right in the face with an entire cupcake. He retaliated by kissing her silly, mashing the cupcake on his face into hers. They were adorable and so in love, everyone could see that they were going to have a long and happy life together.

The rest of the night was filled with laughter, love, and the sisterhood. Each of my sisters would pop over to chat with us where Omar had placed me in a little safe corner of the deck, my man's arms curving around my back keeping me close. We were tucked away, but still able to view and feel connected the party. Most importantly, I felt safe.

Tucker MacCreedy, Mac's cousin, was found smoking a cigarette, listening to music, while sitting in the last car they stole. The idiot parked just down the street from Kerrighan

House, which made it easy for the boys in blue and the FBI who were actually attending the wedding to locate him.

It all seemed to happen so fast. One moment I was in a bathroom having my life threatened with a knife, and the next, MacCreedy was being beat to hell and hauled away. Off to jail. Justice would be served.

I was free.

My family was free.

As Simone said, it was the best day ever. And yet, now, two days later, I was still shell-shocked. Freaked out. Uncomfortable in my own skin. Looking over my shoulder wondering when the other shoe was going to drop. The feeling was maddening, and I loathed it. I wasn't sure how to get my normal happy-go-lucky self back to normal.

"You hungry, *mi lirio*? Mama's got a dish planned to woo you," Omar said as we unbuckled our seatbelts. I stared out at his family's restaurant. A brick building in the heart of downtown Chicago. There were pretty yellow awnings that ran the surface, shielding each window from the sun. There were two huge planters that were bursting with lacy-looking trees. Their leaves long and fanning out in every direction, making the double glass door entrance seem welcoming.

I nodded in answer.

Omar's jaw tightened as he ambled out of the car gracefully, came around and opened my door, offering me a hand to help me balance as I got out in my towering, wedge-style cork sandals. The frilly pink dress I wore fell down almost to my knees. I left the cardigan I'd worn over it in the car. I usually kept layers available because in Chicago, you never knew what kind of day you were going to have. The weather changed on a dime and one's only recourse was to be prepared.

"*Chica*, one day you're going to break your neck in those heels you love."

I smirked. "Says the man that likes to fuck me while I'm wearing only my shoes," I teased.

He came up behind me and wrapped his arms around my chest, pressing his face against my neck. "*Sí, mi amor*, but in that circumstance, I am there holding onto you, so you don't fall."

Swoon.

A shiver ran down my spine at the reminder of what occurred just yesterday. When I got home to his apartment after a long day at school, I was met by my man having just exited the shower. He was wrapped in nothing but a towel and these delicious little droplets running all over his magnificent skin. I traced those droplets with my tongue which in turn ended with me having my dress removed within moments, my naked chest pressed against the kitchen table as he bent me over it, wearing only my heels, as he took me from behind.

It was wild.

It was hungry.

It was us.

Losing ourselves to the other was something that occurred pretty regularly in our world, ever since the day I was released from the hospital.

I leaned against his back. "I need a margarita," I sighed.

He kissed my neck, then let me go and took my hand with his. "Then let's get you a margarita."

We entered the restaurant and instead of waiting at the front for a table, Omar strode through until we were at the bar. He pulled out one of the bar stools and I sat on it. He went around the bar and spoke to the young man already there serving drinks. They hugged and clapped one another on the back.

"Liliana, this is my cousin Mateo," Omar called out from the other side of the long bar.

I smiled and waved, then watched as Omar coated a glass in salt and then made me a margarita over ice. He set it in front of me and went back and grabbed himself a Mexican beer.

"Tell Mama we are here, *¿sí, amigo?*"

Mateo nodded and disappeared through a set of double doors that I assumed went back into the kitchen.

Omar came around and sat next to me, lifting up his beer.

"What should we drink to?" I asked.

"Living a happy life, *mi amor*. That is all I could ever want or need."

God, I loved this man.

I clinked my glass with his and we drank.

A basket of warm tortilla chips and salsa was placed in front of us by his cousin.

"Thank you, Mateo," I said and then my gaze caught on the TV across the way. Two men were standing in front of a podium giving a press conference. "Can you turn that up!" I pointed to the TV, surprised to see one of the faces I recognized from my time on the yacht.

"What it is?" Omar asked.

I shook my head, slipped off the stool and went over to where I could hear the TV better. Omar followed me.

"See those words at the bottom. It's about the bank robberies," I said as Mateo turned up the TV. The hair on my arms stood up as goosebumps covered the surface of my skin. My throat went dry, and I bit hard into my bottom lip as I took in the faces attached to a voice I knew all too well.

279

"Hello, everyone. My name is Logan Winston, and this is my brother Kurt Winston. We are grateful for the hard work done by the FBI, the auditors, and everyone involved in the Lake Michigan area bank heists. The situation unfolding has been atrocious. Finding out that our father Gregory Winston was not only embezzling from thousands of people across all of our companies' holdings but framing dozens of innocent people who had worked for our company for years to take the fall for his treachery is beyond incomprehensible. Several former employees wrongly convicted have served over five years in prison already for a crime they didn't commit. Justice must be sought for these individuals."

The blond man frowned and looked at the man standing next to him. "My brother and I are deeply saddened to learn of our father's deception and will work day and night to right the wrongs that have been done to so many innocent lives. We are horrified that the bank robberies that occurred recently ended in the loss of three lives, an injured man, and a woman who was kidnapped."

The man's voice was one I'd never forget.

Logan Winston. The Primary.

Then the man next to him spoke and I knew what voice I'd hear.

Kurt Winston. The Second.

"Our father was not a good man as proven by what has been uncovered. If the bank robberies hadn't occurred, his deceit and reign of horror would have continued. We can't bring back the lives that were lost or take back the experience of those hurt in the process, but we can give back where it counts. My brother and I will work with the families involved in this scandal to help them whatever way we can. Monetarily.

Mentally. Emotionally. We are committed to the task of finding a way to give everyone involved the peace they deserve." I listened intently as I recognized Kurt Winston as the male who was in the water that night. The one who ultimately ended up saving my life before I drowned in those cold, dark waters.

The Primary took to the microphone again. "Once more, we are thankful to the brave men and women who helped capture John and Tucker MacCreedy this past weekend. John MacCreedy has been identified as the single shooter in the bank robberies responsible for all three deaths and the kidnapping of the schoolteacher who was later returned along with all of the money that had been stolen. Tucker MacCreedy will be tried as an accomplice. As far as we've been informed, both men will face charges. Once we know more, we will share any new information with all of you. For now, please give us the time needed to do what we can to make amends for our father's atrocities and move on from these tragedies. My brother and I thank you for your continued support. Good day." The Primary finished and both he and his brother exited the platform as the police chief took their place.

"You can turn it off," I murmured, suddenly not wanting to eat or drink. I just wanted to go back home, crawl into Omar's bed, and hide for the rest of the year.

I didn't know how I felt about those two men. They helped rob their own banks in order to have their father's illegal behavior tracked and brought to light. The intent was noble, but the execution failed.

People died.

Then again, other innocent people went to jail because of their father, while he got away free as a bird. I could sympathize with their need for justice for the people who'd been convicted of a crime they didn't commit, but again, three others died at that bank. Omar was shot. I was *kidnapped* and tied up. Sure, they ultimately treated me pretty well for a kidnapping victim, unlike the torture Addy received by her kidnapper, or the fact that Tabby died in order to save Addy and Simone from the same vile man. I was here. Alive and having a margarita at my man's family's restaurant.

"Baby, what's the matter?" Omar dipped his head and lifted my chin, so I'd look into his eyes. They were so pretty, a golden brown that got darker when he was angry or aroused. Right then there were crinkles at the edges, giving light to his concern for me.

I shook it off. I needed time to think about everything I learned. Let it all simmer and figure out what to do…if anything.

"Nothing, baby, just learning there was more at stake than money in the robbery is a lot to take in," I confided.

He sighed and sipped at his beer. "Why do I get the feeling there's more that you aren't saying?" His tone was soft but held a note of worry.

I cupped his neck with both of my hands. "I just need some time. Let's enjoy my first time at your family restaurant."

He reached out and pressed a wonky curl behind my ear. "You'll share when you're ready?"

"I will," I agreed.

He groaned under his breath just as we heard his mother's voice. "Where's my *ángel*?" Renata burst from behind the kitchen doors with two steaming plates of food. "Ah, there's our beauty!" She came over, put the plates in front of us, and pulled me into a big hug.

I held on to his mother and looked at him over her

shoulder. "I'll be fine," I mouthed then plastered on a smile for Renata. I wasn't about to let the ongoing tragedy or the new information I just learned about the Primary and his Second ruin another important day in my life.

Omar seemed to know I needed this day, and thankfully, he let it go.

The next day I called out of work sick, allowing a substitute teacher to take on my classes for the day. I had come to the conclusion that I wasn't going to be able to continue on with my life as normal if I didn't come face to face with the men who'd ultimately held me captive.

I stood outside of the enormous skyscraper in the downtown financial district. I walked in and went up to a long reception desk. While I waited for the woman to get off a call, I glanced around the lobby. It was lush. All chrome, glass, and modern art sprinkled with greenery. The floors were bright white, gold-veined marble. Classy and elegant.

A pair of machines scanned people walking in and out. A security guard checked ID badges as their purses, briefcases, and whatever other things they carried with them were run through an X-ray machine that another guard was watching.

"How can I help you?" The pretty woman with almond-shaped dark eyes and striking features asked. She wore a serious-looking business suit while I stood in a flirty sundress that Blessing had designed. It wasn't business professional at all but definitely suited the ladies that lunch type vibe. I felt pretty and confident in it and that's what Mama Kerri always taught me mattered. How you felt in what you wore, not what other people thought when they saw you wearing it. That was for them to think, not for you to concern yourself with. Maybe that's why Blessing was so free and creative with her designs. She didn't care what others thought. She designed for her and what she believed would make the people she dressed feel confident and beautiful.

"My name is Liliana Ramírez-Kerrighan, and I wanted to speak with either Logan or Kurt Winston."

Her brows pinched together. "Dr. Kurt Winston does not work in this building. He has his own private practice outside of the city."

"Okay." I shrugged. "Then I'd like to see Logan please."

She jerked her head back surprised. "Do you have an appointment?"

I shook my head. "I didn't think I needed one." I tilted my head. "Is he here?" I pointed up toward the floors above us.

"Yes, of course. He's the owner of the building," she deadpanned.

"Okay, then I'd like for you to ring him and let him know I'm here." I smiled for good measure. Letting her know I wasn't a threat. Not really. I mean, I did know a lot of seriously damaging information about him and his brother, but she didn't need to know that.

She blinked a few times. "I've never called him directly in my five years working here."

I slumped against the counter. "Why? You just said he owned the building."

"And probably fifty more just like it across the globe. You realize the Winston's are one of the richest families in the US."

Wow. That was news. I'd not taken the time to look up

the Winston clan. I was more the meet up with them in person type. Duke it out face to face.

I inhaled fully and let it out slowly. "I actually didn't know that. I'm sure there's someone you can call to notify him that I'm here?"

"I'll try his assistant." She pressed her lips together in a way that told me she did not want to call his assistant. She didn't want to bother the big boss at all. Either way, I wasn't leaving until I sat down with the Primary.

To me, that's who he was. Who'd he'd likely always be.

I shivered as I watched her make a phone call. "Yes, hello this is Selene at the front desk. I have a woman by the name of Liliana Ramírez-Kerrighan here who would like to speak to Mr. Winston. Yes, I can hold."

I pulled out my phone and busied myself scanning Facebook. Oh, my old friend Julia was pregnant. I'd have to send her a gift.

"Excuse me, Ms. Ramírez-Kerrighan. Mr. Winston will see you right away."

I smiled knowingly. I just bet he would.

"I'm to leave the desk and escort you straight away." She sounded nervous and her hands seemed to tremble as she got up, slid her hands down her suit to remove any pesky wrinkles, and tucked her chair in. "Follow me." She opened a hidden door that allowed me to go through her reception area. The security guard lifted his chin as he watched me skip through the process.

"I'm happy to walk through the scanners," I offered.

She shook her head. "He said for you to come now. He'll call the security team."

I watched as the security guard pressed his fingers to his ear as if listening through an earpiece.

"Follow me," Selene commanded and I picked up the pace.

We entered a separate smaller elevator that was off to the side and unavailable to everyone else. It didn't even have a button to push. It magically just opened as we approached. As I entered, I looked up and noted there was a security camera that probably controlled the unit. I imagined the elevator was the personal one just for the boss. Too rich and too busy to take the normal lifts with his staff popping off at the many floors of the skyscraper.

The lift took us to the fortieth floor. There were five more levels above this one and a button at the top labeled P which I assumed was for the Penthouse.

Selene exited the elevator and brought me over to another tall man with burnished, sandy-brown hair that was slicked back at the sides and short on top. He also wore a spectacular suit.

He reached out his hand toward me. "I'm Drew, Mr. Winston's personal assistant. It's good to meet you Ms. Ramírez-Kerrighan. Mr. Winston eagerly awaits your visit."

My brows rose up toward my hairline as I shook his hand. He was *eager* to see me. If I were him, I'd be scared out of my mind. Which was why I was there. Knowing him and his brother and his entire team were still out there made me uneasy. Neither of us knew where the other stood. He'd let me go, but that didn't mean there wasn't a plan to take me out. And in reverse, I could have told the FBI already who my other captors were. As I saw it, we both had a great deal at stake.

My life and sanity.

His life and freedom.

He motioned toward a hallway next to where we stood. "This way."

I followed him down the hall, turning this way and that until we finally reached a large open space that held an empty desk, which I gathered was Drew's desk, and a pair of large wooden doors with chrome handles.

He pushed one open and gestured for me to enter.

When I did, I found the Primary standing in a pristine suit, looking out the wall-to-ceiling windows over the Chicago landscape. It went on for miles from where he stood. The view was breathtaking.

He turned around with his hands still in his pockets. "That will be all, Drew. Cancel any meetings I have for the rest of the day and do not interrupt me for anything."

"As you wish, sir." He nodded and left. The door snicked shut behind me.

The Primary, who I now knew was Logan, gestured to a pair of white leather couches across the room. "Please, have a seat, Lily." He used the nickname I'd given him on the yacht.

I lifted my spine and strode with confidence over to the comfortable-looking couches and sat in one of the smaller ones so he wouldn't think to sit next to me. I wanted space from him, even though I didn't feel scared.

"Would you like a drink? I sure could use one," he admitted.

I nodded. "Anything is fine."

"I'm drinking whiskey."

"Whiskey's fine," I murmured, and sat bone-straight at the edge of the seat with my purse pressed to my thighs, my hands resting on it so I wouldn't fidget.

"Isn't today a school day?" he asked conversationally, proving he'd looked me up. He very likely knew everything there was to know about me, when I knew next to nothing about him in return.

"It is. I took the day off. I'm sorry you had to cancel your meetings," I said, but it didn't sound genuine, because I wasn't sorry.

He brought over a crystal tumbler with a couple fingers of golden liquid in it and then sat on the couch opposite mine. He crossed his long legs over one another and eased back against the leather, stretching one of his arms along the back of the couch.

"Let's get right to it, Lily. What is it you want out of this meeting? Is it to see me, my brother and my crew go down with the MacCreedys?"

I jolted where I sat, surprised at the audacity of his direct manner. "Is that what you want?"

He smiled slyly and sipped at his whiskey. "Now you know I am not in the driver's seat here. It doesn't matter what I want. What matters is what you are going to do with the information you hold on me and my brother."

"I know why you did what you did. I watched your press conference yesterday," I stated.

He inhaled sharply and let it out just as fast. "My father had to be stopped. We tried for years to find another way, but he had so many auditors and risk assessors in his back pockets. I could have walked into the IRS and shown them everything we had accumulated about his illegal activity, and he still would have walked away unharmed. Sometimes having more money than one can spend in a hundred lifetimes has unforeseen repercussions. In this case, we had to do something extremely drastic to get other agencies involved in order to make things right."

"People died," I reminded him.

"Yes. And that fact will haunt my brother and me for the rest of our lives. We didn't pull the trigger, but we set the plan into motion. We hired the MacCreedys and believed we had a solid team. Every detail was worked out to our exact specifications so that everything would go off without a hitch. What we didn't plan for was human error. I had no idea that the moment John MacCreedy was handed a weapon, he'd turn into a different person. I had not been given the information that he'd been dishonorably discharged for a mental breakdown. He threatened to kill two members of his team who he believed were spies. That information didn't come until much later when everything had already gone to hell."

I closed my eyes as that information washed over me.

"I trusted the wrong people and that ended in lives lost," Logan admitted then sucked back the rest of the whiskey in one go.

"You didn't know," I said, realizing for the first time that I didn't blame him or his brother for those people's deaths. It truly was the fault of one crazed ex-soldier who was mentally ill.

"I should have let you go right away, but I needed time to think. To figure out how we were going to ensure the takedown of my father and free all those people from jail. Twenty-three people serving time for embezzling from my family's company. My grandfather on my mother's side built this business from the ground up. My father was not only making a mockery of all the good he did, but he was destroying all of us in the process. He created fake charities to donate to. Made some of those people the chief financial officers and created impenetrable paper trails. Ultimately, money was being stolen from people's retirement accounts, savings accounts, IRAs, and 401Ks. I can't even begin to tell you how deeply the deceit goes, but thousands of people have been affected. Any time the IRS got wind of a problem, my father would set up one of his people to take the fall. Twenty-three of them. All innocent." He dropped his head down, his chin resting near his chest. "I don't even know if I can truly make amends, but my brother and I are determined to try."

In that moment, I made my decision. My heart filled with light. My chest tightened and I reached out and put my hand to his knee giving it a squeeze in support.

"Which is why I'm not going to tell the authorities anything about you and your brother."

His head shot up. "What do you mean?"

"I didn't tell them anything about either of you. Not that I knew you were brothers. Not that I knew he was a doctor and a swimmer. Nothing. I just told them that I was well taken care of and brought back to the boat when I'd managed to escape. Explained that everyone had worn masks the entire time except when I saw the MacCreedys."

Logan closed his eyes, put his hands to his face, and leaned his entire body over to rest his elbows to his knees.

"Why would you do that? You were kidnapped. Frightened. Almost killed yourself trying to escape." He rubbed his face.

I'd known from the press conference that he was a handsome blond man, but now looking more closely I could tell his eyes were red rimmed, and there were dark smudges under each one. He was unshaven, and his hair looked like it had been tousled a thousand times by his fingers running through it..

"Sometimes in life, the end justifies the means. And besides, everyone deserves a second chance to make things right. You and your brother are doing that. You shouldn't be punished for the sins of your father."

"And what do you want in exchange for your silence?" He looked at me as though he were ravaged by guilt.

I clucked my tongue and sighed. "Nothing."

His brows pinched together. "There has to be *something*. Money. Fame. You're a teacher who's shacked up with a security guard who spends his free time working in his family's Mexican restaurant. You both live in apartments, drive cars that you still owe payments on. I could change your life dramatically."

"Jesus. You did look me up." I frowned.

He smirked. "I'm insanely rich."

"Yes, and insanely unhappy," I retorted.

"Touché. But Lily, there has to be something, *anything* that my brother and I can do in order to make amends."

I pursed my lips and then tapped at them both. I hadn't thought this would be a negotiation. I just wanted to look my captor in the face and tell him what I thought. Turned out, he told me what he thought and why he did what he did. Now that I knew, I mostly agreed with their actions.

Then it came to me.

I pulled out a piece of paper from my purse and a pen. I then wrote down the name of the charitable foundation Charlie worked at. "My sister Charlie runs and operates this charity."

"Charlotte Hagan-Kerrighan?" he asked, knowing her full name.

I gave him the side-eye.

He held up his hands in surrender. "Okay, I won't mention any more of what I know about you and your family. Though I must say, you all fascinate me. You're foster sisters and yet you act as though you are of the same blood."

"We're a tight-knit group. All we've ever had to rely on was one another."

"That's how I feel about my brother Kurt," he admitted.

"Then you understand." I pointed at the paper. "If you want to help out her charity with, I don't know, a donation or something, that would be kind."

He frowned. "It's not enough. What if I do that and put your niece through college? All of your future progeny."

I laughed out loud and shook my head. "My man is old school. He'd never let another man pay his children's way."

"Duly noted."

"My other sister Genesis works for the state. They always need money to help fostered and orphaned children. You could help them too?" I suggested.

"Are you always this generous? You have an endless amount of wealth right at your fingertips and you want to help others. Not yourself."

I stood up and shot back the entire rest of my whiskey before setting the glass down on the glass table. "I'm wealthy in what matters. Love. Friendship. Family." I smiled sadly, wondering if he had that kind of wealth and figuring he likely didn't. "Well, I got what I came for."

"Which was what exactly? A few million to your sisters' charitable offices?" He frowned.

I chuckled and shook my head. "No. To feel safe. To know you weren't coming after me. To know that I made the right decision not telling the authorities what I knew about you and your brother."

"Lily, I feel like we owe you our *lives*." His expression was tortured with the weight he carried.

"I'm sorry you feel that way. You owe me nothing. But please thank your brother for saving me from drowning that second time. I truly believe I would have died in that lake that night."

He lifted his chin. "I will." He cleared his throat and held up a finger. "And one more thing." He moved quickly over to his desk and pulled something out of the drawer then came back to me holding out his hand that was gripping something within his fist.

I put my hand out, palm up.

He set a pair of nail clippers inside my hand. "I found these in a pair of sweats you wore and thought of you. Figured if I ever saw you again, I'd give them to you as a memento of your fierce commitment to surviving against all odds. You truly are an amazing woman, Liliana Ramírez-Kerrighan."

I gripped the clippers tight in my hand. "Thank you."

He put his hands together in a prayer position and bowed slightly at the hips. "No. Thank you."

With my clippers in my hand, I exited his office and left his building with a huge smile.

Now I felt good.

Now I was free to live my life.

EPILOGUE

Six months later…

OPHELIA BURST INTO OUR APARTMENT WITH CISCO ON HER hip and his diaper bag dangling from one shoulder. Cisco was dressed in a pair of jeans, a long-sleeved polo and a little leather bomber jacket. His hair was slicked back and a serious expression was covering his handsome little face.

I reached grabby hands for the baby, now eight months old. "Hey, buddy. How's my big man?" I cooed and tickled his cheeks.

"He's ready for his first time at the zoo! Do you think he looks okay?" She tugged at her son's pant leg and fixed his scrunchy sock. One thing I'd learned about Ophelia was she didn't do anything halfway. The girl was always dressed to the nines as was her son. She and Blessing got along famously for this reason alone.

"He looks amazing, as do you, birthday girl!" I grinned and blew kisses against the baby's neck. He squealed for me, grabbed my curls, and forced my face to his. He gifted me a slobbery baby kiss in return.

"Cisco! You heartbreaker. What did I say about pulling on hair? No, baby love, it hurts." I untangled one fist and then the next from my much longer curls. Turned out Omar liked my hair long. He didn't care when it was short, but he might have a tiny fascination with fisting my longer lengths. I liked my man fisting my hair in the bedroom, so long it was.

Omar entered wearing an outfit almost identical to Cisco's. Only he had on black jeans with a long-sleeved polo and a brown leather jacket that made him look dark and dangerous.

I grinned at the sight of him.

He came over and looped me around the shoulders, kissing me. Cisco slapped at his cheek as he did.

"Happy Birthday, baby," I hummed, staring into the eyes of the most incredible man on the planet.

Ever since I came home from the hospital, I hadn't left his apartment. Slowly without any real discussion, we simply packed up my things and moved them into his house. Now his couches were paired with my pretty lamps. There were family photos and art all over the walls that we'd taken during the past six months together. My clothing and toiletries were mixed with his.

But, the best news was we'd already found a home that we'd put a bid on and were currently waiting to hear back from the realtor. This idea took a lot more discussion and planning because Omar wasn't keen on leaving Ophelia to manage on her own. Both Ophelia and I of course explained that she was a grown woman who had proven she could take care of herself and her son without him being right next door.

Omar eventually agreed to find us a home, one that we could buy together. However, what neither of us knew at the time was he was in cahoots with his younger brother Arturo who also didn't like the idea of his sister being a single mother living in the complex alone. He would be taking over the lease on this apartment when we moved, as he'd been renting a room from a friend and desperately wanted his own place. One he could afford on his salary at the restaurant.

Omar explained it as a win-win to both me and Ophelia but while I was fine with the change because I got a house with Omar out of the deal, Ophelia felt as though she was being treated like a child, not a thirty-year-old woman.

What I'd come to learn in this family was to accept the compromises and move on to fight the battle you wanted to win more. Omar and Arturo saw Ophelia as needing a man around for safety reasons. Having been in a traumatic situation along with all of my sisters, I saw no harm in Arturo moving in next door. It made my man feel better and I was a big fan of him being happy. He genuinely asked for so little.

Unlike today. He was dead set on us taking the family to the zoo for his birthday. The whole family. My sisters, Mama Kerri, Rory, his mama, brother, Ophelia, and Cisco included. Of course it was also Ophelia's birthday, so we'd be going to the restaurant after for a big blowout with food and drinks.

"Happy Birthday, *hermana*." Omar let me go and hugged his twin.

"Happy Birthday to you too, you big lug." She patted his chest and smiled. "I'm ready for Cisco's first zoo experience. I hope he likes the animals."

"All kids like the animals. And besides, he'll have my niece to dote on him." I squeezed him on my hip. "Isn't that right, big guy? You're going to hang out with Rory. Aren't you, baby boy?"

He gurgled and made a bunch of random sounds that I couldn't decipher before shoving four fingers directly into his mouth.

"All right. Let's hit the road." Omar clapped and rubbed his hands together before holding open the door. Ophelia carried the diaper bag and my purse while I carried the baby to Omar's SUV. We already had a car seat for Cisco because I often picked him up from daycare on my way home from school since it was right around the corner from where I worked.

I got our guy buckled up and playing with a toy before getting in the front passenger seat. Ophelia hopped in the back, and Omar in the front, and we were off.

"My family is already at the giraffes," I announced, reading the many text messages from every member of my family. We'd gotten stuck in traffic and had to detour, making us fifteen minutes late.

Omar took my hand in his, and Ophelia pushed the stroller where Cisco was wide-eyed and taking it all in.

The place felt like walking into an outdoor adventure. Tons of lush greenery, interesting wooden enclosures. Flowers, wildlife, you name it, they had it.

"So why did you choose the zoo for your birthday?" I swung Omar's hand back and forth. "Thirty is kind of a big deal. We could have gone to Vegas or New York for the weekend."

He smiled wide. "We had a good time here with Rory. I wanted to give that to Cisco and Ophelia. It's her birthday too."

"I had fun that day as well. It was the first time we *really* kissed." I sighed, dreamily remembering that day. It was an afternoon when we were still in the thick of Addison's situation. It felt like ten years ago when in reality it was maybe a year ago.

"I believe it was a year ago to the day," Omar shared.

I stopped in my tracks not believing what I'd just heard. "No?"

He nodded. "*Mi amor,* it was. I would remember since it was my birthday when I brought you and Rory here."

"You're kidding? That was...that..." I thought back to that time. It had been not long after we'd first met which was at the beginning of Addison's situation. I was still in lust with him and denying it viciously. Then once Addison's tragedy ended and the man who hurt her was dead, I'd made the mistake about Ophelia which allowed another few months to pass. Then of course the bank robbery occurred, and we went through that, then Simone's wedding six months ago, Addison's wedding in December, and now here we were a full year later.

"*¡Dios mío!* You mean to tell me, last year on this *same day* you were taking me and my niece to the zoo and it was your birthday!"

He grinned wickedly. "That kiss, Liliana, that was my present last year. Best present I'd had in a long time."

"But then I was sooooooo mean to you," I griped.

He pulled me into his arms and Ophelia maneuvered the stroller over to a section of the zoo that had barking seals.

"Liliana, you didn't know it, but you gave me everything I could have wanted that day. I spent it with you and little Rory experiencing something new. And that kiss... It cemented you as the one, *chica*. I knew in that moment that I'd do anything to protect you. That I'd give my life in order to keep you safe from harm."

I closed eyes and pressed my forehead to his chest. "I was such a bitch, though."

He snuggled me closer. "You were uncertain. Didn't know which way was up or down. You were in the middle of a crazy situation, and it wasn't even the first or the last. Sure, we had things going against us, but look at us now. We're here, one year later, a couple. Celebrating this day with *nuestra familia.*"

Our family.

"You're amazing, you know that?"

He grinned. "My woman tells me that every day."

I pointed at his chest. "As she should!" I lifted up and kissed him. "Let's go meet up with the family. Everyone has presents for you and Ophelia. It's going to be a blast."

I tugged on his hand, and we found Ophelia, then made our way to the giraffes.

When we arrived, Rory immediately went to greet Cisco, shoving a stuffed lion at his face. "Look what we got you, Cisco! It's a lion! Roooooarrrrr!" She made a face and roared.

Cisco giggled and kicked his feet.

Both Omar and I hugged and greeted the rest of the family. Happy Birthdays were shared with Omar and Ophelia, and then the entire group went over to the giraffes to take a gander at the magical creatures.

I was pointing and showing Rory one when I heard several people gasp. I turned around and found Omar down on one knee with a velvet box held aloft in his outstretched hand.

"Omar, what are you doing?" I stared down at him, completely shocked.

"*Mi amor, mi lirio*, my Liliana, will you make me the happiest man alive by becoming my wife? I promise to love you, cherish you, and never put out your fire, your wild spirit."

I pressed my hands to my face. "Baby, you're asking me

to marry you on your birthday?" The words sounded shaky as a flood of emotion came over me and tears pricked my eyes.

"The only thing I want for my birthday every year is *you* by my side, forever."

"Omar," I choked out.

He opened the ring box and in the center was a ring I'd seen many times in the past six months as it was previously on Renata's finger.

I looked at Renata as tears streaked down my face. "That's yours..." I gasped.

She shook her head. "It is how my Francisco would want it. His children sharing a token of our love through time."

"Liliana Ramírez-Kerrighan, my father presented this ring to my mother when he asked her to be his wife over thirty-five years ago. I am on my knee, in front of those we both love most in the entire world, asking you to be mine. I will love you until I take my last breath. Marry me and make me the happiest man alive?"

Happiness spread from my pounding heart through my chest and poured out each limb. I nodded rapidly. "Yes, I'll marry you, Omar Francisco Alvarado. I'll be your wife until my last breath."

He stood up, put the ring on my finger, and took my mouth in a searing kiss. The kiss went on and on as the sound of cheering and applause eventually filtered into my mind. Omar lifted me up under my bum with both his arms, so I was way above him as he spun me around a few times.

Dizzy with love, excitement, and pure happiness, he let me slide down his body until he held me in his arms.

"Every year, I will look into your beautiful face on my birthday and know I am one lucky man. I love you, baby."

"I love you, too! So much, Omar. Thank you for chasing me. Thank you for committing to us. Thank you for being the man for me." I kissed him and poured my heart and soul into it.

Omar eventually pulled back and shifted us around so that we faced our entire family. "She said yes!"

Not only did our family cheer but all of the patrons near that section of the zoo clapped and hooted.

We'd been through hell the past year but came through it together.

I didn't know what the future would bring with our crazy families, not to mention our jobs and everything in between. What I did know was that I had him, his love, and our families. I couldn't have asked for more.

In my time on this earth, I believed life was meant to be taken one day at a time. And if you were lucky enough to do it holding the hand of the person you loved more than any other...you win.

The End

I am very aware that many of my readers would like to read stories about all the Soul Sisters including Sonia, Blessing, Genesis and Charlie. If that's the case, tell all your friends about the first three books, and if they continue to do well, I'll write more. However, I will only be able to release them as time permits. As a writer, I have to go where the readers and the muse takes me. So I'm going to say this is The End of the Soul Sister universe...for now.

Excerpt from *What the Heart Wants* (A Wish Novel)

MY STOMACH TWISTS AND TURNS, AND I SWEAR IF I THINK too much about the double whammy of seeing Camden after ten years on top of going into business for the first time in my life, I might throw up all over the pristine waiting room floor.

"This will go only one of two ways," Milo declares. "Yes or no."

I close my eyes and lean my head back against the wall. Without warning, flashes of Camden and me together back when we were teenagers rushes through my mind like a spinning wheel of fortune. So much love and laughter. And the smiles. My goodness, when the man smiled, my entire body warmed with light. Until I put that light out.

After I left, I only allowed myself that first year to regret the decision I made to leave Camden and Evie. It was easier with Evie because I knew I'd see and talk to her again. When I walked out on Camden and disappeared, I hadn't planned on ever seeing him again.

I'd spent a full year telling myself that leaving him was the right choice. The only choice. I had to see the world, live life free, and he had to stay here, go to college, and work in his family's steel empire. It was all planned out. There was no wiggle room. He wanted a woman who would keep his home, make his dinner, and raise his children to be the next line of steel empire-running men and women. I wanted to travel, take risks and chances on things I'd only every dreamed of.

We weren't meant to be. No matter how much love we had, my mother was right. She knew what I needed before

I did. Until now. Being here is so far outside of my comfort zone, I'm nowhere in the vicinity of feeling at peace with the decision I made all those years ago or the one I made recently by coming back.

Seeing him again brings it right to the surface. The hope and excitement about the future we shared. It took my mother dying and her letters for me to accept my fate, to have the courage to walk away. And here I am, standing in front of the only man I've ever loved, asking him to commit to my future when I wouldn't do the same for him ten years ago.

"This is horrible." My hands start to shake, and I grip the chair arms so tight my knuckles turn white.

"How so? Unless you're referring to the energy pouring off you and Camden in there. Judging by his familiar greeting as well as the way he couldn't take his eyes off of you, I'm assuming you have a history. Want to fill me in?"

I shake my head. "Not really."

Milo's gaze pierces mine.

"We uh, we knew each other when we were teenagers."

"Knew, meaning…dated?"

I nod. "Yeah. For four years."

The dark slashes that are his eyebrows rise up toward his hairline. "Long time."

"Mmm-hmm."

"Guessing it didn't exactly end well?"

"That would be an understatement."

Milo is about to say something else when the door to the conference room opens and Camden strides into the waiting area.

"Ms. Ross, may I speak to you over here privately?" Camden gestures to another door down the hall.

I stand up, my hands still shaking. Shit. The last thing I want is private time with Camden Bryant. "Um, sure. Can you watch my things, Milo?"

He nods but his gaze is firm and set on Camden.

Camden opens the door to a much smaller room with a round table and four chairs around it. The moment I'm in the room, I hear the door shut, and then my wrist is snagged, and I'm spun around with my back against the door. Camden presses his body a scant inch from mine, arms at the sides of my shoulders, caging me in. He's so close I can feel his warmth hovering over me.

"Why are you back? Why are you here?" he hisses.

I shake my head. "Cam, I had no idea you ran this foundation or were a part of it. Milo was my contact. Apparently, your group helped one of his clients."

"And who is he to you? Your boyfriend?"

"Milo? What on earth? No." I blink rapidly, trying to figure out where this conversation is going.

"Did you plan to come into my company, looking like a million fucking bucks, your hair styled in a way *you know* used to drive me crazy, to what? Show me what I lost out on when you left? Huh, Suda Kaye? You trying to torture me? Trying to drive a stake into my heart?" His tone is raw and angry.

"No! My God, you know me better than that!"

He huffs and I can smell mint and the hint of coffee on his breath. "Do I? Do I really? Maybe ten years ago I would have said so. Though I would have been wrong. Because the woman I loved, wanted to spend my life with, the woman I'd gotten the first damn taste of left the same night I took her innocence," he says crudely.

"C-Camden—" I stutter, desperation lacing the single

word. It feels like a thousand bees are stinging me over and over as waves of hurt barrel through me.

He continues undaunted. "The girl I knew, she never would have left me to wonder what I did wrong. If I'd hurt her that night. If she hated me for what we did. That girl would have *stayed*. This girl—" his gaze runs up and down my body "—this girl, I've never met. So you tell me—why are you here?"

"I-I—"

"Spit it out, Suda Kaye. You've got three seconds before I walk out the door and my foundation's money with me."

"Cam…"

"Three," he says stiffly, his eyes blazing white-hot fire. "Two."

"I just needed an investor for my store. I swear!"

"That's it?" He clenches his jaw and I can see a muscle jumping in his cheek. "No other reason?" He brings his head closer.

I close my eyes and without knowing what the heck I'm doing, I place my hands on his waist. "Camden…I'm…"

He brings his nose close to my neck, and I tremble as the hair from his short-cropped beard grates along my tender skin. While he makes his way up toward my ear, he turns my sadness into something quite different. Hotter. More electric. "Tell me why you're here? The real reason. You have one second left," he whispers almost soothingly.

"I need an investor. I had no idea you'd be here."

"I don't believe you," he says as he dips his head closer to mine and inhales. He closes his eyes before speaking through clenched teeth. "You still smell like cherries." His jaw is tight when his gaze meets mine, but he steps back, making me cold yet relieved at the same time.

I stand there silently, nothing but the air in my lungs sawing in and out of my body. I feel as if I've been on a treadmill at a dead run for the last fifteen minutes, not losing my mind while standing quietly in front of the only man I ever loved.

He shakes his head. "You're not going to tell me the real reason you're here, are you?"

I open and close my mouth, lost in his gaze. The blanket of sadness fills the room and covers us both with its melancholy.

Cam purses his lips, places his hands on his hips while his hazel eyes stare at me. They're filled with that sense of familiarity and something I would have never expected…

Grief.

Loss.

Heartbreak.

After so many years, it's still there, simmering beneath the surface of this beautiful man's gaze. And I'm the reason it's there.

"One," he says cryptically before stepping past me and opening the door, leaving me breathless and speechless. As he retreats, I watch him run his hand through his hair and growl. "Christ…still screwing with my head, even after all these years."

If you'd like to read What the Heart Wants, *it's available now across all retailers.*

AUDREY CARLAN
Titles

International Guy Series

Paris

New York

Copenhagen

Milan

San Francisco

Montreal

London

Berlin

Washington, D.C.

Madrid

Rio

Los Angeles

Lotus House Series

Resisting Roots

Sacred Serenity

Divine Desire

Limitless Love

Silent Sins

Intimate Intuition

Enlightened End

Trinity Trilogy

Body

Mind

Soul

Life

Fate

Calendar Girl
January
February
March
April
May
June
July
August
September
October
November
December

Falling Series
Angel Falling
London Falling
Justice Falling

ACKNOWLEDGMENTS

To my husband, **Eric,** for supporting me in everything I do. I love you more.

To the world's greatest PA, **Jeananna Goodall**, I don't deserve you, but I'm going to keep you anyway. Good luck getting away. All joking aside, I hope you know how much I love and care about you and your entire family. I firmly believe we were meant to be partners in this crazy romance book world. I've never had a better working experience than when you came on to Audrey Carlan, Inc. and made yourself a necessary part of the business and my life. I'm so damn grateful.

To **Jeanne De Vita** my personal editor, I owe you so much. I mean truly you could ask me for just about anything and I'd give it to you. I'll never forget when I came to you after losing my editor of many, many years and you dropped everything and pitched right in. I'm so lucky to have you on my team and can't wait to be a part of your own writing adventure.

To my alpha beta team, I need to say some things so I'm calling each of you out.

Tracey Wilson-Vuolo, you've been my rock. My freakin' diamond. We've survived a lot of loss and amazing times together. Your feedback every chapter makes me feel like I can keep doing this job forever. You have such an incredible ability to lift up those, even when you struggle so much in your own life. You are one of the strongest women I know and the most giving. Thank you for choosing me to be your friend all those years ago. I love you.

Tammy Hamilton-Green, you have to know that I think you're one of the coolest chicks on the planet. You have this ease about you that calls to me. I just love hanging out with you. And your feedback is so well thought out, considerate of my writing process, and always gives me things to think about in my plot. Without you, we'd have some seriously Scooby Doo endings. My goal is always to impress you. And when I do! Whoo-whoo, it's awesome. Thank you, my friend.

Gabby McEachern, all I have to do is think about your smile and I smile. You have that gift of bringing others true joy. Never let that side of yourself go. On this series girl, you have been my go-to. The amount of Spanish in this book was mind-boggling. Having a freakin' Spanish teacher on my beta team… Solid gold, sister! Thank you, thank you, thank you for making sure I represent the Spanish language and that of Mexican-Americans in an honest and accurate light.

Elaine Hennig, my medical professional extraordinaire… I cannot tell you what a relief it is to have someone with your expertise at my back. I make up the craziest stuff sometimes, but having you on the team, a long-time practicing registered nurse, to make sure what I've written is medically accurate is such a blessing. I dedicated this book to you because without your help in this series where everyone was getting hurt left and right, I could have made a fool of myself. But with you on my tribe, I knew you had me covered. Thank you!

Dorothy Bircher, the way you dig into my stories and share your emotions brings me such needed support. I have to know how the readers are going to experience my stories and you don't hold back. I love it. Also having someone who can represent the Asian and Black demographic on my beta team to ensure I don't make stupid or hurtful mistakes is a godsend. Thank you for being there for me, girl. Madlove.

To my literary agent **Amy Tannenbaum,** with Jane Rotrosen Agency, you knew I could make this happen even when I wasn't so sure. Your faith in my ability is a priceless gift. Thank you.

To my foreign literary agent **Sabrina Prestia and Hannah Rody-Wright,** with Jane Rotrosen Agency, who have already secured a foreign deal for this series and continue to find new awesome homes for my book babies. Thank you, ladies!

To **Jenn Watson** and the entire **Social Butterfly** team, you guys blow my mind. Your professionalism, creativity, and business prowess are unprecedented. Thank you for adding me to your clientele. I look forward to teaming up on many more projects in the future.

To the **Readers**, I couldn't do what I love or pay my bills if it weren't for all of you. Thank you for every review, kind word, like and shares of my work on social media and everything in between. You are what make it possible for me to live my dream. #SisterhoodFTW

About AUDREY CARLAN

Audrey Carlan is a No. 1 *New York Times*, *USA Today*, and *Wall Street Journal* best-selling author. She writes stories that help the reader find themselves while falling in love. Some of her works include the worldwide phenomenon Calendar Girl serial, Trinity series and the International Guy series. Her books have been translated into over thirty languages across the globe.

She lives in the California Valley, where she enjoys her two children and the love of her life. When she's not writing, you can find her teaching yoga, sipping wine with her "soul sisters," or with her nose stuck in a sexy romance novel.

NEWSLETTER

For new release updates and giveaway news, sign up for Audrey's newsletter: audreycarlan.com/sign-up

SOCIAL MEDIA

Audrey loves communicating with her readers. You can follow or contact her on any of the following:

Website: www.audreycarlan.com

Email: audrey.carlanpa@gmail.com

Facebook: www.facebook.com/AudreyCarlan

Twitter: twitter.com/AudreyCarlan

Pinterest: www.pinterest.com/audreycarlan1

Instagram: www.instagram.com/audreycarlan

Readers Group: www.facebook.com/groups/
AudreyCarlanWickedHotReaders

Book Bub: www.bookbub.com/authors/audrey-carlan

Goodreads: www.goodreads.com/author/show/7831156.
Audrey_Carlan

Amazon: www.amazon.com/Audrey-Carlan/e/
B00JAVVG8U

TikTok: www.tiktok.com/@audreycarlan